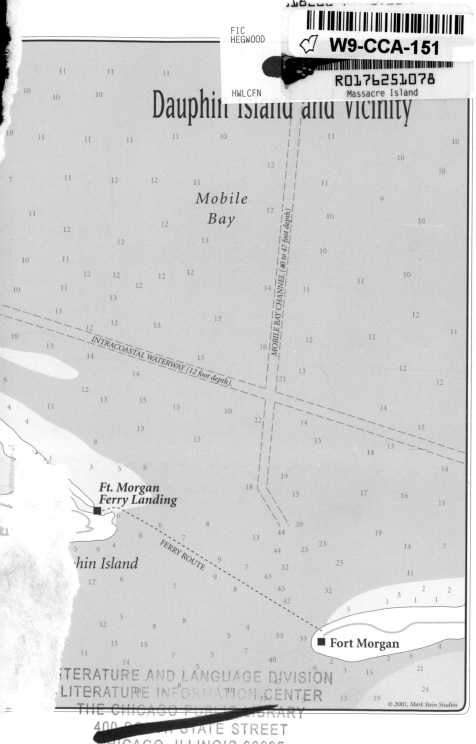

Dauphin Island and vicinity

*Mobile
Bay*

11
11
11
11
10
10
10

10
11
11
11
11
10
11
10
10

7
11
12
12
11
11
9
10
10

11
12
13
12
12
10
10
10

12
12
13
12
10

10
11
12
12
12
12
10

10
11
12
13
10

13
12
13
10

13
13

10
12
13
11
12

14
14
12
12

6
12
13
15
12

4
11
13
15
10
14
14

4
13
15
14
13
13

3
5
8
14

Ft. Morgan
Ferry Landing

18
15
17
16
15

MOBILE BAY CHANNEL (40 to 47 foot depth)

INTRACOASTAL WATERWAY (12 foot depth).

22
14
15
15

16
19

21

20
44
19

44
25
23
14
7

FERRY ROUTE

hin Island

8
7
13
5
9
7
32
25
11

9
43
12
6
9
43
32

42
3
2
2
1
1
1

3

5
8
8
4
53
33

Fort Morgan

12
8
5
5
7
40
2
2
6
4

11
14
5
15
21

7
5
7

13
15
7
5
24

© 2001, Mark Stein Studios

MASSACRE ISLAND

MASSACRE ISLAND

Martin Hegwood

ST. MARTIN'S MINOTAUR ≋ NEW YORK

Massacre Island is a work of fiction. Names, places, characters, and incidents are products of the author's imagination or are used fictitiously. Certain liberties have been taken in changing the landscape of Dauphin Island and Mobile County to fit the story. Any resemblance to actual events at any of the locales depicted in this book are coincidental. Any resemblance to any person, living or dead, is also coincidental.

www.minotaurbooks.com

Library of Congress Cataloging-in-Publication Data

Hegwood, Martin.
    Massacre Island / Martin Hegwood. — 1st ed.
        p. cm.
    ISBN 0-312-28095-5
    1. Private investigators—Alabama—Fiction.   2. Gulf Coast (Ala.)—Fiction.   3.
Islands—Fiction.   I. Title.

PS3558.E4233 M37 2001
813'.54—dc21

                                                                        2001041613

First Edition: October 2001

10   9   8   7   6   5   4   3   2   1

With Love

to Linda, Eliza, and William

for allowing me to chase this dream

ACKNOWLEDGMENTS

I thank the following friends and family members for their assistance:

The Reverend Monsignor John R. Amos of the Mobile Roman Catholic Diocese; Dauphin Island Chief of Police Terry Beasley; Jeff Collier, Mayor of Dauphin Island; my friend Sergeant Chuck Dayton of the Mississippi Highway Patrol; my wife, Linda Hegwood; Tommy Hegwood, my father and my best source for information about the Coast; Jay Higginbotham, lifetime friend, fellow writer, and Director of Archives for the City of Mobile; INS Special Agent Harry Moran; Dean Wallis, friend and expert pilot; Debbie and Jay Willis, my friends since childhood, and their daughters, Katherine, Rachael, and Laura, for allowing me the use of their little piece of heaven on Mobile Bay during the writing of this book; and Judy Winfield of the Mobile Area Chamber of Commerce.

Special thanks go to my editor, Joe Cleemann, for his patience, encouragement, and right-on-target advice.

I remained on the island which I am naming Massacre because we found on it, at the southwest end, a spot where more than sixty men or women had been slain. We found the heads and the rest of the remains along with some of their household goods. As none of these have yet rotted, it appears that this occurred no more than three or four years ago.

—from the journal of Iberville
upon the discovery of present-day
Dauphin Island, Alabama,
February 3, 1699

MASSACRE ISLAND

ONE

I was kneeling on the sand and crushed oyster shells that pass for a parking lot at the Neptune Bar. Down on one knee, running my hand along the bottom edge of the van, feeling for any plastic explosive or dynamite that might have been fastened on to the frame while I was inside. It was a routine that was getting real old real fast, but that letter bomb from the day before had me looking over my shoulder. Somebody had left it propped against the front door of the borrowed beach house I was staying in, and if the training from my old army MP days had not taught me how to spot such things, the Dauphin Island cops would still be out there spraying down the porch with garden hoses to wash what was left of me off the front wall.

If somebody knew explosives—and somebody around the island surely did—it wouldn't take him ten seconds to stick enough dynamite or plastic explosive to that van to blow me into the Gulf of Mexico. All week I had been hearing stories about the Green Guardians, a whacked-out, save-the-Earth group who had just moved in from California and had set up shop in a fenced compound down on the western end of the island; about how they had blown up at least two oil wells in the Western Overthrust. One of the Guardians, a college-aged girl named Heather whom I had met by chance when I first got to the island, had told me she was getting worried about some of the things the leader of the group had been saying, but she was real vague about what he said. I told her to call the sheriff's office, but I don't know if she ever did.

Now that I was tuned in and listening for such talk, I also remembered hearing that when he was in the joint, Bobby Earl Fair, the local bookie, had been a member of the White Resistance, this skinhead group with chapters in all the more prestigious prisons and an active alumni group on the outside. Some members of that same group got caught last year plotting another Oklahoma City–style bombing of an Alcohol, Tobacco, and Firearms office over in Houston. The Resistance had recently set up Bobby Earl in the bookie business after they took over the sports-betting action in Mobile and Pensacola.

But try as I might, I couldn't think of any reason that either the Green Guardians or Bobby Earl would have it in for me. At least, have it in for me *that* bad.

I wasn't all that worried about another bomb getting planted at the beach house. As soon as the neighbors heard about the first one, they started worrying the daylights out of the 911 team, calling them at least two times an hour and reporting what they thought were suspicious characters, most of whom turned out to be families walking past the cabins on their way to the beach.

But as far as being worried about the van I was driving . . . now, *that* was a different matter.

I had started having daytime nightmares about some faceless pyrotechnic maniac and how he could choose where he wanted me to be when he set off the remote-control bomb. Maybe he'd get his jollies over seeing a fireball at the highest point of the bridge as I was driving into the island from the mainland. Or, if he was a real psychopath, he could set it off when I was on the ferry to Fort Morgan and take me out along with a few innocent families on a picnic. The possibilities had made for some white-knuckled driving the past few days, because if the guy really wanted me and really knew what he was doing, there was no way I could guard against it.

Sometimes you just have to hope the bad guys haven't studied the bad-guy business hard enough.

No question about it, I would have been skittish even if the cops and the sheriff's office had the manpower to keep me under a twenty-four-hour protective watch. But every officer on both those forces plus a good number of agents brought in from the Alabama Bureau of Investigation in Montgomery were already tied up trying to get leads into who killed those four kids in that beach house down on the west end a couple of weeks earlier, the same headline-making case that had brought me to Dauphin Island to begin with. So the best the cops could do for me was to tell me to get off the island. And when I told them I couldn't do that, they wished me good luck and told me to watch my backside.

Which is exactly what I was trying to do.

I was kneeling at the rear bumper, the sand and gravel sharp against my knee even through my jeans, looking at the bottom of my gas tank. I could smell some gas, but I had just filled up, so it was probably nothing more than a little spillage. A car eased toward me from behind, its air conditioner compressor working hard, and the engine kept running as the door opened.

"Delmas! I done told you to stop driving that van. You gonna get your ass killed, dammit!" The voice came down as if from a raised pulpit. I turned my head, still on one knee, and from that angle Deputy Jimbo McInnis looked to be ten feet tall.

"I think you just might be right," I said.

"You and me, we need to talk."

I stood and dusted the sand off my jeans. "You hear anything from the crime lab about that bomb?"

"Nothing you don't already know. I ain't here to talk about that. I need to discuss some private business with you."

I leaned against the rear door of my van. "Business? You into some kind of multi-level marketing thing or something?"

He grunted and shook his head. "I'll tell you what. You let ol'

Jimbo get off the clock tonight, and I'll take you someplace we can talk real private. My treat."

"Okay," I said, "but I want you to understand. I tried selling Amway once. Didn't work for me."

We started out right after sunset at the Blackwater Saloon, just six or eight feet across the Alabama state line into Mississippi. The Blackwater is the latest reincarnation of what started out as a steakhouse and lounge back in the fifties when none of us on the coast realized that there was this silly state law against slot machines. The place had been stripped of all the wooden tables and chairs, all the drapes and the carpet, and had been turned into a pure-dee, no frills honky-tonk. According to the flashing portable sign out front at the edge of the highway, a wet-T-shirt contest with cash prizes was scheduled to begin at eight, but I wasn't real sure the message on that sign got changed all that often.

"What kinda test they give for the private investigator's license?" Jimbo asked once we'd gotten to our seats.

"Depends on which state you're talking about. In a lot of them, there's not any test," I said. "All you've got to do is pass a background check."

"This background check, how far back do they go?"

"I don't know. A few years, I guess."

"If the charges on something that happened a few years ago got dropped, you think any record of it would show up?"

I leaned back in my metal folding chair. "You better keep your deputy job and work your way into the business. I started out by checking old newspaper files for this private eye I knew down in New Orleans."

"I don't mind doing stuff like that," he said.

"And you don't need to be working any cases over here in Mobile County, not while you're with the sheriff's department."

"What do you know about bounty hunting?"

I had been having a little trouble picturing Jimbo as a private eye, but I really could see him as a bounty hunter. "I know a little about it. I've met a few."

"How 'bout another beer?" he asked as he rose from his chair.

The place was already half full, but I didn't see any likely candidates for the wet-T-shirt contest. Of course, in a state-line joint, one could break out at any minute. In the South, and for all I know the rest of the country as well, state lines are a natural draw for every bootlegger, crap shooter, road lizard, outlaw biker, and all the other various and assorted honky-tonk types, especially when there is a marked disparity in the liquor laws between the two jurisdictions. The Mississippi-Alabama line down near the coast has the added advantage of being in a swamp, and therefore isolated and generally left alone.

Jimbo was studying the selections on the jukebox and holding two cans of Bud in his huge left hand. He slipped in a couple of quarters and Garth Brooks started singing about all these friends he had in low places. No disrespect to Garth, but I could match him in that particular category on at least a two-to-one basis. Jimbo waved for me to join him over at the pool table.

"I gotta make me a career move," he said. "I can't put up with no more of these political shenanigans."

I nodded as I tested a cue stick by rolling it across the table. It was reasonably straight. "I assume you're talking about this murder case."

"That and a buncha other things. You go ahead and break."

I hit the cue ball good and hard, got a loud pop when it smacked the rack of balls. I hit it head on and didn't get much ball movement; the only one that went in was the twelve, and that was on a lucky carom. But at least it was a loud break, which counts for an awful lot in any pool game in the Blackwater Saloon.

"Looks like I got stripes," I said.

"I guess you heard they took us off the case," Jimbo said. "The boys from Montgomery think we ain't got enough sense to handle something that happens in our own backyard."

I didn't have any open shots on the table, so I tried to bank the ten into the corner. I missed and left Jimbo set up with a straight-on shot at the side pocket.

"Thing that gets me," he said, "the sheriff just stepped aside and let 'em take over without saying the first word."

"From looking at the TV, I thought he was running the whole show," I said. "I mean, every time I turn on the TV, there's Carlton Rice in full uniform holding a press conference about what's going on with the investigation."

Jimbo frowned and took a sip of beer. He was resting the tip of his cue stick on the floor and absentmindedly rolling it between his fingers as he gazed at the table.

"It's your shot," I said.

"They let Carlton be the spokesman so they could get him out of the way," Jimbo said. "When he found out that *Dateline* was coming down to do a story on the murders, he woulda sold out his mama to get in front of that camera."

I chalked the tip of my stick.

"It's fine with me if he wants to get on TV, but, dammit, that was *my* case."

"You've got solids," I said. "I've got stripes."

"I mean, they run around in their suits acting like they know so much more than us ignorant rednecks, and then they waste God-only-knows how much time investigating Scooter Haney."

Scooter Haney was this multimillionaire who had been getting sued in a well-publicized palimony suit by one of the murder victims, this former Miss Global Alabama named Kellie Lee Simmons. Didn't sound like Jimbo thought that lawsuit counted for much as far as a motive was concerned.

"And I don't think they've even talked to all the victims' families yet," Jimbo said. "Shows you how much those experts know."

"I'm just curious, Jimbo. How do you feel about getting taken off the case?"

He glared at me for a second, then slipped into a gap-toothed smile. "You're right. Screw it. No more bitchin'. I'll just play pool and let them solve the case. Whose shot is it?"

Jimbo sank the seven ball in the side pocket and reeled off three more good shots before he missed. A barmaid opened the door to the kitchen and the smell of fried onion rings and hamburger patties drifted across the room.

"I'll get my brother to check on the requirements for an Alabama license," I said. "You ever been bonded?"

"I got out on bond back in college when about half the football team got arrested after this fight out at Len-Lu's. Does that count?" He ran his fingers up and down his cue stick. It looked like an extra-long pencil in those big hands. "Let's finish up this game and head over to Mobile. Don't look like they're gonna have no T-shirt contest."

We were riding in Jimbo's truck since we didn't want to have to keep checking my van for bombs and, as he explained, the department frowns on using a patrol car for the purpose of barhopping. The truck was as fine a cowboy Cadillac as you'll ever see. A three-year-old Ford F-150, Mississippi State maroon with gray cloth seats and jacked up high enough to ride through an acre of fresh-cut pine stumps. It had mud-grip tires, a Warn Winch, fog lights, and a tag on the front bumper that read simply DAWGS.

"You heard anything from any of the Green Guardians lately?" I asked.

He tapped the side of his head three times just above his ear. "My hearing must be going bad. I coulda swore you just asked me if any of Zandro's bunch has reported in to me."

"I'm talking about that good-looking blonde, the one we saw at the Guardians' compound. Didn't you say something about you two being in the first stage of romance?"

"You sound like you know something I oughta know."

"I was just wondering," I said.

We raced along old Highway 90, zipping through Grand Bay and St. Elmo with our windows down and the big mud tires singing. The night air was cool, the smell of new-mown hay strong, and when we crossed the bridges, the bullfrogs in the roadside ditches and ponds bellowed their deep, manly calls to attract any of the lonely frogettes who might be out cruising the pond this fine, romantic, late-summer night in south Mobile County.

The boot heel of Alabama is split evenly into two counties by that great triangular wedge Mobile Bay. The city of Mobile is at the top of the triangle—a saltwater seaport set back a full thirty miles from the Gulf—with Baldwin County to the east and Mobile County to the west. Mobile County's ragged southern shoreline is edged with a carpet of marsh grass veined with shallow, curving bayous, a land so flat that the water moves only when the tides shift, home to the alligator and nutria and great blue heron, and much of it covered by the largest remaining virgin pine savanna in the United States.

It's a land of sprawling live oaks and Spanish moss, of azaleas and dogwoods and wisteria, home of the world-famous Bellingrath Gardens. Major east-west roads, even from the days when the French were in control, have run from what is now the Mississippi border due northeast to Mobile, bypassing and isolating the county's southeast quadrant, those inland truck-farming towns of Grand Bay, St. Elmo, Irvington, and Theodore, and those coastal shrimping villages of Bayou La Batre, Coden, and Heron Bay. Dauphin Island lies due south, three miles offshore.

You don't just pass through these places, you have to be going to them. That part of the county became, and remains, an area of neither great poverty nor great wealth, peopled by hardy, self-reliant folk. Hospitable, yet a bit wary of the outsider. You can party with them, but you don't dare mess with them. They work hard, and they play even harder.

And, man, do they *ever* party hard!

"Are we through talking business?" I asked.

"I might wanna ask you some more stuff later on."

"Well, since we've taken care of yours, now let me take care of some of my business. How well did you know Rebecca Jordan?"

He reached for a can of Skoal on the dashboard and put a pinch between his cheek and gums. "Is this an interview?"

"That depends on you."

"I gotta start learning this kinda stuff if I'm gonna go into the business."

"Okay," I said, "let's call it an interview. How much did you know about Rebecca?"

"Mighty fine gal," he said. "Out of the four what got killed, she was the best by far. Her mama's the one you working for, ain't she?"

"She wants me to find out if what they've been saying in the tabloids is true."

"Of course it ain't! Rebecca wasn't no drug addict, sex addict, devil worshiper, or any of that other bullshit they been putting in those rags. She spoke to everybody she saw, never gave nobody no trouble. A lot of them girls who grow up rich can look at you like they think you need to be scrubbed with a steel-wire brush and sprayed down with Lysol. But not her."

"The papers are saying they did a lot of drugs at Jason's beach house," I said. "You know anything about that?"

"Don't know what other people did at that house. But that Jason, he warn't running no drugs, I can tell you that. Last year the narc sharks up at the Bureau of Narcotics sent a new guy down here and he figured it was time to move up in the agency. They got this confiscation law. You heard of it?"

"I've heard of it."

"Cars, boats, planes. Anything they claim was used to haul drugs. They just outright steal 'em sometimes. But you notice they ain't never confiscated one of them two-hundred-million-dollar cruise ships out of Miami. You put a bunch of rich kids on vacation on one of *those* things and tell me you couldn't run a dog through and turn up some nose candy." He reached below the seat for a Styrofoam cup, stuffed in a paper napkin, and spit into it. "Anyhow, this new guy was a real cowboy. He found out Jason was bringing Mexicans in and out of here and figured he'd make a run through that plane and find enough Acapulco Gold to get his young ass named as bureau chief at the very least."

"Where did all this happen?" I asked.

"Right there on the island. Right at the airstrip. This new agent had three narcs out there with guns, a dog, the whole bit. They sat there and waited for him to land. But ol' Jason warn't no fool. He found out they was waiting for him, and he wouldn't let 'em on the plane until his lawyer got there."

"Didn't you say these narcs were carrying weapons?"

"Son, there was way too many witnesses around for them to be firing shots at a grounded civilian plane. The guy at the airport called me, and by the time I got there, Jason had started steering that plane in circles around the tarmac with those three narcs running beside it shoutin' at him. I just sat back and watched the show until his lawyer, Bob Sanchez, got there. Now, Jason, he was smart enough I reckon, but Sanchez, he was the brains behind Jason's business. And let me tell you, Sanchez was some kinda hot that day."

I was having trouble hearing him, so I rolled up my window.

"They run that dog up and down that plane half a dozen times. But me and Sanchez were with them, so there warn't no way they could plant anything. Only thing they found was some Cuban cigars. And by the time Sanchez got through chewin' on their ass, they didn't even take the cigars. That guy is one scary dude. I'd hate to go up against him in court. But, don't you see, if there hadda been drugs in that plane anytime in the past year, them dogs woulda smelled the residue. I don't know what Jason was doing, but I'm here to tell you he warn't running no drugs."

We pulled into the parking lot of a warehouse-sized club near the Mobile airport called Shirley's Country Music Palace and found a space close in. The lot was at least two acres, paved, and nearly full. It was a new sheet-metal building with a pink-and-green neon sign up at the roofline big enough and bright enough to be seen for a mile in any direction. He wiped the Skoal out of his mouth with a napkin and spit out the window.

"This interview over?" he asked.

"One more question. The other two kids who got murdered, Kellie Lee Simmons and Rod Eubanks, what did you know about them?"

"I stopped Kellie Lee on a DUI in Theodore one time. She started cussing me and shoutin' that she'd have my badge, all kinda stuff like that. Hell, I was just gonna give her a ride home before she started all that. She didn't get my badge, but some-body—I figure Scooter Haney—must have made a phone call. The charges sure got dropped. Now, that Eubanks guy, to me he was just a face on the TV reading the news. Never met him."

The music from the band inside came through the thin walls, especially the bass guitar. Two guys sat on bar stools outside the door, checking IDs and making folks pour out their drinks before going in. Before we got so close to the front door that it would be hard to hear each other talk, Jimbo stopped.

"I mighta made it sound like I thought Jason Summers was clean," he said. "That ain't exactly what I meant to say. Jason was doing *something* shady, you can write that on the wall. The boy was making too much money not to be. I just don't think he was flying no drugs in on that plane of his."

The two bouncers were weight-lifter types with shaved heads and black T-shirts with *Security* written across the front and their names above the chest pockets; one was named Mike, the other Tony. They recognized Jimbo, and Tony squared off with him in a fake boxing match for a few seconds.

"You working undercover tonight?" Mike asked.

"I'm tryin' to work my way under somebody's covers," Jimbo said. "Any likely candidates walked through tonight?"

"Always, man. If you can't find it at Shirley's, you just ain't lookin'."

"You been taking steroids, Mike?" Jimbo asked.

"Naw. Them steroids might pump your arms up, but I hear they shrink you up in some other places I'd just as soon not be shrinking."

They stamped the back of my hand with a little round rubber stamp and the red ink blurred immediately from the sweat. We stepped through this tunnel that led to the big dance hall.

"Them two back there, they're good boys," Jimbo said. "Do anything in the world for you."

When we opened the main doors, the music was so loud I could feel it, as if the sound waves were little puffs of air. Jimbo led the way toward a table at the front, set to the side so we wouldn't be in front of the big amplifiers. Before we got there he grabbed this waitress around the waist from behind and kissed her cheek and sort of buried his face in the side of her neck. When we got to the table, he pushed it against the wall.

"How's this?" he shouted at me over the music.

"Kind of hot in here."

The music stopped and the sudden quiet set my ears ringing. The band announced they were taking a short break.

"Check out that pair over there." He pointed with his head toward two hoochie-mamas sitting a couple of tables away from us. They had a Crown Royal bottle, still in the purple felt bag, set on their table. Both were blondes, but the source of the color was questionable, and both favored heavy makeup and vivid colors. It didn't appear to be their first time at Shirley's Country Music Palace.

"I better take that big one," Jimbo said. "I don't know if you could handle that much woman without pulling a muscle or something."

The waitress came with a clear glass pitcher and two mugs. Jimbo must have ordered them when he was nuzzling next to her ear; I never saw him order anything. He poured himself a beer with an inch of foamy head and, without a word, walked over to the table where the two blondes sat, leaving me and the pitcher alone at our table. The beer wasn't all that cold, but the room was stuffy, so it was cold enough. He talked to them for a few minutes before he waved for me to come over to their table.

"Are you really a private investigator?" one of the women asked. She was busty, I mean real busty, and wrapped tight in a white Spandex top. Had a pretty face and big red lips with just a slight overbite. The overbite was kind of cute. Neither of them had wedding rings, but Shirley's wasn't the kind of place you're likely to see any wedding rings, whether folks have got them or not.

"Yeah," I said, "I'm an investigator."

"Ol' Jimbo ain't lying to y'all," he said. "My man here's on an undercover case that's getting national headlines. He's one of the best in the whole country."

The busty woman smiled at me and sized me up with a quick once-over.

"Jack, this here's Darla," Jimbo said. "She's a big Harrison Ford fan."

"Do you really know him?" she asked.

"Of course he does," Jimbo said. "Jack here was Harrison's body double in that movie *What Lies Beneath*. You know what a body double is, don't you, honey? I'd say you'd be a pretty good one for Dolly Parton."

She giggled with obvious pride.

"My name is Lila," the other woman said. I could see that she was tall, even though she was seated. She had a narrow, well-shaped face, high cheeks and a strong jawline accented by the fact that she was chewing gum.

"Lila likes Harrison Ford, too," Jimbo said.

"What's he really like?" Darla asked.

"Well, I don't really know," I said.

"What Jack means is, ol' Harrison, he's kind of a private person," Jimbo said. "Hard to get to know much about him."

The band, which had been on a break, started up and Jimbo

practically pulled Lila out of her chair. He stood to the side as she led the way to the dance floor. Darla fell in behind her. Jimbo leaned his head in close to my ear.

"Work with me on this, son," he stage-whispered. "If the girl wants Harrison Ford, then by God, give her Harrison Ford."

I knew at that instant that Jimbo McInnis had that one element that will take you farther in the pursuit of poon than anything else. He wasn't overly handsome, wasn't polished a bit, obviously wasn't rich. But Jimbo had plenty of what it takes for success with women. He had a complete inability to be embarrassed, a total lack of shame.

Darla grabbed my hand and pulled me into the middle of a big crowd of dancers, lots of black cowboy hats and ostrich-skin boots. We danced a clumsy version of Western swing to a trio of old Bob Wills tunes from the fifties. For all that most of that young crowd knew, those songs could have been written last week. Jimbo wasn't a dancer, but he made up for it with enthusiasm and laughter and whoops and hollers. Lila and Darla were giggling and eating it up.

We sat back down at their table after the band's third number. We were hot and sweaty and thirsty. The waitress came by and announced that there was a special on Jose Cuervo Gold; everybody ordered a round of shooters, everybody except me. I've had some bad experiences with tequila.

"You girls live around here?" Jimbo asked.

"We live in Bayou La Batre," Darla said.

"Y'all know where Bayou La Batre is?" Lila asked.

"Honey," Jimbo said, "I practically grew up there. You go into the Catalina Restaurant and ask them if they know ol' Jimbo."

"Lila!" Darla said. "Look at who just walked in!"

"Oh, my God!" Lila said.

I recognized him from the tabloids and the TV. Scooter Haney himself. Lifted off the front page and reconstituted into human form and walking among us. A month earlier I wouldn't have noticed him in that crowd or any other, but Scooter had been singled out in my consciousness, and that of the whole country, by the supermarket tabloids. And it now seemed as if he glowed, as if some nimbus surrounded him, and the crowd parted to let him through.

Scooter wasn't a tall man—five-nine, maybe five-ten—but he was broad shouldered and thick necked and had the self-assured strut of a natural leader, an attitude of confidence and entitlement manifested in the way he moved, the almost imperceptible smirk when he looked over the room, taking measure of the place as if he were there to take over, that cockiness that takes some men to great heights not so much on any ability they may have but simply because they act without hesitation. Some would say without conscience.

"Y'all think he killed those people?" Darla asked.

"He just don't look like the type," Lila said.

"You're an investigator," Darla said. "You think he did?"

"We can't tell y'all anything about that case," Jimbo said. "We ain't supposed to be talking to civilians about it." He placed a touch of emphasis on the word *civilians.*

The two girls exchanged glances and Darla's mouth dropped open. "Y'all really do know something about it, don't you?"

"Can't talk about it," Jimbo said.

Darla looked at me in an appeal of Jimbo's pronouncement, but I just shook my head and backed him up. The waitress brought our drinks and Jimbo began staring at Scooter, making an obvious show of it, frowning, and putting on a steely-eyed glare that would have made Humphrey Bogart proud. Darla and Lila fell silent as they watched Jimbo with wide-eyed wonder and a touch of fear.

They had somehow stumbled into the middle of this murder case, the same murder case they had been reading about in the tabloids at the beauty shops and hearing about on *Hard Copy,* and you could see the excitement building in their faces. Jimbo tossed back a shot of Jose Cuervo, keeping his eyes on Haney the whole time, and began breathing through clenched teeth, looking as if he was ready to spring at Scooter. Darla started fidgeting like she was about to wet her pants.

"Uh, y'all excuse us for just a minute," Lila said. She popped up out of her chair and motioned for Darla to do the same. "We've gotta go to the little girls' room."

They walked off toward the back of the dance hall, their boot heels clicking, giggling and whispering to each other and looking over at Scooter. Jimbo held his Bogart pose until they blended into the crowd and we lost sight of them.

"What in the world are you getting us into?" I asked.

"A little late-night trip to Bayou La Batre," he said, "and maybe a little breakfast in bed tomorrow morning. Man, the women just love this private eye stuff, don't they? You gotta get me into it."

"What are you going to tell them when they get back?"

"I'll have to play it by ear. You just keep acting like the strong, silent type and ol' Jimbo'll do all the talking."

"*Acting* like the silent type? The reason I'm not talking is because I don't have any idea what you want me to say."

"You're doing just fine, son."

I killed what was left of my beer and leaned back in my chair. I poured myself the last of the pitcher, and this calm came over me for the first time since I found that bomb, and I decided to kick back and let Jimbo take me on this ride. I started looking around for the waitress and noticed that Scooter was walking in our direction. He got a little closer and I realized that he was headed toward our table.

"Look who's coming," I said.

"Good thing the girls went to the bathroom. Darla woulda peed all over herself."

"Jimbo! My main man!" Scooter broke into a big smile and slapped his hand into Jimbo's for one of those arm-wrestling contests that pass for handshakes at a deer camp or a golf course.

"Scooter, I want you to meet this friend of mine. This is Jack Delmas from over at Bay St. Louis."

The man had a crunching grip; he had done some outdoor work sometime in his life. "I go over to Bay St. Louis pretty often," he said. "We play the Diamondhead course about once a year."

"Been reading about you, Scooter," Jimbo said.

"Don't believe everything you read."

"You here by yourself?" Jimbo asked.

"Was when I walked in. But I ain't no more."

"I would ask you to join us," Jimbo said, "but Jack and me, we're working on a little project right now."

"So I saw. I was just on my way out and thought I'd say hi. Let me know if I can do anything for you." He pointed his finger at Jimbo as if it were a pistol and winked at him. He turned and walked back to where this tall redhead in tight jeans was standing, purse in hand, next to the service bar across the room. Scooter stuck out his arm and she took it and they walked toward the door. Most of the people in the place had stopped what they were doing and watched the couple in awe, the way medieval peasants must have watched the king's carriage as it passed through the village.

"You didn't tell me you knew Scooter Haney," I said.

"You didn't ask. Everybody down here knows him. He's been a regular at every bar in Mobile for the past twenty years. I knew him before he got rich. He ain't changed a whole lot. I kinda admire that."

"I'm not telling you how to run your business," I said. "But he's a prime suspect in a murder case your department is—or was—investigating."

"So?"

"So you think you ought to be socializing with him?"

The waitress came with a fresh pitcher. If Jimbo was ordering these things, I sure wasn't seeing it. He poured himself a glass, took a big gulp, and belched.

"I know some things about this case you wouldn't have no way of knowing," he said. "Let me tell you this. Scooter Haney didn't kill nobody in that beach house or nowhere else. He ain't got it in

him. He don't get into fights like he used to. He's more into lovin'
nowadays. You ever heard the saying 'So many women, so little
time'? Well, that's Scooter's motto."

"But what about that threat he made to Kellie Lee on the telephone?"

"It's a fake, son. It probably did come from Kellie Lee's answering machine. But somebody spliced it together. We knew the second we heard it that it was bogus. But them TV folks, they got a
copy of it, and they're in such a feeding frenzy right now they
didn't check it out too good."

"Where'd y'all get this tape?"

"Kellie Lee's daddy," Jimbo said. "He's the one who put it
together, sure as I'm sittin' here. He's this old sorry two-bit con
artist who walked out on Kellie Lee's mama twenty years ago. I
guarantee you he's trying to work up a wrongful death suit against
Scooter. Probably got the idea from that O. J. Simpson lawsuit. He
wouldn't have enough sense to think it up hisself."

"But you still don't know that Scooter didn't do it."

Jimbo chugged down the rest of the glass and wiped his mouth
with the back of his hand. "One time when I had just moved down
here, a bunch of us went to the Dauphin Island Fishing Rodeo.
Scooter was there. Now, you can't believe how many people come
to that thing. I'm talking maybe twenty thousand people walking
around where the weigh-in station is. And it was hot, let me tell
you. Well, we're over at the pier looking at this tarpon somebody
had landed when we hear these tires squeal out at the street and
there's this thud. Somebody had hit a stray dog.

"Poor old thing had a broke leg and was scared to death.
Limped up under this cabin and was just whimpering and crying.
It was enough to break your heart. Well, Scooter climbs up under
there and picks it up. The dog was bleeding all over him and
ruined this brand-new Izod shirt he was wearing. And don't you
know he puts the dog in his car and takes it all the way into Mobile
to the vet. He's probably still got that dog."

Across the room, Lila and Darla were making their way back toward us. Darla had put on a fresh coat of lipstick.

"A man who'd do that," Jimbo said as he stood, "you think he'd murder four people?"

"Sorry we took so long," Darla said. "That place was so crowded you wouldn't believe it."

"Where'd Scooter Haney go?" Lila asked.

"He left right after y'all walked off. I don't think he felt all that comfortable in here."

"Does he know you two are on the case?" Lila asked.

"All I can say is when he saw us, he didn't hang around very long."

Darla scooted her chair close to me and pressed her thigh against the side of my leg. The girl was beginning to give off heat. "I'll bet you get a lot of good cases, don't you?"

"Why don't we get away from all these people and go somewhere quiet and talk about them," Jimbo said. "Some of this stuff we don't need to be telling to the whole world. You girls can keep a secret, can't you?"

Darla reached for my hand and gave it a light squeeze. "I won't tell." She had the softest little voice.

"We'd need to tell Mike and Tony something before we leave," Lila said to Darla.

"Mike and Tony?" Jimbo asked. "You mean the Mike and Tony out at the front door?"

"Just tell them you're not feeling good," Darla said. "We can see them again anytime."

Jimbo slapped his hand against his side pocket. "Uh-oh, Jack. I think the call just came in. I gotta get to the phone." He stood and walked toward the front of the hall in a big hurry.

"What call's he talking about?" Lila asked.

"I'd like to tell you," I said. "But I really can't."

We sat and listened to the band as Darla rubbed my hand in both of hers and gazed at me with her big gray eyes, her ample chest rising and falling in a steady, quick rhythm. She had a permanent, slight part to her lips. Jimbo came back toward us across the dance floor, almost trotting.

"We gotta go, Jack."

"Was it an important call?" Lila asked.

Jimbo frowned and nodded his head. He poured another shot of Jose Cuervo and knocked it back. He made a face as he swallowed and opened and closed his eyes real hard three times. Then he smiled with his lips closed and squinted at Lila, his eyes mere slits, Clint Eastwood style.

"Can't we go with you?" Darla asked.

"Yeah," I said. "Can't they go with us?"

"I'm afraid not. Too dangerous."

"Oh, *no!*" Darla looked like she was about to cry.

"Are you sure we've got to go?" I asked.

"We need to get moving."

When I stood, Darla was still holding my hand. "Y'all be careful. Please."

"I'm sorry we gotta run like this," Jimbo said. "We'll tell you all about it next time."

As we rushed across the big floor, the girls sat waving at us, Darla's white, rounded Spandex top glowing under the purple lights from the bandstand. Jimbo had this grin, the same tight-lipped smile that came on right after that last shot of tequila.

"What in the world did you just do?" I said as we walked across the parking lot to the truck. "I had thought up enough stories to keep those two entertained for the next month."

"Mike and Tony, those two bouncers, were going to meet them later on."

"But those girls wanted to go with *us*. Especially Darla."

"You can call her some other time."

"But I don't know her last name."

"I can find it for you. Don't worry about it."

He started the truck and raced the engine twice before popping the clutch and squealing out of the parking lot.

"Are you okay?" I asked.

"Let's go have us some fun!"

We launched onto the interstate from the entrance ramp like an F-14 catapulted from a flight deck. Jimbo stuck a Lynard Skynard CD in and turned up "Sweet Home Alabama" to window-rattling pitch as we raced down I-10 toward Mobile, blowing past everything else on the road until we got to the Dauphin Island exit.

"You up for some more pool?" The wind whipping through the open windows was so loud he was almost shouting.

"Pool? I just left a Dolly Parton look-alike who was rubbing up against my leg, and I did it for a game of eight ball?"

"I'll get you her phone number, no problem. You can pick up right where you left off. You wanna play pool or not?"

We took the next corner with two wheels almost leaving the ground, the jacked-up cab of the truck leaning enough to press me against the door. Got onto this two-laned road running through low marshy country, thin stands of skinny pines stretching out to either side and cattails in the ditches, and rode it for miles. There was a constant rising and falling of the buzz of locusts and a rotten-egg smell from exposed mud where narrow bridges spanned the bogs and bayous.

The place we finally turned in to didn't have any name that I could see. A streetlight on a pole in the parking light cast enough light for me to see on the front outside wall this rectangular patch where the yellow paint on the cinder blocks was a little brighter and less sun faded. A sign or board, probably bearing the name of the place, had been there until recently. Kids like to steal things like that to use as wall decorations. Along the roofline a long strand of Christmas-tree lights blinked red and green and blue.

The parking lot, a shell-covered and rutted patch of hard-packed sand, was covered with puddles of milky, standing rainwater. To the rear of the place and beyond the parking lot there was low, marshy ground thick with bull rushes and palmettos, the kind of muck favored by cottonmouths and alligators. This marsh circled the parking lot like a moat, stretching out fifty yards in all directions. Beyond this marsh were sparse stands of skinny pines on what looked like semi-solid ground. We stepped out of the truck and the smell of salt water was strong in the breeze.

"Smells like the beach," I said.

"That's because it's right there through them pines," he said, pointing past the back of the building. "We ain't but about three foot above sea level here."

Through the trees, I caught a glimpse of moonlight shimmering on the Gulf, and when I stood still I could hear the steady lapping of waves through the constant whirring of insects.

"You ready for some fun?" he said.

"I was ready for that back at Shirley's."

He stepped back to the driver's side door and re-opened it. The truck was jacked up so high that the door was at waist level. He reached to the floorboard under his seat and came up with a bottle of Jim Beam. "You ever read any Ernest Hemingway?"

"What?"

"Hemingway. He wrote *For Whom the Bell Tolls* and a bunch of other books."

"I know who he was."

"Back at State, I took this English course. First time I'd ever read all that much except for newspapers and stuff. This professor, he really liked Hemingway. So I got started reading some of his stuff and got to where I liked it. But the thing I liked best about Hemingway was not so much his books; it was the man hisself, his own real life."

"Has this got anything to do with Darla? 'Cause right now, I'm having a hard time getting past that."

"Hemingway, he was a lot like me. Liked to fight, liked to drink, liked women. Liked to do stuff just for the hell of it. But he had something I didn't have. He had this code he come up with." Jimbo twisted the top off the bottle of whiskey and held it out to me. I shook my head. One of us was going to have to drive home. He turned it up and took a swig. "It hit me one day that I needed me a code. Far as I can tell, that's what separates the good guys from the bad guys. So I come up with one. Got it written down back at the house."

I sat on the back bumper, resting my hands on my knees. A bullfrog started its deep croaking over in the marsh a few feet away. I wondered what Darla and Lila were doing. Jimbo twisted the top back onto the bottle.

"One thing I put in the code," he said, "is that I don't never snake another man's woman."

"Snake?"

"Steal her away. She goes out with some man, she stays out with him for that night. Lila and Darla, they were supposed to meet Tony and Mike and go out to a movie. That's what Mike told me. Now, he did say that him and Darla, they ain't all that serious or nothing. But, still, they did have a date later on."

A damned code. An Ernest-by-God-Hemingway code. I would have never dreamed it, not from Jimbo McInnis of Waynesboro, Mississippi. You just never know.

"Can you handle yourself all right?" he asked.

"Usually."

"Good." He unbuttoned his shirt, took it off, and tossed it on the seat. Beneath it he was wearing a Mississippi State T-shirt with a bulldog face on it, its tongue hanging out the side of its mouth. The slogan "Dawg Pound Rock" was emblazoned beneath the dog. "What do you think?"

"Elegant understatement," I said. "I didn't realize the new J. Crew catalog had come out."

"J what?"

"Never mind. The shirt looks just fine."

"You don't have on no Ole Miss shirt underneath, do you?"

"I'm afraid not."

"Well, this oughta be enough to do the trick."

"The trick?" I asked.

"A private eye, he got to know karate and stuff like that?"

"What are we about to get into?"

"We gonna rock and roll a little. I noticed you ain't drinking much." He flipped me the truck keys and we walked across the lot, the gravel and oyster shells grinding beneath our feet.

The trucks parked beside the honky-tonk were working trucks, fishermen's trucks, not like the show trucks back at Shirley's. In the beds of these pickups there were cast nets and trawl boards and chicken-wire crab traps. The bumpers and fenders were scratched and dented, and the paint was for the most part faded. One truck had a tag on the front bumper supporting the Hurricanes, the high school team out of Bayou La Batre. There was one Camaro, recently sanded down and unpainted except for a flat coat of red-orange primer. It had extra-wide back tires and a big, black number 3 decal—the number was slanted to the left—in the center of the rear windshield. Dale Earnhart's number, God rest his soul. The only other car in the lot, a champagne-colored Crown Victoria, seemed out of place because it was new and clean and free of decals or bumper stickers. At the far end of the building, the end opposite the front door, right up against the building, was a dark green Plymouth Barracuda I had earlier seen around the island. It belonged to the local bookie.

"They used to keep the riffraff outta this place," Jimbo said, pointing at the Barracuda. "They keep lettin' the lowlifes in and they're gonna lose their four-star rating."

The tonk was dark inside with a low ceiling, a concrete floor, and cheap paneling on the walls. There was the customary array of lighted beer signs and posters. The bar was to our right, a rough-cut, homemade counter with a top made of varnished plywood, stained by years' worth of spilled drinks and spotted with burn marks, two to five inches in length, made by a hundred cigarettes laid on the surface. The woman behind it was a high-mileage model with jet black hair teased up high and eyebrows that looked as if she'd painted them with a Magic Marker. She had a cigarette stuck in the corner of her mouth as she drew a couple of draft beers into clear, heavy mugs. Behind the bar, taped to the rear wall, was a sign that read IF YOU WANT TO ARGUE, GO TO LAW SCHOOL—IF YOU WANT TO FIGHT, GO JOIN THE DAMN MARINES! Other wall decorations included an Alabama football schedule, an Auburn War Eagle flag, and a faded poster of Bear Bryant wearing a plaid sports coat and his famous checked hat. He was walking across the calm surface of a pond.

We stepped to the bar and Jimbo ordered a setup for himself and a draft for me. At the far end of the bar, I caught Bobby Earl Fair, the owner of the Barracuda, looking at us. He was on the other side of this guy who was wearing dirty blue jeans and white rubber shrimper boots. Bobby Earl kept peeking around the guy to watch Jimbo. He and the guy in the shrimper boots seemed to be examining a sheet of paper laid out on the bar.

"Looks like Bobby Earl's set up shop," I said.

Jimbo set his bottle on the bar, raised up on his stool, and looked over the top of the shrimper. "You know him other than by sight?"

"He got in my face the second day I was here and told me to quit going around the island asking questions."

"What did you say?"

"I told him he had a smart mouth and that he was ugly. Then a few days after that, I saw him taking bets at the Pelican Pub. I understand Jason Summers used to bet pretty heavy with him."

"Yeah. Bobby Earl's a suspect all right. Far as I'm concerned, he's one of the front-runners. Course, they ain't asking my opinion these days. You know I said how Scooter, he wouldn't kill nobody? Well, that scumbag down there, I wouldn't put nothing past him. And that white-trash group he's tied in with is worse than he is."

"You think they could have planted that bomb on my porch?"

"About half of them are anti-government types who study that shit on the Internet day and night. Timothy McVeigh didn't have nothing on the White Resistance. Hell, McVeigh might have even been a member. Yeah, they coulda planted a bomb."

The shrimper sitting beside Bobby Earl had never looked around. He reached into his pocket and pulled out a wad of bills and laid them on the bar. Jimbo turned his face toward me and acted like he wasn't interested in what Bobby Earl and the shrimper were doing.

"You see that sheet of paper in front of those guys down the bar?" he said. "Let me know when Bobby Earl touches it."

"Are you planning on doing something in here? You think it's a good idea to try to roust a suspect when you've been shooting tequila?"

"I'll let those tight-asses with the Alabama Bureau of Investigation worry about stuff like that. You in for some fun or not?"

Bobby Earl smoothed out the wadded bills and put them into a stack. He put the stack on the sheet of paper, pressed his forefinger down on it, and pulled it toward him across the bar. The shrimper pointed to something written on the paper and Bobby Earl started shaking his head.

"He just touched the betting sheet," I said.

Jimbo sprang off the stool. In two quick strides he was at the other end of the bar. He stabbed the bar with this Buck knife that came out of nowhere and impaled both the betting sheet and the stack of money. He pushed aside the shrimper and I broke the guy's fall as he stumbled backward. Jimbo grabbed Bobby Earl's wrist and put him in a half-Nelson so quickly I completely missed the move.

"How many times I gotta tell you gambling's against the law in Alabama?"

"Turn me a-loose, Jimbo!" Bobby Earl shouted. "I got witnesses here!"

"And I got me some evidence here. Right here on the bar."

"Hey!" the woman shouted. "Y'all read that sign back there!"

"Now, just take it easy," Jimbo said. "We'll be through here in a minute."

"Aw, come on, Jimbo," the shrimper said. "Don't take my money."

"You just sit your ass over there in that chair by the pool table. And don't you go nowhere until I tell you to."

"When did the sheriff's department start giving a shit about gambling, anyhow?" the woman said.

"When these unsavory elements started moving in."

Jimbo walked Bobby Earl over to the wall and pushed his chest against it. He ordered him to put his hands against it and gave him a quick pat-down. I kept an eye on the shrimper and the money and spread sheet stuck to the bar. The shrimper kept shaking his head and drawing in big breaths and blowing them out, completely disgusted by the whole deal.

Three kids who had been at the pool table eased toward the door a step or two at a time in an effort to go unnoticed. When they got close enough and had a clear shot at the door, they broke for it. Everybody else sat frozen where they were, watching the unfolding action to see if it was going to spread.

"All right, Bobby Earl," Jimbo said as he let go and stepped back three paces, "get the hell outta my sight."

Bobby Earl hitched his belt and tucked his shirt back in his pants. "You ain't got no right to be rousting me."

"The hell I don't! I heard about that threat you made the other day at the Sea House. You want a piece of me, you know where to find me. I better not ever hear no more about you saying out in public how you gonna try to whip my ass."

Bobby Earl gave him a venomous look. The muscles in his jaw were working so hard I could see them rippling even from where I stood at the bar. He looked at me and curled his lip and snorted before swaggering out the door at a deliberately slow pace.

"You think you ought to be rubbing his face in it?" I asked. "He looks like he'd take a sniper shot at you in a second if he ever catches you out on one of these backroads."

"Not at me, son. That White Resistance group that's done set

Bobby Earl up with this territory, they all got felony records. They damn sure ain't gonna pop a cap at some deputy, not just because one of their bookies got rousted. That spells death penalty." He turned to me with that slit-eyed smile. "But you ain't no deputy. You might oughta watch your backside for a while." He looked around the room, which had become as quiet and still as a wake. "Show's over, folks!" Jimbo shouted. "It's time to party!"

"Come on, Jimbo," the shrimper said. "Give me my money back, man. It took me all night dragging them nets to make that."

"I still don't know why all of a sudden the sheriff cares about a little gambling," the woman said.

"Let me have one of them little garbage bags," Jimbo said.

"You done run all my customers off."

He pulled the knife out of the bar and picked up the betting sheet, taking pains to avoid the corner Bobby Earl had touched. He dropped it in the white plastic garbage bag and pulled the twist tie closed. Then he folded the whole thing and stuck it in his back pocket.

"You still want a beer?" the woman asked me. "Least y'all can do after running my customers off is buy a beer."

"Come here, Tee Jay," Jimbo said to the shrimper. "Here's your money. You ought to thank me for saving you from throwing it away. I saw on that sheet where you had picked Mississippi State to get beat. Hey, give this man here a beer on me."

The shrimper smiled and the woman handed him a can of Busch. He asked her for change for the Alabama Redemption machine. The front door opened and four guys in jeans came in shouting and laughing, a loud bunch, already drunk. That seemed to lift the woman's spirits some.

"I don't know if they can lift Bobby Earl's prints off this betting sheet or not," Jimbo said. "They claim they can, but it don't seem to me like you could do something like that. Anyhow, I got a buddy who can match them up with the ones they say they took off that envelope they found at your place."

"Are you telling me they have prints from that letter bomb?"

"Some. But they probably ain't the bomber's prints. They might just be from some clerk at the store where he bought the envelope. But who knows. Sometimes criminals slip up."

"So why is Bobby Earl a suspect?"

"He was Jason's bookie, and you never know how deep in hock Jason might have been in to him."

"You believe that's what happened?"

"It's believable," he said. "Especially when you consider that Bobby Earl Fair is a friggin' psychopath and I think he's already been in on one killing since he took over the bookmaking operations in Mobile County. You remember reading about this car salesman who was at a red light in Theodore and this car pulls up beside him and unloads two barrels of number-four shot into the side of his face? We can't prove nothin', but that guy was in to the tune of two grand to Bobby Earl."

"They killed a man over a measly two thousand dollars?"

"It's a new bunch who moved in since the old bookie retired. They don't know how to handle it. I believe they outted somebody over two grand, and sometimes Jason would lay more than that on just one game."

Over at the pool table, one of the guys who had just walked in lined up to break. He got under it with his cue stick and the ball went airborne and bounced off the bumper and onto the floor. He yelled "Shit!" real loud and popped the door of the ladies' bathroom with his fist. All his buddies laughed and hooted.

"Told you this was a fun place," Jimbo said. "Why don't you go over to that pool table and lay a quarter on the bumper?"

"I'm out of practice. I don't know how good I'll play."

"When was the last time you broke and missed the whole damn table?"

We sat at the bar, stools turned around and elbows propped on the edge, so we could stretch out while we watched. Two couples walked in and sat at a booth along the wall. The barmaid stepped around the bar and went to take their orders. The game we were waiting on took forever. These guys were really bad, or drunk, or, more likely, both.

Jimbo traded in his almost-full bottle of Jack Daniel's to the barmaid in exchange for two shriveled-up limes, a half-full bottle of some off-brand tequila with a miniature sombrero attached to the neck, and the free use of a salt shaker. I asked Jimbo about possible state regulations against bar patrons trading in already-opened bottles of liquor. He pointed out, with some accuracy, that this wasn't exactly the Court of Two Sisters we were sitting in.

Jimbo quartered one of the limes while we waited for the pool match to end. He licked the fleshy part of his hand where the thumb and forefinger join and sprinkled it with salt. Then he licked the salt, took a swig of tequila out of the bottle, and bit down on the wedge of lime in a smooth three-step operation. That droopy-eyed, tight-lipped smile crept back up his face.

Over at the pool table, the winners gave each other the high five and the losers bought another round. They all chugged the remainder of the beers they already had to make room for the new ones.

"Who's next?" one of the winners shouted.

"You ready?" Jimbo said.

"We're just playing pool, right?"

"Lighten up, man."

We grabbed two sticks out of the rack up on the wall, didn't even sight down them to see if they were crooked. Jimbo set his tequila bottle on a nearby table, and we flipped a quarter to determine which team got to break. The game was eight ball. They won the toss, and their break was truly bad. The two we were playing against both worked as roofers and both had been out in the sun all day. They smelled like it. Not a strong odor, but the smell of stale sweat dried into their shirts and pants, the scent of the working man. They had light sunburns, their hands were rough and dirt stained, and one of them had a ponytail. The other one could have also put his hair into a ponytail if only he had a rubber band.

Jimbo lined up the four ball, a gimme shot straight at the side pocket. He hit it just a little to the side and it rattled against both sides of the hole before dropping in. He left himself a tough shot, the six in the corner. He had to run it down the edge of the table, but it hit a little hard and bounced away from the edge. It rolled to a spot six inches out from the pocket.

The two roofers high-fived each other. "Too bad, bulldog," one of them said. He then sank the eleven on a show-off shot, an extra-hard pop that slammed the ball into the pocket. But he left himself in terrible shape when it ricocheted back to the middle of the table. He missed the next shot.

"Your shot, bulldog."

From back at the bar where the two others were seated came a loud, "Roll, Tide!" Jimbo's smile got a little bigger as he winked at me. These were some serious Alabama football fans, and that's a group that doesn't take kindly to criticism of the Crimson Tide or of anything remotely associated with the program, especially when they've been drinking.

Jimbo bent over the table and laid his face almost down on the felt as he lined up his next shot. He made it, and walked around the corner of the table to where the cue ball had come to rest. As he walked in front of me, he whispered to me, "You ready to rock and roll?"

"Not over a football game," I said.

He cleared his throat and looked at me. His smile looked just like Stan Laurel's of the old Laurel and Hardy comedy team. "You guys must be Alabama fans."

"Roll, Tide," the guy with the ponytail said.

"What they got this year?" Jimbo studied two possible shots and decided on the comeback carom to the side. "Besides probation, I mean."

"Well, they gonna kick Mississippi State's ass," this roofer up at the bar shouted. I didn't realize our voices were carrying so well that the guys at the bar could hear us.

"That so?" Jimbo pointed in my direction. "What they gonna do against Ole Miss?"

All four of them laughed to make it clear they didn't think the prospect of Ole Miss beating Alabama was worth serious discussion. I thought the Rebels were going to be pretty good, and we were playing Bama in Oxford that year. But I didn't say anything. Football talk in a strange bar, especially in Alabama, can get real tricky, real fast. I had the feeling Jimbo was trying to start a war here.

"Well, I think you boys are in for a surprise this year." Jimbo hit the ball with a soft touch and it banked off the opposite bumper right into the side pocket in front of him. "Because I been studying the situation real close. And you know what? Bama sucks."

Oh, God, I thought. This is not good. Not in some honky-tonk in the middle of a swamp in Alabama. I swear, I could feel the barometric pressure going up. The two other roofers at the bar got up and eased toward us. I backed up a little to make sure nobody was behind me.

"Jimbo!" the woman warned. "You better read that sign again!"

"Can't I give a simple opinion about something?"

"Hey!" one of the pool players said. "Bama *rules,* man!"

"They used to," Jimbo said. "But they're going down. They living on reputation. I noticed they had to drop Louisiana Tech off the schedule 'cause they couldn't beat 'em."

The woman behind the bar, no doubt an expert at spotting storm clouds, picked up a telephone and started dialing some familiar number. Since the pool game started, a fairly good crowd had come in, mostly kids. There were two tables of them on what was sometimes a dance floor. They were drinking pitchers of beer and eating popcorn. Jimbo missed the next shot.

"It's all yours," he said to the nearest roofer.

All four of them were now lined up at the pool table eyeing Jimbo. They tried to look grim. But their eyes showed that they were anything but angry; they were excited. And I knew then we were in for one hell of a fight. These guys had spotted their chance to make this a south Mobile County evening to remember. We were just playing out the same old familiar scripted play to its inevitable conclusion, which is a knock-down, drag-out brawl. I could delay it, but I damn sure wasn't going to be able to stop it.

The one closest to me stepped over beside me, keeping his eyes on Jimbo the whole time. "You better tell your friend to watch his mouth."

I shrugged. Jimbo knocked back another shot of tequila; didn't even bother with the lime. I stepped around the table and walked toward him, making sure I kept the four roofers in front of me.

"Your shot," Jimbo said to them.

"I think they're taking your remarks personally," I whispered.

"I mean for them to. We need to liven this party up some."

"Why don't we just go home? I think the barmaid has already called the sheriff for backups."

"Man, you are no fun at all."

"Let's just let it go," I said. "That tequila's started talking."

None of the four roofers was stepping away from the table. "At least Bama's *got* a reputation," one of them said.

"You're absolutely right," I said. "Alabama is a great team. They'll probably win the national championship. Let's play pool."

"Yeah, and Ole Miss sucks, too."

"Let's just let it drop," I said. But I'd taken just about enough from that guy. You don't talk like that about another man's team.

One of the roofers stepped to the table to take a shot, but he kept his eyes on Jimbo and me. And so did his three companions. The music stopped and I thought I could hear a faint, high-pitched, undulating sound coming from outside the building, far away through the woods. The barmaid kept glaring at us. Everybody else in the place, the two married couples and the kids with the pitchers, were unaware of any tension.

The guy naturally missed the shot, and I stepped up to survey the table. "Table seems to lean to this side a little, doesn't it?"

"You talk about Louisiana Tech," a roofer said. "How about Alabama beatin' the shit outta Florida?"

"Yeah," another one said. "Twice!"

I sank the six ball and stepped back around the table. "Why don't I buy you guys a pitcher?"

"How many national championships has State won?"

Jimbo chuckled and started nodding his head as he walked over to where they stood. He was half a head taller than the biggest of them, but they were a tough-looking bunch. He licked his lips and smiled. His eyes were glazed and almost closed.

"You know," he said. "You guys are right. I shouldn't be talking bad about the Crimson Tide. So I ain't gonna say another word about 'em."

Outside the faint wailing sound I had earlier heard was growing louder. Sirens. Sounded like more than one.

"You hear that, Jimbo?" I said.

He glanced back at me over his shoulder and held up his hand in the okay sign. "So let's play pool, and y'all forget I ever said anything."

I leaned over to see the angle on the eight ball to win. Looked like the best shot was in the far corner. The cops had made it to the parking lot and killed their sirens. The barmaid let out a big breath, stepped around from behind the bar, and rushed toward the front door to let them in and show them who the troublemakers were.

"Yeah," Jimbo said. "I take back what I said about the Tide."

"Corner pocket." I pointed with the stick and lined up the shot.

"But what pisses me off is that ugly-assed checked hat the Bear always wore." He pointed to the picture of Coach Bryant that was hanging behind the bar. "I mean, what French Quarter queer joint you reckon he was cruising when he found *that* piece of shit?"

The guy with the ponytail threw the first punch. Caught Jimbo square on the jaw. Didn't even knock that wide, thin smile off. In fact, it grew bigger.

Jimbo counter-punched, a blind, instinctive return swing. Hit the breastbone of the ponytailed guy and staggered him. The long-hair beside him didn't realize what had happened before Jimbo's second punch caught him at the hinge of the jaw. It dropped him like he had fallen out of his bed.

I had been stretched over the table aiming for the eight ball when that first swing came. And it came so fast that I was still in that same position when I saw this cue stick whipping down at me. I rolled to the side. It barely missed. Smacked against the table and broke in half.

About the time that cue stick snapped, the deputies hit the front door and the barmaid screamed. It was a painful wail, a realization that she had not quite made it, hadn't called for the cops soon enough. The couples at the table were standing, one wife holding her husband by his arm to keep him from jumping into the fight and the other wife pinning hers against the wall to do the same thing.

I hit the floor and rolled under the table to the other side in case another pool stick was coming. I crashed into the table of kids, knocking it over, setting off screams and shouts and shattering a pitcher of beer.

The two cops raced to the middle of the fight, pulling people apart only to have them jump right back in. The cops were having a hell of a time trying to figure out who was on what side. The barmaid stood behind the bar, her eyes as big as Ping-Pong balls, gripping a full-sized Louisville Slugger in front of her, pointing it straight up.

One of the roofers was struggling to get up off of the floor. He kept slipping on a wet spot. This other guy picked up a chair and came running at me holding it over his head. I grabbed his forearm, fell to one knee, and flipped him forward. The momentum of his run launched him and the chair skyward. He hit the floor on his side, and the chair cracked when it hit the wall.

I popped up looking for Jimbo. He stood like the biggest kid on the block in a game of King of the Hill, tossing grown men around like so many sacks of feed. He ducked this roundhouse punch by one of the roofers, a punch thrown with so much force it spun the guy around like a top. He landed in Jimbo's arms. Jimbo grabbed the guy under the armpits from behind. He spotted a deputy coming at him and threw the roofer like a medicine ball straight into the approaching lawman and knocked them both to the floor.

The barmaid kept stepping from the back of the bar around to the front, the bat held in front of her like a parade rifle in the Present Arms position. She kept looking for an opening to get into the scrap, but talked herself out of it each time.

One of the kids at the knocked-over table, a big, soft kid with the beginnings of a beer gut, jumped in between one of his friends and that same roofer who had tried to hit me with the pool stick. He got popped in the nose for his troubles. The blood started gushing and a girl who was with him screamed and started swinging at the roofer with her purse.

The smell of spilled beer was strong, and the floor was sticky. One of the cops crouched low to make a run at Jimbo, but when he made his move, his foot slipped and he hit the floor. He rolled over on his side holding his shoulder and reaching for his radio.

The girl swinging the purse was really pissed. She started cussing in this shrill voice and kicking anybody she could in the shin. I tried to get to Jimbo, but somebody grabbed my shoulder from behind and spun me around. It was the ponytailed guy. The fool tried to hold me in place as he cocked back his fist, like I was going to sit still for him to plant his fist into my face or something. He came forward with his fist aimed at my nose. I ducked and it grazed me right at the eye socket. I planted an uppercut into his rib cage. The air blasted out of his lungs. I hopped to the side and let him hit the floor. My eye watered and I wiped it with the back of my hand as I scooted to Jimbo's side. I grabbed him at the arm, staying low to avoid one of his wild swings.

"Let's go!" I shouted as I pointed to the cop on the floor. "He's calling for backups!"

"I saw you flip that guy. Damn, you're pretty good."

"Hey, man, let's do the play-by-play later. We gotta get out of here."

I dragged him toward the door. The fight had taken on a life of its own by this time. The cop on the floor had managed to rise to one knee. He was talking into the radio and holding his shoulder, rubbing it round and round. The other cop was pinning one of the roofers against the wall, trying to slap some cuffs on him.

I got in front of Jimbo and shoved him toward the rear door, sliding him like I was pushing against a blocking sled at football practice. He kept looking over my head at the panoramic battle that had spread throughout the room, admiring it as if it were some wall-sized mural in the Louvre.

"Move, Jimbo!"

"I'm going, I'm going." He spotted the bottle of tequila, still intact on the table where he had set it. He grabbed it as I pushed him past it.

"They're about to run everybody in," I said. "I don't want to wake up in the jailhouse."

"Look at that little gal swinging that purse, would you. She ain't no bigger'n a minute."

I pushed him back into the emergency bar on the door and it popped open. We fell forward to the quiet of the shell-covered parking lot. I shut the door behind us. The frogs in the mud and bogs and bulrushes all around us had set up a contrapuntal series of croaks and bellows. Lightning bugs twinkled among the skinny, straight pines. The wind whistled through the high needles and the air was a blend of brine from the nearby gulf and a sweet, clean fragrance of pine.

There was a cracked and dried-out two-by-six plank propped against the rear wall. I grabbed it and wedged one end against the door handle and stomped the other end into the sand with the heel of my shoe.

We ran to the pickup. A whine of far-off sirens rose, like a

mosquito flying close to my ear. We climbed in. I had trouble finding the right key to start the truck. Jimbo calmly unscrewed the
top off the bottle of tequila. The cop with the hurt shoulder
appeared at the corner of the building and fumbled for his service
revolver as I started the engine.

"That way!" Jimbo shouted. "Right through there!"

"That's a damn swamp!"

"Stop!" the cop yelled.

"What are you doing, man?" Jimbo said as he reached over and
flipped the headlights off. "Don't turn the lights on!"

"We can't go through there!"

"Stomp on it, son!"

I mashed the accelerator to the floor. The big F-150 roared and
lifted as if about to leave the ground. The tires spun and kicked up
a cloud of sand and bits of oyster shell that rattled against the
floorboard at our feet. We raced toward the swamp under the light
of a strong moon, across the white glow of the shells. Jimbo
reached under the seat and pulled out this big cowbell. It had an
eighteen-inch length of lead pipe welded to the handle. The whole
thing had been painted white, and there was a Mississippi State
Bulldogs decal plastered on its side. It looked like a heavy-duty,
oversized version of what a Bavarian bell choir would use, or as
much like that as a cowbell can look. He rolled down his window
and started swinging the thing with all his might as we left the
solid ground and launched into the swamp like Thelma and
Louise did at the end of that movie.

CLANG-A-LANG-A-LANG-A-LANG-A-LANG-A!!!

The nose of the truck splatted into the bog and the tires sank
into the mushy, dark mud. But the four-wheel drive kicked in and
we churned through the black, smelly ooze with all four wheels
spinning faster than we were actually going, like riverboat paddle-
wheels on calm water. As we bounced from mudhole to mudhole,
the windshield got splattered with the tar-like globs and the light
of the moon that had been guiding us got blocked out as we

entered the canopy of the pines. I flipped on the overhead KC searchlights and turned the wipers on high, but that only smeared the mud, so I stuck my head out the side window and tried to weave through the spindly trees as the ringing of the cowbell echoed through the woods.

"You can slow down now," Jimbo said when we got a hundred feet into the swamp. "They can't come after us in this quicksand." He reached over and hit the wiper fluid switch and the spread of mud began clearing, but it smelled as if we had been low-riding in some sewage lagoon.

"I assume there's solid ground somewhere on the other side of this," I said.

"Trust me, son. Head toward that clearing over there."

"Jimbo, those stumps are going to take off our oil pan."

He turned and looked out the rear window. Another patrol car had pulled into the parking lot, its light bar sending blue-and-white pulses through the swamp.

"You realize that those deputies know who you are," I said.

"That's the reason we're staying at your place tonight."

"We?"

"Well," he said, "you are planning to stay there, ain't you?"

We reached the clearing and climbed onto solid ground. The tires gripped the firm dirt and I slowed down and he pointed me through this field, which was somebody's cow pasture. There were dried-out cowpies, some as big as antbeds, scattered around and we squashed a few of them. That further added to the truck's ambiance.

"Jack, this stuff tonight, if some report gets filed and it mentions my name, the private eye people gonna look at that in a background check?"

"I guess it depends on whether somebody actually files charges."

"Well, that Crimson Tide son of a bitch, he was the one who threw the first punch."

The far side of the pasture was fenced with a cattle gap at the open gate. We rattled across it and that shook off some of the bigger globs of mud, and we got onto the rough and cracked pavement of some unmarked county road, which Jimbo said would lead to the Dauphin Island Parkway if I stayed on it, and took a left every time we came to a crossroad. As I drove, searching the shoulders for anything that could pass for a crossroad, Jimbo scrunched down in his seat, rested his chin on his chest, and slipped into a smiling, almost angelic, sleep.

A few years earlier I would have been using this drive time to dream up some way to explain to my now ex-wife, Sandy, why I was coming in at sunrise with swelling around my right eye and smelling like a turned-over beer truck. But she had heard one too many such explanations. That's one of the reasons she left me and took our daughter and moved back home to Memphis. So now, all I had to do was come up with a story that made sense to myself. But since somebody had tried, just the day before, to blast me into bite-sized pieces, and every sheriff's deputy in Mobile County was now after my ass, making sense even to myself wasn't as easy as it sounds.

I wanted to blame it all on my brother, Neal. He was the one who had told the woman I might be able to help her. He was the one who had sent her to see me. But, by God—and I could kick myself for this—I was the one who agreed to take the case.

I took the case even though I knew better. Knew it as soon as she sat down on my front deck and started talking to me. Knew good and well that I'd be a fool to get into such a damned mess.

TWO

M r. Delmas," the woman had said, "you just can't imagine what it's like to open up one of those sleazy tabloids and read that your daughter's been snorting cocaine and sleeping with half the men in Mobile."

I immediately had this bad feeling. An instinctive realization that I didn't need to be getting into this. I mean, there I was, minding my own business, which is already hard enough to do in Bay St. Louis, when this poor woman I had never laid eyes on before drives up to my front door and within five minutes is giving me this blow-by-blow account of every parent's worst nightmare. And she hadn't even gotten to the bad part. It was exactly the kind of thing my brother is always tossing me right in the middle of. The woman's voice dragged and her fingers quivered as she pushed her honey-blond hair behind her ears and gazed down at the three children in front of us.

She had an aristocratic bearing and an almost military posture. Her voice had a cosmopolitan inflection that could fit as well on the French Riviera as it did here on the Mississippi Gulf Coast, a voice that masked the anxiety I knew she was experiencing during the well-publicized hell she was going through. Her eyes were gray, flecked with blue. Strong, but beginning to show the effects of the ordeal of the past three weeks. Her bottom eyelids were puffy and shadowed with dark crescents. Might have been from lack of sleep, but I suspected she had been hitting the bottle pretty hard the past few days. That's what I'd be doing if I were in her place.

"Are any of those children yours?" she asked.

I nodded. "One of them; the little blond girl with the pony-tail."

"Wouldn't it be wonderful if you could keep them that age for-ever?"

Fifteen feet below the wooden deck on which we sat, my eight-year-old daughter, Peyton, and her two little cousins, Billy and Lisa, were playing a no-rules version of kickball. They squealed and laughed as they scampered across what I call my front lawn, a scattering of weeds and wildflowers poking through the stalky tendrils of St. Augustine grass that run along the ground and keep the sand from blowing away. Steamy afternoon breezes blew in toward us from the gulf, carrying a hint of salt across Beach Boule-vard and stirring gray strands of Spanish moss in the live oak beside my driveway.

The woman sat rigid on the edge of the white rattan chair, both hands gripping the top of the oversized straw purse resting across her knees. Her arms were deeply tanned and showed some effects from a lifetime in the sun. But she had taken care over the years to protect her face. On her right hand was an heirloom diamond ring in a setting worn smooth with age. Out over the dimpled surface of the water, a flat-bottomed cloud that had been hiding the sun drifted off to the east. The ensuing glare lit up the front wall of my camp house, and she slipped on a pair of Gloria Vanderbilt sun-shades.

"Your brother, Neal, said you might be able to help me, Mr. Delmas."

"Are you one of his clients?"

She shook her head no. "I met Neal last year when I was leading a group trying to stop Gulf Quest Oil from drilling a well out by Petit Bois Island. He was representing the oil company."

"You've got to understand, Mrs. Caviss. My brother is a lawyer. He represents oil companies and contractors and—"

"I'm not criticizing him," she said, "not at all. He worked up a compromise that I thought was reasonable. Of course, the Green Guardians didn't like it. In fact, they hated it. But they're crazy; they'd hate anything he came up with. Your brother's a good man, Mr. Delmas."

Yeah, sometimes a little too damn good.

Trouble often finds its way into Neal's office. When it's something that can't be handled with a quick look into the law books, he frequently sends it my way. Such trouble usually comes from Bay St. Louis, our hometown, but this time it came from Pascagoula, fifty miles along the Mississippi Gulf Coast to the east, and it was sitting across from me in the person of Carolyn Caviss. It was an even stickier situation than he usually passes off to me.

I knew all about the tragedy Carolyn Caviss was living through, but so did every other person in the world who had a television or a radio. I had even seen the story earlier that day on the front page of *The National Standard* when I was in the check-out line at the Sav-A-Center buying the spare ribs, charcoal, coleslaw, and ice for the cookout that evening. And because I knew her story, I knew I couldn't help her.

The football season was kicking off up in Memphis that evening at seven o'clock—the Ole Miss Rebels against the University of Memphis Tigers. Any other year I would have been in the lobby of the Peabody Hotel, sipping Heinekens and waiting for the Ole Miss alumni bus to take me to the game. But Peyton was down from Memphis for the annual two-week summer visitation that her mother and I had agreed to some years earlier. So I had rented a pay-for-view TV converter and invited some people over to watch the game.

"How do you think I can help you, Mrs. Caviss?"

"Please, call me Carolyn."

"Only if you'll call me Jack."

Her smile was pinched, labored, and short lived. "I need someone to find out why my daughter was killed. Someone who's involved with the case for some reason other than the headlines."

"I'm afraid I can't do you much good. I'm a private investigator. This is a matter for the police."

She snorted and looked as if she had bitten into a lemon. Her voice came to life. "If you'll recall, those TV reporters stayed in Colorado for two years after that poor little girl was murdered. Then they flocked down to Miami when somebody pulled that little Cuban boy out of the ocean. Now those same vultures have converged on Dauphin Island, and that prissy sheriff—that Carlton Rice—is milking it for all he can."

"Is the sheriff in charge? I thought it'd be the Dauphin Island Police."

"They have concurrent jurisdiction," she said. "But the chief of police for Dauphin Island doesn't like to talk to the press. The sheriff, on the other hand, couldn't care less if they ever get to the bottom of this case, just as long as the TV show lasts through election day."

I felt the same way Carolyn did about Carlton Rice, even though I'd never met the man. I had caught one of his press conferences on the evening news, and that was enough for me. And she was absolutely right: The TV talking heads had occupied Dauphin Island like an invading army.

"I can't jump into the middle of a police investigation," I said, "especially one that's on the front page every day. They won't tell me anything you can't get from reading the newspaper."

"I've had a grand total of one deputy sheriff from Alabama who's bothered to talk to me. The only other people who seem the least bit interested in my daughter are the TV reporters from *Hard Copy*. I want you to find out why these murders happened."

"I don't know if Neal told you what kind of work I do," I said. "I'm a private investigator, a one-man operation. I mainly check out questionable claims for insurance companies. Sometimes I find a missing heir or two, and when things get tight, I track down cheating spouses or deadbeat dads. The closest I ever came to being a cop was when I was in the military police in the army over in Germany. None of that qualifies me to do the job of the police force on Dauphin Island or anywhere else."

She held her stare as she looked at me through the opaque sunshades. I felt as if I were being observed through a two-way mirror. Her mouth tightened and the corners of her eyes crinkled. I could hear her breathing through her nose. She pulled a folded newspaper out of her purse and spread it on the table in front of me.

"The case has become nothing more than fodder for trash like this," she said. "Think about having your child libeled in every corner of this country for the benefit of any gum-smacking gossip who has a dollar bill to spare when she checks out at the supermarket."

The front page was almost covered by a head shot of a woman in her twenties, a classic beauty with luminous blue eyes and platinum hair in long waves that curled under at the shoulders. She wore a rhinestone tiara and long, sparkling earrings. The teeth and lips showed a full smile, but the eyes were slightly disengaged, a bit out of sync with the smile. The face looked familiar, but I couldn't place it. The headline announced in two-inch letters PALIMONY PRINCESS MURDERED IN ALABAMA! In a shaded box in the lower-right-hand corner was the subhead "D.A. Vows to Track Down Beauty Queen's Killers—Page Four."

The inside pages showed photos of all four victims. Rod Eubanks, the TV anchor, was featured in an airbrushed portrait, the kind they put in the lobbies of TV studios. He was blond with a strong jawline and high cheekbones. Looked like every country club lifeguard you've ever seen. Jason Summers was thick necked and slightly round-faced, with dark eyes, a full head of black hair, and the smile of a natural-born salesman.

The photo of Carolyn's daughter Rebecca came from some school yearbook. She didn't seem to fit with the rest of the group.

She was a thin girl with shoulder-length hair, brown with light currents of red. Her hair was flat and combed straight back, held in place by a white hairband. Her lips were full—surely her best feature—but she wasn't smiling, and her sparrow brown eyes were so wide open she appeared to be alarmed. She was pale and wore no makeup, not even powder, and the flash of the camera made her forehead shine.

"You see what they say in there about Rebecca?" Carolyn said. "College dropout! She was laying out a semester and working as an employment counselor for this reputable firm at the Belair Mall. Just trying to make the next year's tuition. And they make Jason sound as if he was some worthless playboy. You'd think he was a professional gambler."

"Professionals don't get into trouble with gambling," I said. "It's the amateurs who get in too deep."

"Jason was high spirited, I'll say that. But Rebecca would have known if he was a problem gambler. I know that wasn't the case. Jason was making good money with his import business and was planning to go to law school. Didn't have any money problems. But none of that fits in with what they want their story to be. And, believe me, that's not the worst I've seen."

"Now I remember where I've seen that girl on the cover." I pointed at the headline. "Palimony. She was the one who was suing Scooter Haney."

"Yes, she's the one." Carolyn sighed and ran the tip of her tongue across her bottom lip. "Kellie Lee Simmons. She wasn't actually suing Mr. Haney. The rumor was out that she had retained a Mobile lawyer named Bob Sanchez to represent her in this suit." I could hear in her voice that she didn't like Bob Sanchez even a little bit. "Jason was in the import business with Sanchez. I met him one time when I was visiting Rebecca. It was about the same time the tabloids started running stories about the palimony suit."

Scooter Haney is a go-getter around Mobile, an open-collar

kind of guy well known along the coast because he likes to do his own TV ads for the various ventures he has tried over the years. Started out as a car salesman and salted enough away to get in on the land boom over at Gulf Shores fifteen years ago. He had gone through two fortunes and three wives before he hit on the idea of an upscale commuter bus line complete with croissants and espresso in the morning and wine and cheese on the return trip in the evening. Started in Birmingham with a line running from Mountain Brook into the downtown district. He soon had his busses in every big city in the South. And now, even Scooter isn't able to spend all the money he's taking in.

"I think Kellie Lee planted most of those palimony stories," Carolyn said. "She and Bob Sanchez were getting so much mileage out of the publicity about a possible suit that they weren't all that eager to actually file one."

"This Kellie Lee Simmons, was she a friend of your daughter's?"

"Kellie Lee and Rod Eubanks and Jason had known each other since they were in high school together in Mobile. Rod and Jason were pretty close. Kellie Lee would date Rod when she'd come back home from New York between married boyfriends. I doubt that she and Rebecca knew each other very well."

"Do you know why Kellie Lee and the Eubanks guy were at Jason's beach house?"

"I don't know anything, Jack. That's why I want to hire you."

I propped my feet on the bottom rung of the railing and watched a group of brown pelicans facing into the light wind, suspended ten feet above the gulf. I reached into the bowl on the table for a handful of salted peanuts. I shook a few into my mouth and licked the salt off my lips and thought about the best way to tell her I wouldn't take the case.

"I don't have access to the evidence, the crime scene, nothing. They'd run me in on an obstructing charge if I even so much as smiled at a witness. Besides, you still don't know what the cops might come up with."

"Do you think they're handling the case well?" she asked.

I shrugged to say I didn't know.

"Carlton Rice is being interviewed on *Larry King Live, Nightline, Dateline,* every one of those talk shows," she said. "I drove over to Mobile to ask him about the investigation. Waited for an hour, and don't you know that arrogant prima donna handed me off to a deputy who hadn't even reviewed the file? Didn't even introduce me to the deputy, just turned to him and told him to take care of me. And he was standing there glancing at his wristwatch the whole time. I found out later he was on his way to a press conference about the case."

"It sounds as if you've got a bigger problem with Sheriff Rice than you do with the investigation. I can understand that. But there's nothing I can—"

"My daughter deserves better than what she's getting."

Doggone Neal's sorry hide! I had been having a great time with Peyton for the past ten days. The first college football game of the season was starting in two hours. The air had cooled and dried just enough to suggest the start of fall, but there were still plenty of beach days left. And I was several thousand bucks to the good after settling with Bayou Casualty on a case I had worked in Biloxi.

But thanks to my busybody brother, I couldn't enjoy any of these things because I was having to tell a mother who had just buried her daughter why I wasn't going to help her. I was gearing up to hang tough, to tell Carolyn no and save us both some heartache, when she let out a long sigh. Her shoulders sagged and it seemed as if the air was escaping from her as she examined the back of her crossed hands. She swallowed and started breathing through her mouth and pulled a pink tissue from her purse.

"Why don't you just tell me what you know about the case." I closed my eyes as I massaged both temples with my index fingers and asked myself why I was prolonging this agony.

"May I have some of that tea?" she asked.

"Have you talked to anybody with the police?"

"Just that one deputy who drove over from Alabama and asked me some questions." She sniffed and wiped her nose with the tissue. "He was a broad man with big, rough hands. But he was very polite, almost gentle. He's the only person involved in the case who seems to care about Rebecca's death."

I handed Carolyn the glass, a plastic stadium cup left over from last year's LSU game. A soccer ball thudded against the rail near my feet, and I leaned forward and shouted at the kids not to kick the ball in our direction. Peyton stuck her tongue out and laughed at me before tossing the ball over Billy's head to Lisa. She gets that kind of stuff from her mama.

"They're saying that Jason was a gambler," Carolyn said. "The deputy asked me whether Rebecca ever mentioned his gambling to me."

"You say gambling wasn't a problem. But it keeps coming up."

"They're trying to come up with something sexy enough to satisfy the tabloids. Once I shot that theory down, he asked me whether Rebecca had any enemies, if anybody had any reason to wish her dead. Then he asked some more about Jason, about his import business."

"From what I've read, I can't tell exactly what his business was."

"Jason bought spices, clothes, jewelry, whatever he could find a market for. Most of it was from Mexico and Central America, so all the newspapers are saying he was involved in drugs. But that's ridiculous. He was as visible as you can get. He flew clients in from Mexico all the time, and he'd take them charter fishing, take them to the outlet mall in Foley to go shopping; he'd take them everywhere." She dabbed at her upper lip. "He never tried to hide anything. Does that sound like a drug smuggler? Besides that, he would go to his mother's house every Sunday for dinner after church."

The breeze died and my T-shirt started to cling to my shoulder and chest. I touched my forehead with my fingertips to hide my eye so I could sneak a glance at my watch. An hour and forty-five minutes until kickoff, time to light the charcoal and get the food read

"I'd like to help, Carolyn. But I can't solve a mass homicide over in Alabama."

"I don't expect you to."

She fished a packet of photographs out of her purse and handed them to me. There were about ten color shots of a brunette with an hourglass figure in a yellow bikini on a beach. She was bronzed and had a glittering smile and thick, full lips. In one close-up, a stock glamour pose, she tilted her face forward and to the side and her hair fell across one eye, a brunette Greta Garbo.

"As you can see," she said, "when Rebecca met Jason the world opened up for her."

"You mean this is Rebecca?"

Carolyn nodded. "The difference was amazing, wasn't it? She had started smiling for the first time since junior high school."

I opened the tabloid to the picture of the plain Rebecca and laid the glamour shot beside it. If Carolyn hadn't told me, I would have never realized that the knockout in the later photos was the same person as that mousey little girl in the yearbook. The hair, no longer stuck under a hair band, was thick and long. The lips seemed even more moist and full, and the indoor pallor was replaced with a healthy outdoor glow. But the biggest difference was in the eyes. In the school photo there was a small and timid person behind them; in the photos Carolyn brought, the chestnut eyes glowed, unveiling a sensuous young woman ready to devour every one of life's goodies.

"She had just started to live," Carolyn said. "And despite his faults, I owe that to Jason. He made her feel like a queen."

I flipped through the stack of photos one more time and shook my head. "I agree; the difference is remarkable. But the police in Alabama are still your best bet to find out who killed them. I can't do any better than a hundred-man team of investigators."

"I've already said I don't expect you to find the killers."

"I thought that's exactly what you wanted."

"I said I wanted to find out why she was killed. I need to know

what she or the other three people in that beach house did that was serious enough to cause four murders. I've heard or read a dozen theories. Rod Eubanks was a drug dealer, Jason and Rebecca were drug dealers, Kellie Lee was a blackmailer, Jason and Rod were in hock to the mob for gambling debts. I've heard all that and more. Rebecca is being linked to every sleazy rumor you can imagine. I need to clear her name if for no other reason than to shut her stepfather up once and for all."

"Her stepfather?"

"My husband. At least my husband for the time being."

I shifted around in my chair and rubbed my back against it to scratch an itch on my shoulder. A bank of clouds parked in front of the sun and cooled the air, causing a light shift in the direction of the wind and pulling in the smell of chicken being roasted on a charcoal grill a few houses down the road.

"All I could do is an extended background check," I said. "I can turn up credit reports, buying habits, and the names of some friends and acquaintances. If I get lucky, I'll be able to tell you what they drank, ate, smoked, or snorted. I can tell you where they went on trips and which magazines they read. But unless the moon and stars are lined up just right, I won't be able to tell you who killed them."

Carolyn removed the sunshades and leaned back in her chair. She looked to the east and her eyes searched far past the shrimp boats six or eight miles out, far past the gathering of wispy clouds on the horizon, seemingly all the way to Dauphin Island. She cleared her throat and took a sip of her tea.

"I do insurance investigations. I just don't think I can help—"

"These murders could have happened for any number of reasons," she said in a low voice, still looking across the water. "Most of the reasons involve money. And it's dirty money, not the type of thing I want my daughter's memory associated with. The Dauphin Island Police and the sheriff's department will never find the killers; whoever did it is a thousand miles away by now. So the TV and the newspapers and the gossip rags will have a field day for a few months, and all people will remember later are the sleazy innuendos and outright lies about Rebecca. I want you to find out what kinds of things these kids did or didn't do. I'm going to need to clear Rebecca's name, and I'm going to have to do it very soon. I can't wait until the press poisons everybody's perception of her, if they haven't already done that."

I scratched my chin and grabbed another handful of peanuts. A flock of killdees tweeted and chirped as they ran along the beach at the edge of the water, dodging the waves when they rolled in. Peyton and her two little cousins were pulling up dandelions and blowing on them, scattering the feathery seeds into the sunlight. My heart was telling me to say yes to Carolyn, but that clear voice of hard experience kept saying no.

"What makes you think I can handle this?" I asked.

She ran her eyes from my face to my feet and back in an instant appraisal, and it felt as if she were seeing me for the first time, as if she had been so intent on telling me her story that she forgot to check me out when she first walked up my front steps and for the fifteen minutes we had just spent talking to each other. She tilted her head and examined my face and rubbed her index finger across her bottom lip several times and paused before she spoke.

"Your brother tells me you can," she said. "I guess I'll just have to take his word for it."

"That's not exactly a ringing endorsement."

"I didn't mean it as an insult. I don't know you, so if someone I trust tells me you're a reputable private investigator, that's all the endorsement I can get."

"I understand that," I said, "but before I take your case, is there anything else I need to know?"

She looked over the railing toward the island out on the horizon and clutched her handbag even tighter. "After we settled the dispute over drilling at Petit Bois Island, I received a number of death threats. I believe they all came from the Green Guardians."

THREE

My sister-in-law, Kathy, had just bought a new car, so she let me take the Windstar van she had been driving the past four years over to Dauphin Island two days later to start working on the case. It turned out that Varner, my ex-wife's fiancé, had this med-school roommate, Randall Chapman, who had just moved to the island, and it was no problem for them to fly there—in Varner's private plane—rather than to fly to Bay St. Louis.

I was using Kathy's van because somebody stole my pickup a few weeks earlier over near Biloxi. I was just sick about somebody stealing my truck, actually having nightmares about the poor old thing, helpless and in the hands of some pervert with a cutting torch in some backwoods chop shop. But even if no lowlife had stolen it, I would have still borrowed Kathy's van while Peyton was down for her visitation. All the accessories—especially the air conditioner—work on the Windstar. Not to mention the brakes.

Neal's got this idea that when he buys a new car, he can sell the old one himself, instead of trading it in, and come out ahead. Trouble is, he parks the old cars out on the front yard and he tapes on the windshield these red FOR SALE signs that he buys at the Dollar General store. Everybody on Beach Boulevard hates for him to do that, especially Kathy. When my truck was stolen, Kathy had just bought a new Volvo, and she gladly let me take her old van out of her front yard until I could either find my truck or get me another one. For the trip over to Dauphin Island, I took the FOR SALE signs out of the windows.

Peyton and I left that last stretch of solid ground southbound on Dauphin Island Parkway, and a vast expanse of marsh grass on both sides of the road replaced the tall pines. A mile ahead of us, just past the marsh, sunlight sparkled on the gulf. Lazy white sea birds took the place of the busy sparrows and robins and mockingbirds of the mainland, those dark, land-based birds that seem to work so hard at flying compared to the graceful gulls. The road was bordered to our right by a bayou barely wide enough for two skiffs to pass each other and so straight it looked man-made. The sulphuric smell of swamp gas whipped through the open windows as we zipped along.

"What kind of bird is that?" Peyton asked.

"That's a pelican, honey. See how long its bill is?"

"What's a bill?"

"It's like the bird's mouth. It's that hard part they peck you with. Like this." I poked her ribs lightly and she flinched and started laughing. Peyton's real ticklish. She told me to quit and brushed my hand away and kept watching the slow, graceful sweeps of the pelican's wings as it trailed off away from us.

"Why don't they have pelicans in Memphis?" she asked.

"Pelicans live on the ocean. But you've got ducks in Memphis. You remember the ducks?"

"At the Peabody! They are so cool! Mama and Varner took me there last week."

I immediately wished I hadn't brought up the subject. "Does Varner take you to a lot of places?"

She nodded her head vigorously. I could tell she liked that. Well, what could I expect? I made a mental note not to say anything bad about Varner, Sandy, or anybody else up in Memphis.

We passed a long, tall wooden pier, which was open to the public for fishing. At the base of the pier, a bait shop sold live shrimp, ice, beer, sunscreen, hooks, sinkers, bobbers, and fishing line, all of which would be needed throughout the day by the landlocked and boatless patrons who had come to fish at three dollars a head for mullets, croakers, redfish, and the occasional flounder.

It was Monday, the first day of the last week of summer, the week before Labor Day. Even at ten in the morning, there was a good bit of traffic headed to the island, mostly kids wanting to milk the most out of these last few vacation days. The road was built on sand and shells and sat low, barely above high tide. Straight ahead, the huge white concrete hump of the Dauphin Island bridge rose like a mountain over the horizon. Under the early-morning glare, it glowed like white marble.

"Is Mama coming over here?" Peyton asked.

"She'll be here tomorrow."

"What is that big thing up there, Daddy?"

"That's the bridge that goes to the island."

The bridge runs north and south and ties the island to the mainland on the western shore of Mobile Bay. There is also a day-time ferry that runs east and west from the eastern tip of the island across the wide mouth of Mobile Bay to Fort Morgan, but most people get to the island by way of the bridge.

"Do we *have* to go over that?" she said.

"It's okay."

"What if we fall off the side?"

"It's got walls on both sides. It'll be okay."

The bridge is wider than the road leading to it. It's really four lanes, but you're supposed to use only the two inside lanes. The outside shoulders are kept clear for emergency vehicles. The glare off the surface from the mid-morning sun made us squint. It felt rock solid under the tires compared to the sun-softened asphalt I had been driving on. The concrete ran level for a mile or so, a steady ten feet above the surface of the water, before it began a sharp upward slope to the crest at the point where the bridge crossed the Intracoastal Waterway. The long rise felt like that first tension-filled ascent that every good roller coaster has. Peyton tightened her grip on her doll, and her eyes grew wide as silver dollars.

"Don't worry, baby." I reached over and squeezed her hand. "I've gone over this bridge a hundred times."

The island is shoaling northward as the currents pile up sand on the lee side and fill in the gap between the island and the mainland. Another thousand years and you'll probably be able to walk out there and hardly get your feet wet. Right now, the water near the island is so shallow that it is almost always calm and barely covers the bottom in many places. A dozen sandbars poke through the surface, and serve as rest stops for hundreds of sea birds. You get careless with your boat in these shallows, and you pay. You've got to know where the sandbars and the cuts are. One familiar Dauphin Island landmark as you drive in is this shrimp boat off to the right that grounded itself not fifty yards outside the channel. It has been stuck there for years, sitting high and cantered to one side, a warning to all sailors to stay inside the markers.

As we topped the bridge, a pair of pelicans flew toward us, banked when they approached the bridge, soared high in the air, and crossed our path. Peyton watched them with the intensity that only an eight-year-old can have. We were over the peak of the bridge and going down the other side before she realized what was happening.

"See," I said, "that wasn't scary, was it?"

"That was cool! Can we do it again?"

"Maybe later, honey. We need to get to the beach."

Dauphin Island is only a dozen miles or so on a straight line across the Mississippi Sound south-southeast from Pascagoula, but it is about a thirty-five-mile drive on land. It has been Mobile's playground ever since the bridge was built in the mid-fifties. Besides Dauphin, there are four other barrier islands between Mobile and New Orleans: Petit Bois, Horn, Ship, and Cat. Together they are laid out end to end, a hundred-mile-long chain that breaks the waves of the gulf and serves as the southern border of the Mississippi Sound. Dauphin, the first one in the chain, is also the closest to the mainland.

I was surprised that with all of the reporters on the island, none of them had yet done a story on the history of the place. A pair of brothers, the French Canadians Bienville and Iberville, led an expedition in 1699 that claimed a good part of the northern coast of the Gulf of Mexico for France, and while doing so named each place they discovered. Some years earlier LaSalle had been in the area and discovered the mouth of the Mississippi. He had claimed for France all the land drained by that huge river, an area that stretched all the way to Montana. When Iberville and Bienville got there, they named this territory "Louisiana" in honor of Louis XIV, king of France at the time. As big as Louisiana was, it still couldn't contain the Sun King's gigantic ego.

Most of the place names they chose in 1699 are still used today. But when the French Canadians put ashore on what is now Dauphin Island, they found a pile of bleached-out human bones, and, understandably, called the place Massacre Island. The name didn't stick for long. Twelve years later, Bienville, who had become Governor of Louisiana, came up with an idea to encourage Louis XIV to continue funding the struggling colony. He changed the name of Massacre Island to Isle Dauphine in honor of a young duchess whom King Louis really liked and who had just married one of his grandsons. Dauphine is the title she got when she married into the family. The name has over the years been Anglicized to Dauphin.

This name change served two purposes. First, it was a blatant suck-up to Louis XIV. In the France of the early 1700s, you had to do that at least once a month or so if you hoped to get one red franc from the government. Second, it helped some in attracting settlers. Seems Bienville was having a tough time getting folks interested in moving to a place named Massacre Island.

From all accounts, Bienville's idea was a success. If he were alive today, he could be knocking down megabucks as a spin doctor in some Madison Avenue PR firm up in New York.

Historians today doubt that the pile of bones were the result of a massacre. More likely it was the site of the community burial ground. The Indians who lived in the area were a somewhat docile group—at least before the Europeans got there—and there is no indication that any massacre ever occurred on Dauphin Island.

At least that's the way it was until two weeks earlier.

Once on the island, we slowed as we passed the piers where the charter fishing boats were tied off. The strong smell of fish, salt water, diesel fuel, and exhaust from the boat engines combined in that familiar aroma of saltwater docks. I was low on gas, so I turned into the parking lot of the Double Quick, the one at the main intersection. That intersection, a three-way stop where the highway from the mainland dead ends into Bienville Boulevard, is at the heart of the island. That's where the trees are tall, almost all of them pines, and the woods are too thick to see through. Bienville Boulevard is the east-west drag, the only one that runs the length of the island, the point of reference from which all directions start when you ask someone how to get somewhere. The intersection has only stop signs. There are no traffic lights. Not there, not anywhere on the island.

That alone is enough to make you fall in love with the place.

As we pulled into an open space right at the front door, I looked at my rearview mirror and caught a glimpse of a fifty-one-foot tractor-trailer rig with the ABC News logo emblazoned on the side. The truck itself was an independent driver-owned Peterbilt with a Confederate flag painted across the grille and the owner's name and hometown painted on the driver's door.

"What kind of ICEE do you want, Daddy?"

"Let's see what they've got."

"If I get strawberry, will you get strawberry, too?"

"We'll see."

"You order first, okay?"

At a round, concrete patio table two guys and a young woman sat drinking Budweisers out of cans. One guy had a beard which showed a little gray. His hair was pulled back into a short ponytail, and he was wearing faded cutoff jeans and a tank top. The girl, also in cutoffs, wore John Lennon sunshades with purple lenses, black lipstick, and a CBS News T-shirt. She had a scruffy pair of Timberlands on her feet, no socks. The other guy, about college age, was squirting sunscreen into his hand and rubbing it on his face and neck.

The clerk was on his tiptoes searching for something on the shelves that lined the rear walls. A pretty, slender young woman was waiting at the checkout counter, her light blond hair gathered under her bill cap and her face hidden behind a pair of yellow-lens Oakley sunglasses. She smiled down at Peyton.

"We're going to get an ICEE," Peyton said.

"Oooo," the woman said, "I love ICEEs."

"Here you are," said the clerk as he handed her the little green medicine bottle. "This is the last bottle of extra-strength we got. You might oughtta try some of that BC Powder. Tastes like hell, but it works."

"I like strawberry," Peyton said to her.

"Me, too. But I really love tutti-frutti." She reached down and stroked Peyton's hair. "I gotta go. Bye-bye." She looked back as she stepped through the door and gave Peyton a little wave. Peyton followed the woman with wide eyes and the same open-mouthed wonder with which she had watched Big Bird just a couple of years earlier. Followed her all the way to her car.

The store had a grill inside and a serving table for the plate lunches they sold in carry-out Styrofoam trays. There was an aisle along the back wall reserved for inflatable floats, ice chests, sunscreen, sunshades, souvenir T-shirts, flip-flops, beach towels, and beach umbrellas. The place had an overworked air conditioner, which couldn't hold its own against the sun radiating through the plate glass and the front door that opened every few seconds. The clerk had cleared off the motor oil and paper funnels from the top ledge of the nearest display rack, set a big box fan there, and aimed it at the checkout counter.

The smell of hot grease blended with the sweet scent of syrups in the ICEE machine and over-ripe bananas and fresh cantaloupe in a bin on the center aisle. Peyton took her time studying the selections, trying to reach a final decision on whether to get tutti-frutti or strawberry.

"Oh, for the love of Mike!" a man shouted up front. "This beer is hot again today!"

"Look," the clerk said, "it's like I told you yesterday. There's so many of y'all down here we can't keep the stuff on the shelves long enough for it to cool. The crew from CNN beat you to it today. Get one of those iced-down bottles there in that foot tub."

"I don't drink that cheap stuff."

"Well, buy you one of them Styrofoam chests and ice some down. Why don't you just buy a case and keep some around 'stead of coming in here ten times a day?"

"God, I'm about to melt." The man reached into the ice and pulled out a brown quart bottle of Schlitz. "How much for a cup of ice?"

"It's already cold."

"I need a cup."

"Just go back there and get one."

He stepped toward us gripping the neck of the bottle. The brown paper sack the clerk had put it in was already darkening as the water from condensation and flecks of ice began to soak through. He was a distinguished-looking guy, vaguely familiar, with black hair going gray at the sideburns and temples and strong features—jaw, nose, and chin—but with the first hint of jowls.

"I want tutti-frutti," Peyton said.

"Good choice," the man said. "At least it's cold." He winked at Peyton as he pulled a red and blue ICEE cup out of the aluminum sleeve. "You're a mighty pretty girl."

"What do you say?" I said.

"Thank you," she said.

"How'd you like to be on TV?"

She looked down at her feet and shook her head.

"She's a little camera shy," I said.

"Well, stay that way, honey. There's some bad people on TV." He rubbed her head, smiled at me, and stepped toward the front. He plunked a quarter on the counter as he walked out and went over to the table with the umbrella.

"Anything else for you?" the clerk said as Peyton and I stepped to the counter.

"Where have I seen that guy who was just in here?"

"He's a TV reporter for Fox News. Name's Darren Wright. Comes in here every day after they shoot their report. Complains about the beer being hot every time. He does love his beer. He ain't a bad guy, though. I'm gonna stick him a six-pack of Heinekens back in the cooler for tomorrow. He'll get a kick outta that."

"They got a full crew down here?" I asked.

"Man, they done took over the island. They got ever' TV network in the world down here. Them killin's, that's big news. Ain't nothin' like that ever happened before, least not around here."

Dauphin Island is the only one of the barrier islands off the Mississippi-Alabama coast connected to the mainland by a bridge and, therefore, the only one with permanent residents. Twelve hundred people year round and nearly triple that during the summer. Some of them have money, like the full-time residents who have retired there and the well-paid professionals who commute into Mobile. These rich ones live in the new houses—which are genteel but hardly opulent—on the island's higher, eastern end (although many of the raised houses on the narrow, treeless western end are equally fine). But mostly there are beach cabins set on stilts with rough wooden porches and catchy names. These cabins are usually vacant most of the year. It's no Palm Beach, never will be, and the Dauphin Islanders like that just fine.

The economy of the island is based on fishing (commercial and sport), government work (the Marine Resources Sea Lab and the Coast Guard), and tourism. Most of the people who make their living on the island either work in one of those three areas or provide services to folks who do. You have to keep your eyes open for hurricanes, but other than that, it's a regular community with a beautiful, clean, crime-free existence. Or at least it was.

When we got to the beach house, Carolyn was waiting for us, sitting on the wooden steps and sipping a Diet Coke in a foam cooler. She was wearing a lime green one-piece bathing suit and a long-billed white cap and she was rubbing suntan lotion onto her arms.

The cabin was tall and airy with white shutters around plate-glass windows, giving the whole place the look of a glassed-in porch. The wind from the Gulf blew in on us, bending the sea oats. A flock of seagulls rode wind currents at the level of the second floor. The roar of incoming surf drifted over the dunes, and the sunlight bouncing off the white sand could blind you if you weren't wearing sunshades.

"Were my directions okay?" Carolyn shouted. "Come on and we'll get you moved in."

"Who is that lady?" Peyton asked.

"That's Miss Carolyn. This is her cabin."

I stepped out and opened the side door to get our suitcases off the backseat.

"I saw this precious little thing at your house the other day," Carolyn said.

"This is Peyton."

"You're very pretty, Peyton."

"Nice place," I said.

"We were lucky we could get it. I'm afraid we would have never found a place for you to stay if we hadn't. There's not a hotel room between here and Mobile. In fact, we had to bump Admiral Pace and his wife to get it. They were scheduled to come down here for their annual week of bird-watching." She stood and brushed the sand off her seat and the back of her legs and started walking up the steps. "Peter raised hell about me bumping any Navy brass for something as trivial as trying to defend the reputation of my daughter. But he can just kiss my lily white—" She looked down at Peyton. "I mean, that's just tough toenails. Isn't it, honey?"

Peyton laughed and started saying the phrase out loud, laughing each time.

"Carolyn," I said, "I could stay somewhere else if it's going to cause trouble between Peter and you."

"Oh, no indeed. I want you to be here and talk to people first-hand. The wife of the president of Mayson Marine is a good friend of mine and she was the one who insisted that the admiral can come back for a week in October. She can't stand Robert Pace or his wife any more than I can. They're the kind who expect the whole world to jump when they say so. They can just wait for two months. And if it causes Peter any problems, at this point I couldn't care less." She rubbed Peyton's head. "That's just tough what, honey?"

"Toenails!" Peyton shouted.

"You take as much time as you need," Carolyn said. "Every single day there's some new salacious report about Rebecca and the rest of the kids who got killed. Any interest in the truth has long since died. They've even started interviewing store clerks now. The trouble is, some of these people will make up a story just so they can get on TV."

"Can I go to the beach, Daddy?"

"Only if you stay on the sand where I can keep an eye on you. Don't get in the water."

"Can I look for shells?"

"That'd be a great idea."

She bounced down the steps, kicked off her shoes when she got to the bottom, and took off, squealing and running barefoot over the hot sand.

"They're hard to keep up with, aren't they?" Carolyn stood and stared as Peyton ran along the edge of the water, splashing through the incoming waves and occasionally bending down to pick up a seashell.

"Again, Carolyn, I don't want to get your hopes up. I can't solve this case."

"I know that. I just want to salvage Rebecca's reputation."

"I can't promise that either."

"You find out the truth, and I'll live with it."

Down at the beach, Peyton was holding a seashell up to her ear.

"I know it might be tough," I said, "but I need to ask you some questions about Rebecca's personal life. I can save you a lot of time and money if you'll shoot straight with me."

She gazed down at the beach and cleared her throat. A passing flock of seagulls had spotted a school of shiners fifty yards off-shore and had started circling and squawking and diving at them.

"Did Rebecca use drugs?" I asked. "I'm not talking about a little pot now and then. Was she into any heavy stuff?"

"No. I would have known that."

"Did she ever say she was in any kind of trouble? Was there any-one who may have wanted to hurt her?"

Carolyn shrugged. "She did mention this one man who made her feel uncomfortable. This gambler named Billy Ray, Bobby Joe . . . one of those double names. I hear he was Jason's bookie."

"Anybody else?"

"Of course there are the Green Guardians," she said. "But you already know about them."

"I've got some people back in Pascagoula who can tell me about them," I said. "Right now I'm concentrating on what was going on here on Dauphin Island."

"So am I," she said. "You just got here, so I guess you haven't heard. The Green Guardians set up their Gulf Coast headquarters on Dauphin Island a month ago. In fact, they're right down the street."

FOUR

Whispering Dunes is a zero–lot line subdivision beside the Dauphin Island golf course. It is shaded by native slash and long-leaf pines and a few imported palms. It features a swimming pool, tennis court, golf course, and a clubhouse. There is one entrance, blocked by an electronically controlled gate, and Peyton and I were parked at the curb just outside that gate because I had forgotten the access code that my ex-wife, Sandy, gave me to get past it. I was searching through scraps of paper for the one on which I had scribbled the four magic numbers that would let us inside.

Why in the world did they have a gated community on this island, anyway? With only the one bridge leading in and out, the whole place is already a semi-gated community. I never have understood why people who live in such places figure it's worth the price they pay. Some snob-appeal developer throws together this overpriced subdivision and puts this guardhouse at the road leading in. Looks good at first. But pretty soon the residents find out it's a pain in the neck to have to fool with having the gate open and close every time you want to run down to the store. So after three or four months they just leave the gate open all the time and the security guy waves at you as you drive by. At least he does those few times he's not asleep.

But I guess it's like the ceremonial guards in front of Buckingham Palace. There's no way they're going to stop any armed terrorist squad from storming the front doors, but they do add a lot of class to the place.

I was still searching through my wallet when a delivery van eased past me and stopped and the driver punched in the secret numbers. The gate swung open and I slipped in right behind him.

Sandy and Varner—his full name, preferably said in one breath, is "John-Varner-Keyes-the-third-the-prominent-Memphis-radiologist"—were flying down that afternoon to the little airstrip on the island and staying the evening with one of Varner's classmates, an endocrinologist who had recently bought a unit in Whispering Dunes. The endocrinologist, Randall Chapman, had a seven-year-old son and they had invited Peyton to go to Mobile to see a movie that afternoon with the little boy and one of his friends. After two weeks with me, Peyton had seen enough of the beach, and I needed some time to check out things on the island, so I agreed it would be a good idea.

It was just past noon and stifling hot. There was no breeze and the entire island shimmered under a superheated haze. The lawn sprinklers were running on the yards and over on the golf course where the club had also set up fans to blow on each of the greens in an effort to save the bent grass from shriveling up. There was a faint odor of barbecue from some neighborhood backyard and the constant noise of central-air-conditioning units running at top speed. We followed Sandy's directions and had no problem finding the Chapman house.

The woman who greeted us at the door was tennis tanned with muscles developed from a lot of time on the court or at the spa. Her hair was close cropped and sun streaked. She had a pleasant face, a pretty smile, and a diamond tennis bracelet. She gave me a quick appraisal, smiling the whole time, no doubt trying to see how I had matched up to Sandy's description.

"I'm Susan Chapman," she said, extending her hand. "Please come in."

I introduced myself and then Peyton. As soon as I did, a little boy came running into the room. He was barefoot and was wearing green shorts and a St. Michael's Day School T-shirt.

"Harper, this is Peyton," Susan said. "She'll be going to the movies with us this afternoon. Why don't you take her in to your room and show her your new game?"

The little boy wheeled around and gave Peyton a sign to follow him and started running into the next room with Peyton right behind him.

"Sandy tells me you've been hired by the parents of one of those murder victims to find out who killed them."

"Say what?"

"You know, those killings in that beach house over on the west end."

"The police are handling that."

She studied me for a minute and decided to let the matter drop.

"I guess I'd better be going," I said.

"You don't have to leave so soon."

"Well, I know you're busy getting ready for this evening," I said. "I really appreciate your taking Peyton with you. I think she's about ready to see some children her own age."

"You're coming back for the party, aren't you?"

"I don't think I'll be able to," I said. "I've got—"

"Oh, of course you can. We're having some of the Fox News crew over. Darren Wright will be here. Maybe he can tell you something about the murder case. And of course Sandy and Varner will be here."

Sometimes I don't understand people. That's exactly the reason I didn't want to go to the party.

"They ought to be here any minute," she said. "In fact, I think I see the car coming now."

A Land Rover, British racing green, pulled into the drive right behind my van. The driver was a tall man with salt-and-pepper hair, skinny legs, and a light tan. His front-seat passenger was a blondish man, a few inches shorter than the driver, but twenty pounds heavier, a muscled, broad-shouldered guy. He wore white tennis shorts and a yellow knit shirt that clung to him and accented his pecs. Sandy emerged from the rear door of the Land Rover. She smiled broadly and waved in our direction.

Sandy looked great. She had on a light blue dress, sleeveless, split up the side past her knees, revealing a long stretch of well-shaped leg. She was tanned and as firm as a swimmer. Her auburn hair had grown out to shoulder length and glistened in the sunlight. I always told her that her hair looked great when she wore it long, but she always kept it cut short when we were married. Said it was too much trouble to wash it each day.

It was easy to tell when Sandy realized it was me up on the porch. The smile stayed, but it lost its life. She recovered quickly, however, and bounced toward us, squealing the way women do by way of greeting. Susan bolted past me and ran toward her, also calling out in a voice a full octave above normal. They hugged and moved in a little circle before stepping back and looking each other up and down for the ritual compliments. Susan took Sandy's hand and stepped toward the house. For an instant, Sandy hesitated, not resisting Susan's pull toward the house but not going with it either, as it ran through her mind just how she would handle me.

"Hello, Jack," she said. Didn't sound as if her heart was in it.

"Hi, Sandy. You look great."

"Oh, doesn't she?" Susan said. "You just look wonderful. I'm just so jealous of that tan."

Now just what do you do when you see your ex-wife for the first time in months and when her new fiancé and a pair of old friends are watching? As far as I've been able to tell, the thing to do is to act about the same way you would if you ran into an ex-coworker. Do you shake hands? I mean, this is the woman you made a baby with not all that long ago, a woman you shared your thoughts and dreams with, who saw you at your worst a lot more times than you'd care to remember. At least there ought to be a hug. But what kind of hug? Should it be one of these things from the side where you reach across her back and pull her toward you? That's the kind of thing you do with some guy after your team makes a field goal. No, it definitely had to be full frontal. But how tight? And who starts it? This was tricky. The wrong move and I get pegged in a different class from the clubhouse crowd.

I was trying to picture what my father would do if he were in a similar situation with Mama. Just couldn't picture that. While I was straining to imagine that scene, Sandy leaned to me and gave me a pre-emptive kiss on the cheek. It was one of those kind two women give each other after they've been to France for vacation, like touching with your lips.

"I didn't expect to see you here," Sandy said. "When did you get a van?"

"It belongs to Kathy," I said. "She's letting me use it for a few days."

"So you don't have your pickup truck back yet?"

"Not yet."

"Oh, Lord," Susan said. "What is it about men and trucks. Randall's about to have a fit to buy one of those big pickups. He'd love to talk with you about it, I'm sure. Maybe you can sell him yours."

Sandy gave me a look that let me know she'd rather I not say too much about my truck. She always knows how to make me feel like a loser in any situation. After we had been married a few years, it sank in that she was never going to have as much money with me as a boat builder as she would have with me working in a bank. Once that connection was made, nothing I ever did seemed to be good enough. The assorted pickup trucks I drove around Bay St. Louis were particular sources of embarrassment for her.

But that's okay now. And I doubt that my truck was what Randall had in mind anyhow. I'm sure he'd prefer one of those leather-upholstered models they name after some city out West or maybe some mountain range. The kind the desk jockeys fork over forty grand for. The kind that makes a statement from the guy behind the wheel: "Don't let my eighty-dollar Ralph Lauren tie fool you. I'm a rough, tough outdoorsman at heart." But somehow, Saturday mornings always seem to find the guy driving the thing to the Red Arrow Car Wash instead of the woods.

"I'm afraid the truck isn't available right now," I said. "I had an unfortunate incident."

"Come on inside and get out of this heat," Susan said as she stepped through the door, leaving us outside, alone, while Varner and Randall were pulling the luggage from the back of the Land Rover.

"I heard about your incident," Sandy said. "Kathy called and told me all about it."

"It goes with the job. Sometimes things happen you don't count on. Makes it fun."

"Yeah. When you were twenty-five years old, I'm sure stuff like that was fun."

"As I remember, you seemed to enjoy a little adventure now and then."

"Now and then is one thing, but from what I hear you seem to be having more than your share of adventures these days. Or do you now call them incidents?"

"Maybe if I went back into banking I wouldn't have so many. Of course, it gets a little tricky having to walk around all day with your nose stuck up somebody's ass, but some people get used to it."

"Oh, yeah. I forgot," she said, "you've got this thing about structured environments. You'd rather work where there aren't any rules. Like every low-class honky-tonk from Pascagoula to Baton Rouge."

"I met more honest and decent men in two days at the loading dock in New Orleans than I met in two years at that damned bank."

"Well, maybe if you had stayed there, some of this honesty and decency you talk about would have rubbed off on those mean old bankers."

"I know it looks like we're moving in," a male voice said, "but I promise we're only staying tonight."

It was the blond-haired guy in the yellow shirt. He had come up on us without either of us realizing it. Had two big suitcases, one in each hand. Sandy immediately shifted to a smile, but all I could do was try to not make my anger obvious. She's a lot better at doing that than I am; comes from her upbringing.

"I told Sandy the Cessna has a weight limit," he said, grinning, "but she just couldn't decide which dress to wear tonight, so she brought them all." He set down the suitcases and held out his hand. "You must be Jack."

Varner Keyes had a California look about him. Tan, blond, athletic. He had a broad, white smile and, except for an accent of white hair at the temples, looked like a college rush chairman. The touch of white hair only made him look rich.

"Sandy's told me all about you," he said.

Susan stepped back outside. "Come on, Sandy. You haven't seen Peyton yet."

As Sandy moved toward the door, I had this micro-second of realization that I had missed a rare chance to chew her out about something. She had obviously let it be known to Susan Randall that I was coming to the island as the hired investigator of Carolyn Caviss to look into the murders, and that's a big-time no-no. It's not often in my dealings with Sandy that I get the chance to be on the side of righteous indignation, I'd say one chance for me to every ten chances she has. And I had just let a good one slip by.

Sandy glanced at me over her shoulder as they stepped inside: a stormy look, a warning for me to back off, to avoid infecting this new guy with whatever male disease I was carrying, that sickness that takes over some of us and to which I had succumbed long ago. As if Varner could catch it through casual contact with me, like maybe we shake hands and he forgets to wash his hands before he rubs his lips or something, and suddenly he would quit being a radiologist and go into scuba-diving instruction or stock-car racing. I had seen that look from her many times. Her eyes grow dark and the blood flows to her face and her pupils and even her lips seem to swell. Looks pretty good, to tell you the truth.

"You bring your clubs, Jack? Randall and I are planning to get in a round this afternoon."

The tall, skinny guy reached out and shook my hand. "We've got a great little course here," he said. "Great place to work on your short game."

"I've got some work I've got to get in."

"I heard about your case over here," Varner said.

"You heard what?"

"Are you a lawyer?" Randall said.

"Jack's a private investigator," Varner said. "Now it was the mother of this Jason's girlfriend who hired you, wasn't it?"

"I can't talk about any cases."

"So it's got something to do with the murders," Randall said. "Of course it would have to. That's the only thing that's happened here in years. You've got to come to the party tonight and tell us all about it."

"I can't talk about it."

"Well, why don't you come anyway?" Varner said. "Maybe you can give me a few pointers on how to deal with Sandy."

I know that I'll never filter out all my redneck tendencies. But the way the country clubbers out in east Memphis deal with their ex-spouses has always seemed a bit much. Like this one guy up there I used to work with in Sandy's daddy's bank: He got a divorce, and then his ex-wife married one of his golfing buddies. Then he got remarried himself, and now all four of them go on vacation together. If you're that good of a buddy with your ex, why did you get the divorce to begin with?

Must be a British thing. You could get those people up there to walk down Beale Street naked with their hair dyed purple if the British upper class started doing something like that in London and some stockbroker from east Memphis over there on vacation happened to see it.

It just doesn't seem right to be closer to a woman when she's your ex-wife than you were when she was your wife. I mean, I guess I'll always have feelings for Sandy. I'll probably always love her. We had some great times together and she is Peyton's mother.

But, dammit, does that mean I have to like this Varner guy?

FIVE

A lot of the lumber that comes on barges down the Tombigbee River to Mobile is shipped to Mexico. Mexico City is already twice as big as New York and swelling each day with more and more dirt farmers who have nothing in the world except a fuzzy idea that there's something waiting for them in Mexico City, something that can't be any worse than what they've got back home. This migration takes up a lot of lumber. Several of the Mexican companies who come to Mobile to get this lumber use the same law firm. In order to handle this business, that law firm sent Roberto Sanchez to Mobile to set up a one-man office.

Neal did a background check for me on Sanchez and on the law firm in Mexico City. Graduate of the University of West Florida, did a stint in the Nicaraguan Army under the latest Somoza before going to law school at Samford in Birmingham. The firm set him up in an office in the Waterman Building, the tallest building in the city, standing alone and towering over any of the other structures downtown, just a few blocks from the state docks.

The firm itself was one of the five largest in Mexico. It did a lot of oil and gas work, a lot of admiralty work, and a lot of work for banks, specializing in the import/export trade. But this firm handled a lot more than that. From what Neal found, the law firms in Mexico are not restricted to the practice of law. They had a real-estate division, an investment division, and a division that handled employment. And these divisions didn't just deal with the law governing these areas. The firm bought and sold real estate on behalf of their clients. They acted as stock and bond brokers. And they had a job-placement service, actually went out and found jobs for people. The firm was so big, they occupied eight floors of a skyscraper in Mexico City's financial district.

The lady at the desk in the anteroom of Sanchez's office had the look of a woman with children, I guessed three of them. She was a cheerful, thirty-something type losing her figure to a lot of hours behind the desk and too many trips with the kids to Baskin-Robbins. You've seen the type selling hot dogs and filling cups from two-liter bottles of Coke at every eighth-grade football game you've ever gone to. Her hair was cut short, but for utility, not style. The clothes were of a fashion that could best be called American housedress. She had a pretty face, smooth and clear, and big, blue eyes with the start of laugh lines at the corners from that smile she no doubt kept even when she slept.

"Is Mr. Sanchez expecting you?"

"I left a voice mail message," I said, "but I'm afraid I didn't follow up. I was hoping he'd have a few minutes sometime today."

"Oh, I'm sure he'd love to see you if he can. Let me step into his office and tell him you're here. I'm afraid I didn't get your name."

"Jack Delmas. My brother, Neal Delmas, said he was going to call and try to set up an appointment."

"Oh, yes. I talked with him. He's just the nicest man."

She stepped into the next room and pulled the door behind her. I stood at the desk looking at the framed photograph on the credenza. An airbrushed group photo from some church directory. I had guessed wrong; there were four kids. The husband didn't look like he was passing on many of those trips to Baskin-Robbins himself. Looked like a happy family. Well-respected folks in their town. Doing the best things, so conserva-tively. Every time I see something like that I wonder what I'm missing. But then, I'll bet the guy in that picture sometimes wonders the same thing about himself. I didn't notice when the door opened.

"Jack Delmas," Sanchez said, "come in, my frien'." He walked toward me and gave me a power handshake and a smile. "I'm honored that you have come to visit me."

He was a dark man, broad shouldered and bull necked, in a seersucker suit, white with blue stripes. He had the posture of the career soldier. His eyes were hard and his full, black mustache turned down at the ends. In his left hand he held a long cigar, thick as a broom handle. He wore a heavy gold ring with a large, clear, purple stone encircled by tiny diamonds. Sounded for all the world like Ricky Ricardo with a scratchy throat.

"I'm sorry to drop in unannounced," I said.

"That is no problem at all. Your brother called me and told me you would be visiting. Margaret, please bring us some refreshments."

His office had a view of upper Mobile Bay all the way over to Spanish Fort and Fairhope on the eastern shore. The stately battleship USS *Alabama* lay before us, as awesome as ever. Closer to us was the Alabama State Docks, where three freighters were snugged in at the wharf. A crane was lowering pallets stacked with heavy-duty sacks into the huge square openings on the deck of the middle ship, sacks of grain judging from the brown clouds of dust billowing out from the cargo hold. The office was nice but nothing fancy, top-of-the-line stuff from Office Depot but nothing like some of the more plush digs I've seen at the World Trade Center over in New Orleans. The room smelled like cigar smoke. He seated me in an armchair and walked back behind his desk.

"Are you also a lawyer, Mr. Delmas?"

"Private investigator. I'm doing a background investigation on the four people who were murdered in Jason Summers's beach house."

He raised an eyebrow in question.

"Rebecca Jordan's mother hired me."

Sanchez fingered the corner of his mustache and studied my face. He had the piercing eyes of an interrogator. I could see how Carolyn might feel uncomfortable around him.

Margaret walked in and set a tray on Sanchez's desk in front of me. There were two bottled waters, a Diet Pepsi, regular Pepsi, and a Seven-Up along with a bowl of ice. There was also an open wooden cigar box with ten or twelve fat, deep brown cigars stacked inside.

"Please help yourself as you wish," Sanchez said as he dismissed Margaret with a slight wave. "What can I do for you today?"

"I need some background information on those four people on Dauphin Island."

"Are you investigating the murders?"

"I'm only doing a background check. I need to find out personal information on the victims."

"I don' quite understand. If you are not with the police, why are you in this case?"

"The police have to keep their investigation secret until it's concluded. I don't. I've been hired to find out what the four victims did for a living; what they owned; who they owed money to; what their personal habits were; what they drank, ate, or smoked; and who they slept with. The press is ripping up the reputations of these four, and Rebecca Jordan's mother wants to be able to set the record straight. If she waits until the police release their report, it may be too late. Once the story is over and the press coverage ends, the harm is done and there's no way to undo it. If her daughter was living a fairly clean life and not doing all the things they are saying about her in the tabloids, she wants to be able to go public with it while the public is still tuned in."

"So what does this have to do with Jason? Why are you looking into his affairs?"

"Jason and Rebecca were in love, maybe on their way to marriage. That's a close relationship. If Jason was doing something wrong, folks might assume Rebecca was in on it, too."

Sanchez regarded me with a slight smile of amusement. "I wish you luck, my frien'. There are dozens of policemen trying to solve this case. What makes you think you will succeed when they cannot?"

"I'm not trying to solve a murder. I'm trying to write a character sketch. I'm going to find out more about Jason's business than he knew himself. The police are more concerned right now with fingerprints and blood spatters and physical evidence. They just don't have the time right now to go into the areas I plan to go into. Besides, I don't have to play by the rules," I said. "And I don't have news reporters watching me every minute and second-guessing me every time they have a broadcast. I don't have the forensics lab at my disposal, but I don't need it."

He bit off the end of his cigar and spit it into the wastebasket beside his chair. He pulled a gold lighter from the top drawer of his desk. "I cannot tell you anything about any of the four dead people except for Jason."

"What was your relationship with him?"

"He was like my little brother. But, Mr. Delmas, sometimes little brothers will not listen to what you have to say." He lit the cigar and took a few puffs to get it started. "He just wouldn't listen."

"Didn't you also have a business relationship with him?"

He shook his head. "No, no. I was only his lawyer. He heard of my firm from some of his clients in Mexico. He came to me to draw up the articles of incorporation for his business. That's how we met."

"I never have known exactly what Jason's business was."

"Imports. Pottery, yard art, garden heaters, fountains, all that stuff you see for sale in garden centers. He would send a lot of it up to Boaz, where they have this huge outlet mall. There's a store up in Mississippi in a town called Canton where he would sell tons of it. Jason had made a lot of contacts in Mexico. For an Anglo, he had a very good understanding of how business works in Mexico. It is based on personal relationships, friendships, if you will. He spent most of his time developing these friendships with his suppliers. That's what he used his beach house for. He brought clients up here all the time."

Outside a cloud slipped across the face of the sun, dimming the harsh glare of midday. I didn't realize that I had been squinting, but I felt the muscles around my eyes relax. "Why would these clients come up here to Alabama?"

"They loved Dauphin Island. Loved Mobile. Jason took them charter fishing, took them to the big outlet mall in Foley. They were an hour away from the casinos over in Mississippi. They enjoyed coming up here." He swiveled his chair halfway and looked out the window as he took a drag on the cigar and blew out the smoke in a thin, white plume. "And Jason knew how to party." Sanchez smiled at the memory. "They liked his parties."

"There's a lot of talk that maybe Jason had been importing more than pottery."

"Yes," he said, "I've heard it. You can hardly miss it, this talk. It is one of the prejudices we Mexicans face. The Anglos assume the only business that is done with my country is the drug business. They tried one time to take his plane away, but they could find no drugs. The police would have planted drugs, but I was there. The dogs that ran through the plane, they found nothing. All that talk of drugs is a lie, my frien'."

"But did they use drugs at the beach house?"

"There were a lot of young people in and out of that house. Too young sometimes. Jason was like my little brother, but he did not use good judgment sometimes. I gave him advice when he asked, but he didn't always accept it."

A rainstorm, gray and poorly defined, was making its way up the opposite side of the bay blowing in from the gulf. The leading edge had reached Fairhope. To the south, the horizon was covered with a haze that was closing behind an outgoing tanker headed down to Dauphin Island Pass.

"Who did Jason bank with?" I asked.

"I think he used several banks."

"Do you have any of his records?"

"Some copies of contracts he signed with some of his suppliers. Not much else."

"Could I see them?"

He frowned and took another draw on the cigar. "I can let you see some things. I'll have to go through the files. But some things, I cannot let you see unless I have permission."

"Permission? Who can give permission?"

"Right now, no one. Soon we will make the necessary arrangements for his mother to take over his affairs. She has no experience in business, and it will take some time."

The rainstorm five miles across the bay had thickened; its bottom rim was now slate gray. A single bolt of lightning flashed along the ridge on which Fairhope sits. There was a break in the clouds above us and the shafts of sunlight created a short segment of rainbow over the eastern shore.

"Is there any truth to the rumors of Jason's gambling?" I asked.

Sanchez pursed his lips and nodded. "He once got in over his head with the bookmaker who used to operate here in Mobile. I had to give him some money to pay his debts. But there is a new bookie now. This new one has a bad reputation. He is not the type of man you wish to get into debt with."

SIX

Carolyn was gone when I got back to the cabin. It would have been a great day for a round of golf. It was hot, but there were plenty of clouds and a good breeze off the gulf. However, I was going to have to go back to Randall's place later that evening to pick up Peyton for the last night of our visitation, and I didn't care anything about playing golf with the two doctors and listening to all their inside jokes and putting Varner through a couple of hours of trying to make me feel comfortable.

Varner struck me as a natural-born pleaser. He wanted me to like him, and was sure going to try to make me do just that. And in another setting, I probably would. But it just wasn't in the cards.

For one thing, Sandy was right. I had been hanging around with bail bondsmen, skip tracers, paid informants, barflies, and various down-and-outers a long time. I didn't know what to talk to the east Memphis crowd about. Besides, they're so dull. And on top of that, most of them are a whole lot better at golf than I'll ever be.

The inhabited part of the island isn't all that big, maybe six miles long east to west and maybe a mile wide at the fattest part. But it's only that wide on the eastern end, back where town is, where the churches, the cemeteries, the stores, the marinas, the restaurants, and the naval base are, where the pines are tall and dense. The long, thin western end is a sandy needle maybe a thousand feet wide, a treeless stretch of sand and sea oats pointing back toward Mississippi with a long road running down the middle and little finger roads branching off from it. On each of the little roads are groupings of cabins set on poles, hoping to withstand the tidal surge and the backwash of the next hurricane.

I needed to take a look around the island and to get my bearings, so I'd slipped on some gym shorts and a pair of Nikes and stepped down to the road. I don't guess I'll ever get to the point where I enjoy jogging. I mean, I don't hate it, but I do it out of habit more than anything else. For so many years I got by without it, but the metabolism doesn't eat everything up the way it used to and I had crossed that two-hundred-pound barrier earlier that summer. I wasn't ready to cross that line yet. I know I'll never be a flatbelly like I was when I was playing outfield up at Ole Miss. But that office job in Memphis, if it didn't do anything else for me, made me determined not to get soft.

In my line of work, getting soft can be downright hazardous. Yeah, most of what I do involves nothing more than sitting in cars with a set of binoculars for hours at a time, or looking into files and old newspapers, or sitting on a stool picking the brain of some bartender. But you do make a certain number of enemies, and some of them try to respond in a physical manner. And you never know where that's coming from. The tiny white scar I've got just below my chin came when I had tracked down this guy who was getting it on with one of his co-workers, and the wife, of all people, got mad because I had taken some zoom photos and shown them to her. Threw a dinner plate at me. I mean, it was just like in those old cartoons. The plate caught me right above the collar bone and sliced my chin like a knife would. I thought she'd be happy about getting the damn pictures, that's what she hired me for.

Okay, so maybe staying in shape wouldn't have helped me much there, but there are a bunch of other times it's kept me out of the emergency room.

I had been running west about fifteen minutes when a pebble somehow got into my shoe. I stopped and knelt down and took the shoe off to shake out the rock. About the time I put it back on and stood up, I was face to face with this BMW that was speeding toward me. It veered off the road on a course straight for me.

When you think there's a good chance you'll die in the next few seconds, your brain puts all its lieutenants on alert. Smell, hearing, taste, sight, and touch are all pressed into instant service. Later you think everything happened in slow motion, but it only seems that way because, unlike almost every other unremarkable second of our lives, in those moments when we face imminent death we get a full report from each of our senses. Such moments seem slower because there's so much more stuff we can remember about them.

The driver wasn't going all that fast, but I was caught flat-footed, so it seemed that she was at top speed. She had spread out a map and laid it across the top of the steering wheel, studying it as she held a car phone cradled between her shoulder and ear. The sun shone full on her face and she was reaching up to pull her sunshades down.

She was a pretty young woman with a long jawline, high cheeks, and an aquiline nose, light blond hair pulled back over both ears. She was wearing a pair of yellow sunglasses. Appeared to be fairly tall, hard to tell since she was sitting. She looked familiar, but my brain was engaged on other matters than trying to recall where I had seen her. Like I said, all these details didn't appear in my view for more than a fraction of a second, but I took them all in.

My pulse pounded in my ears and I was panting like I had run a set of wind-sprints. I pushed hard with my left foot and hopped onto the shoulder of the road. With a push of my right leg, I lunged for the sand.

The car whipped by me, its left tires kicking up sand from the ill-defined edge of the pavement. I hit the ground with a shoulder roll. I popped up and wheeled around and I saw the flash of the

Beemer's taillights. The rear end of the car rose from forward momentum, and the tires squealed and smeared two black strips of seared rubber along the gray pavement.

She twisted around and laid her arm across the seat. The white backup lights came on as she eased back to where I stood. The car had a Tennessee tag, Davidson County.

I felt light-headed and a little queasy. Sweat had popped out all over and I could feel it running down my neck. I put my hands on my hips and walked around in a slow circle and contemplated deep thoughts like why the good Lord would pull me through gun battles, knife fights, and collisions at sea, and then almost let me get squashed by some rich gal in a BMW who's running late for a brunch or something. Guess every once in a while He wants to show me who's in charge.

I think it was the fact that it was a BMW that pissed me off the most. I wouldn't mind getting squashed nearly as much if it was some guy who fell asleep at the wheel of his pickup after pulling a double shift at the plant. At least he'd have a good excuse. But like I always say, you never know when you're going to get your ticket punched.

"Are you all right?" Her voice was sheepish, embarrassed. "I didn't mean to crowd you."

"I'm really sorry. I just looked off for a second and when I looked back up, there you were."

"Yeah, well, no harm done."

"You sure you're okay?"

"Yeah. I'm okay. Forget it."

I brushed the sand off my face, knees, and elbows and the back of my T-shirt as best I could and started off at a walk to let the adrenaline work its way out. When I had gone twenty feet or so, I glanced back at the car. She was watching me in her side rearview. I wiggled my fingers in a good-bye wave. She sat there for a few seconds, still watching the mirror.

I jogged backward for a few steps and raised my arm and waved it back and forth. Now that I had my wits back about me, I realized where I had seen her. She was the young woman who had spoken to Peyton in the convenience store earlier that day. If she recognized me, she didn't show it. She put the Beemer in gear and went on, the tires scratching off quietly in the sand before gaining traction on the asphalt. She drove maybe two hundred yards, took a left toward the bay side of the island, and disappeared behind a cabin.

My run was pretty much ruined, so I reversed my direction and started trotting back to the beach house. A Fox 10 News van, a white Chevy Astro, passed me on its way back to Mobile. I wasn't running into the wind anymore, so it was doubly hot. At the next cross street I looked to the left, toward the bay side of the island, down the street the woman had turned on.

The street dead-ended at a double gate and far beyond the gate was a dormitory-style building on a lot that took up a good three acres. The whole compound was surrounded by an eight-foot-high chain-link fence. There was a sign on the gate, and, of course, it was just small enough to where I couldn't read it from where I stood, so I walked toward it.

I figured it was a government building, probably the EPA or the National Park Service, since the grounds enclosed by the fence were spacious and, from what I'd heard about Dauphin Island property values, mighty expensive. The fence had a looping border of razor wire across the top. Along the bottom of the fence a low dune of wind-driven sand had begun to pile up. Weeds and sea oats and rockachaws had spread across the sand inside the gate and a hundred low-flying terns, thick as a swarm of mosquitos, rose above the nests they had made down in that sparse ground cover.

The sign on the gate looked official enough, a professionally painted, plywood-backed poster with a sea green and sky blue logo showing a leaping dolphin against a backdrop of a globe. PROPERTY OF THE GREEN GUARDIANS was written across the top of the poster, and across the bottom in a bright red, NO TRESPASSING.

As I neared the gate, the front door of the building flew open and a German shepherd came bounding out, dragging at the end of its chain a young woman in khaki shorts and this beret, the kind the Army Special Forces wore in Vietnam. Right behind her this kid, a boy, trim, tan, and wearing the same get-up, bolted out the door and caught up with her. The German shepherd had spotted me by this time and strained to charge at me, barely restrained by the chain and the weight of the young woman.

"This is private property!" the young man shouted, being as firm as he could. He didn't worry me, but that dog had my attention. It had started snarling and snapping at me. I scanned the fence trying to spot any holes the beast could slip through.

The kid rushed to the fence. His eyes had the fanatic's gleam, that rigid, clear sense of purpose, that self-assurance that kids have before the years bring the failures. The girl was desperately trying to keep the dog from pulling her to the ground.

"You'll have to leave," the girl said. Tried to make it sound like an order.

"Cute dog, darling," I said. "Don't I know you?"

"Move along, please," the young man said.

"Didn't you almost run over me with a car about ten minutes ago?"

"Hush, Cousteau!" she shouted at the dog.

"I'm going to have to ask you to leave," the young man said.

"Are you sure you're all right?" she asked. "I'm really sorry about running you off the road."

"Take Cousteau back to his pen, Heather," the young man said.

"I've just been kind of out of it the past few days," she said.

"You'll have to leave," the young man said.

"Oh, shit!" Heather said. "Here comes Jimbo!"

I heard the roar of an engine and the squeal of spinning tires and turned toward the sound. It was a police car and the damn thing was racing straight at me. The driver flipped on the blue lights in the grill and on the overhead light bar and hit the siren. I froze, not knowing whether to go right or left. A shot of adrenaline nearly lifted me straight up. My eyes focused on the tag on the front bumper as it zoomed straight at me, swelling in size until it seemed as big as a roadside billboard.

It was a Jimmy Buffett Margaritaville tag. Swear to goodness.

The tires screeched as the big car slammed on brakes. It slid off to my right. Came to a stop, barely missing me, with its bumper about a foot beyond me and its fender close enough for me to touch it. The car might not have killed me had it struck me, but it would have damn sure bounced me off that chain-link fence. I just stood there, shaking like a short-haired dog in a snowstorm.

And I promised myself I wouldn't be doing any more jogging around Dauphin Island, Alabama.

The deputy threw the door open, grabbed the sedan's center post, and pulled himself slowly out of the car. I don't know how he got into the thing to begin with. It was like watching a hot-air balloon filling up. When he finally got all the way out, he laid an arm across the roof of the car—the roof wasn't much higher than his waist—and held a VHF microphone with his other hand.

The two Guardians had already turned and headed toward the dormitory. I could tell they wanted to break and run, but the dog was barking and lunging toward the deputy and me. Heather, who had wrapped the dog's chain around her wrist, was pulled backward hard and landed on her butt in the soft sand.

"Awright, children! Y'all stop runnin' and get your asses back over here!" the deputy said in a calm voice, amplified by the speakers mounted in the grill. "Y'all can either talk to me here or I can drive right through that fence and jerk Zandro out of his yoga class." He looked at me through a pair of silver, mirrored cop shades. "Are you with those two?"

I shook my head from side to side, stunned into silence, breathing through my mouth and shaking with each breath. I was feeling light-headed, so I sat down on the sand and propped my forearms on my knees. This had been one hell of a jog so far.

"Can we help you, officer?" the young man said, his voice a lot more tentative than it had been with me.

The huge deputy stepped to the trunk of his patrol car, opened it, and scooped up a double armload of cardboard signs nailed to wooden stakes. He was a pleasant-looking giant. Round, not fat, and jolly. If not jolly, at least smiling a lot. Looked for all the world like a deep-water tanned version of Hoss Cartwright of the old *Bonanza* show. Even had a tiny gap between his two front teeth.

The cardboard signs looked like yard signs for a political campaign. They bore the same sea green and light blue logo that was on the fence. Across the face of each sign was the slogan STOP THE KILLING, NO OFFSHORE DRILLING! The deputy walked to the gate, furiously working over a jawful of bubble gum. He dropped the signs to the ground, reached down for one, and tossed it over the fence with a hook shot. He kept slinging the signs over the fence as he smiled at the thoroughly intimidated kids. The dog, which had pulled free from the girl, ran up and down the fence barking a playful bark, trying to catch each sign like one of those dogs at a football game catching a Frisbee.

"I told y'all that we got an ordinance on this island about sticking signs on the side of the road."

"Whatever happened to freedom of speech?" Heather asked.

"I don't hear these signs sayin' nothing, sweetheart. When you gonna go on back to school and leave these losers alone?"

The young man's jaw tightened, but he didn't say anything. Heather stood and brushed the sand off her seat.

"Now y'all go back in there and tell Zandro I ain't about to let him trash up this place just because he's got some political movement or whatever it is gnawing away at his ass. It don't matter whether we got TV cameras down here or not. And tell him I better not watch the news tonight and see a bunch of these signs all over the place."

"You watch the news, Jimbo?" Heather said. "I'm impressed."

"I watch the sports, the weather, and the fishing report, darling.

And if you want to be really impressed you need to let ol' Jimbo take you out on the town one night. It'll make you wanna quit hangin' out with these tree huggers, I guarantee you."

She glanced at her young companion, who by this time was four miles past angry, glaring at Jimbo in helpless, sputtering—but very quiet—rage. "I think I'll pass on that," she said.

"Suit yourself," Jimbo said.

The young man had managed to get hold of the dog's leash and calm him down. He gave the girl a signal with his head and they started walking back toward the big house. Jimbo stood with his beefy arms crossed, smiling from behind the mirrored shades and chewing his gum like he was trying to bite it in half.

"You know Zandro?" I asked.

"Huh?" He snapped his head toward me. "Hell, I plumb forgot you was down there. Yeah, I know him. He's a pain in the ass who thinks he's gonna save the world from mankind by holing up behind this fence and dropping acid. You know him?"

"I was just out jogging and figured I'd get a closer look at this place. I thought it was a Coast Guard station or something."

He turned back to look at the kids. "Take a look at that, would you? Saw her out on the beach the other day in a bikini, one of those thong things from Victoria's Secret. Man, I'm tellin' you she is some kinda fine."

"So you do know her?"

"I introduced myself. We're sorta in that first stage of romance right now."

"First stage?"

"The one where they pretend they can't stand the sight of you."

Jimbo was a specimen, six foot three at least and a good two sixty. Arms about like a normal guy's legs. A big, beefy guy with dishwater blond hair cut short all around; every feature about him was oversized. I had this feeling I knew him from somewhere, but couldn't remember where. He wore a short-sleeved, light blue shirt, amulets on each shoulder, and the shield of the Mobile

County Sheriff's Department on each sleeve. No tie, open collar, and the top two buttons loose. He wore a pair of khaki shorts held up by a drawstring, the kind with pockets on the sides of the pant legs. Not any cop issue I'd ever seen before. He wasn't wearing a pistol or holster; no belt-mounted radio. For that matter, no badge.

"You staying here on the island?" he asked, still watching the slow, pleasant, animated retreat of the girl in the beret and tight shorts.

I nodded and stood and wiped the sweat out of my eyes with the dry edge along the bottom of my T-shirt. "I'm staying over at the Mayson cabin."

"So you're the private eye? The one that Rebecca's mama hired?"

I wondered if maybe Sandy had put ads in the newspaper or something. "I'm doing some background checks. But that's all."

"You might want to avoid messing with the official investigation. Those guys already know all there is to know about solving crimes. If you don't believe it, just ask them."

"They?" I asked. "You're not in on it?"

"The boys from Montgomery are handling it now."

"The Alabama Bureau of Investigation?"

"They let me know real fast that I was gonna be directing traffic while they did all the heavy lifting. So it's their show now. Them and Sheriff Carlton Rice. Hey, now, would you look at that?"

Heather was bending forward at the waist to undo the leash from the dog's collar, turning her well-shaped bottom in our direction, her long blond hair hanging down to where it almost touched the ground. She pushed her hair behind her ear, turned her head while still leaning forward, and looked at us over her shoulder. Jimbo grunted in appreciation, chewing the gum at a furious pace and flashing a big, toothy smile.

"They know just what they're doing, don't they?" he said.

She straightened up, stuck her tightly packed tush out at us, kissed the fingertips of her right hand as if ready to blow a kiss, and gave herself a single sharp pat on the right cheek of her bottom. Jimbo howled with delight as she stepped into the compound and slammed the door behind her.

"She's crazy about me," he said. "What can I say?" Jimbo took the last of the yard signs and tossed them all over the fence. "You probably ought to stay away from this place. Those toy soldiers Zandro's got running around ain't gonna hurt nobody but theirselves. But he's got a coupla German shepherds inside that place that you could put a saddle on."

"You know this Zandro?"

"He's the leader of this whole group. You probably won't see him; he stays in that barracks they got there. That, or out in their boat. But he's already got you on file."

Jimbo must have seen the question on my face.

"He's been watching you the whole time you been sitting there," he said. "Probably got some good long-distance shots. He's a camera bug and got more equipment than any one of those TV crews down at the other end. He's got a dozen pictures of you by now. Why don't you look up there at that top window and smile for him?"

SEVEN

T his crab dip is absolutely to die for!" the woman in the orange
sundress said. "Susan and Randall always manage to find the
best caterers."

"And I understand you're a detective?" the red-haired woman
beside her said. "That must be so very exciting."

"Private investigator," I said. "It's usually fairly routine stuff. I
do a lot of fire-scene investigations and background checks." The
dip really was pretty good.

"I saw this Robin Leach TV special the other day about this private investigator the stars use out in Hollywood," the woman in
orange said. "He drove this white Jag and had the most *gorgeous*
apartment right off Rodeo Drive."

"So do you handle big cases like that?" her friend asked. "I hear
you've been hired by the Caviss woman to investigate the murders
here on the island."

"Are you serious?" the one in orange said. "Oh, please, tell us all
about them. I'm just dying to know what really happened."

They were apparently both unattached; at least there were no
rings. I've always heard that a woman can spot a man's wedding
band at a thousand yards. But I've got to admit that I've started
noticing rings myself—on women's hands, that is—a lot quicker
than I used to. Kathy tells me that's a subliminal sign that I'm

accepting the divorce psychologically. Everyone I know thinks he's either a psychologist or a detective.

In addition to being unmarried, these two were knockouts. Each of them had a penchant for big diamond earrings and diamond-studded tennis watches. It was hard to tell how old they were. They were past the girl stage, but neither had started showing much age other than to say they were broken in. That showed in their eyes. No little girls there. In fact, both had the look of experienced, highly skilled, professional divorcees.

"Did it have anything to do with Kellie Lee Simmons and that palimony suit she was about to file against Scooter Haney?"

"I'm not really investigating the murders. I'm just trying to find some background information."

The woman in the orange dress looked puzzled for a moment, but then broke into a broad smile and started nodding her head. "Oh, I see." She winked at the redhead and touched her on the forearm. "He can't talk about it."

"Oh, of course," the redhead said. "Well, maybe you could tell us if you're looking into background on Scooter."

"I've heard the name."

"I'll bet you have. If you need to know anything about him, you just ask Jennifer here."

Jennifer, the woman in the orange dress, stiffened. Her lips tightened and she sniffed in a short breath. The redhead winced and assumed an "Oops!" sort of smile and put her finger on her lips.

"I know Scooter Haney," Jennifer said. "Actually I used to date him some. Of course, you could probably find a dozen women in this room who could say the same thing. As I recall, you may be talking with another one right now."

"I rode on his yacht to Destin one time," the redhead said. "That's not exactly dating him."

"Well, whatever," Jennifer said. "Scooter and I went out some back before he made all that money with those bus lines. He was still driving the Porsches and going out on the town every night. But back then he was doing it on credit cards and investors' money. God, I still can't believe I couldn't see through him, even back then."

"Well he's hit the big time now," the redhead said. "You ought to see that house he's building up in Mobile. Who'd have ever dreamed you could make so many millions with busses?"

"But from what I hear, he hasn't changed," Jennifer said. "He apparently still can't keep his pants zipped. Sure as I'm standing here, that Kellie Lee Simmons was fixing to pop him with a palimony suit. He finally met his match there. She was every bit as money hungry as he is and every bit as ruthless."

"And she had the tools to bait a trap for him, too," the redhead said. "I'll give her that."

"Yeah, well, from what I remember about Scooter, he wasn't one to take too kindly to getting trapped. He may come across as everybody's good buddy, but, God, did that man have a temper."

"Jennifer," the redhead said, "look over there for a second." She leaned her head toward a blond woman at the door. "I heard about her surgery, but that's unbelievable. I wonder who did it."

"I heard it was some doctor in Stockholm."

"Stockholm?"

"Well, they can certainly afford it." Jennifer looked at me and touched the side of her nose twice and mouthed the words "nose job." She looked past my shoulder and, using only her fingers, waved at the owner of the nose in question. I turned and saw Varner coming up behind me.

"Jack," he said, "you can't be greedy. You can't occupy more than one beautiful woman at a time."

"Jack's been telling us about his case here on the island," the redhead said.

"We think Scooter Haney did it," Jennifer said.

"Well, I understand Jack's got a lot of stories he could tell," Varner said. "Did he tell you he used to play baseball up at Ole Miss?"

"I went to a baseball game in Atlanta one time," the redhead said. "I loved it."

"And he used to be in the Army Military Police," he said, "and he's a black belt in karate—"

"It's judo," I said. "I'm surprised Sandy didn't explain the difference. She seems to have told a lot of my old secrets."

"And he used to be the vice president of one of the largest banks in Memphis."

"You were vice president of a bank?" Jennifer asked.

"I quit."

"To become a private eye?"

"Sort of."

"How long does it usually take somebody to make as much in the private eye business as they would being a lawyer or a stockbroker or something like that?"

"Until you told me about that guy you saw on Robin Leach," I said, "I had never heard of one who made all that much. And I know firsthand that private eyes don't make as much as bankers."

"Really?" She gave me a quizzical look. "Well then, why would you . . ."

I smiled and winked at her.

"Jennifer," the redhead said, "I hate to interrupt, but it looks like that person you said you wanted me to introduce you to is getting ready to leave."

"What person?"

The redhead cut her eyes toward the other side of the room as she tilted her head in that direction.

"Oh!" Jennifer said. "*That* person. Oh, sure, *that* person. Jack, it was very nice to meet you."

"It sure was," the redhead said as she lightly grasped Jennifer's arm and steered her away. "Good luck on your case."

They set down their hors d'oeuvre plates, picked up their drinks, and slipped into the crowd. But it didn't appear that they were going to meet anybody in particular.

"I saw that Jennifer and Laura had you cornered," Varner said. "Thought you could use an escape hatch."

"Laura?"

"The redhead. I knew them when they were both married. They're regulars on the party circuit around Mobile."

"I'll just bet they are," I said.

"They're waiting for a couple of Randall's friends to meet them here. Two real estate developers from over in Biloxi who've been out charter fishing all day. I hear these two have made a ton of money on a casino deal over there."

"My kind of guys," I said. "Why don't you come on over to the bar and let me buy you a drink."

We weaved our way through the crowd, a crowd that had grown large enough to heat up the room and loud enough to drown out Mozart's greatest hits on the built-in entertainment center's CD player. The room was white—walls, ceiling, and carpet—and trimmed in the cool tropical tones of coral, aqua, and seafoam green, which you dare to use only in a beach house. The wall facing the water was floor-to-ceiling plateglass. The bartender, a broad, olive-skinned man, handed a Heineken to me and a Perrier to Varner.

"Peyton's been having a really good time today," Varner said. "We were wondering if it'd be all right if she stayed over here tonight. The kids want to have a pallet party."

I shook my head no. "That'd be fine any other time, but this is the last night I'm going to see her for a while."

"I understand. Sandy just wanted me to ask."

"Sandy could have asked me herself."

"She would have if she had gotten to you first."

I started to say something I'd regret and caught myself. "If I would have known sooner, we could have worked it out."

"Excuse me, gentlemen," said a familiar voice from behind us. "I wan' to get to the bar, if you don' mind."

"Mr. Sanchez," I said. "Good to see you again."

He gave me a solid handshake. His palms were as dry and rough as a dried-out plank. He was wearing that same seersucker suit he was wearing when I was in his office.

"You're Bob Sanchez?" Varner said. "I'm Varner Keyes from Memphis. I've heard a lot about you."

"I'm afraid I have been in the news a lot more than I wan' to be," he said. He got a rum and Coke, nodded a silent good-bye, and slipped back into the crowd.

"Gotta like a guy who wears seersucker," Varner said.

"Do Randall and Susan know Bob Sanchez?"

"It's a small island. I hear Sanchez and Jason Summers were friends." He twisted the top off his bottled water. "Randall told me he doesn't know Sanchez all that well. But you got to admit, the man adds a certain flair to the party."

Sandy stepped up behind us and slipped her arm around Varner's waist. It was a sight that made my gut tighten, but I didn't let it show. At least I don't think I did.

"Hi, honey," he said. "I was just talking to Jack about foreign adventures."

Honey? Now how was I supposed to take that? I took a deep breath and let it out slowly.

"Jack's always been attracted to adventures," she said, "foreign and otherwise. Have you two talked about Peyton?"

"I think she needs to stay with me tonight," I said.

"Why won't you let her stay over here?" Sandy said. "She's having such a good time with her new friends."

"But I won't see her again for two months."

"She's been down here with you for two weeks. She's ready to play with somebody closer to her own age."

"She'll have all the playmates she can handle in a week," I said. "At least all those whose parents can spring for twenty grand a year for tuition."

Sandy gave me a frosty stare. "I'm sure you want the best for your daughter. And it's twenty-*four* grand."

"And so that proves it's the best?"

"Of course it is! The admissions standards are among the highest in the country."

"The admissions standard for Seeley Academy is the same as it is for any other one of those brat academies. If the check clears, the kid gets in the friggin' school. Period."

She drew up as tall as she could stretch. Her lips got tight and her eyes blazed.

"I'm sorry you feel that way," she said, her voice dripping with contempt. "But I do wish you'd put Peyton's interests first for at least this evening." She wheeled around and stomped off. Varner cut his eyes toward me and shook his head.

"Did I say something wrong?"

"She's sensitive about Seeley Academy," Varner said. "She spent weeks trying to pick out the school she thought would be best for Peyton."

"Sandy knows full well what I think about those overpriced snob schools. She's known it for years, so that's nothing new. It's more than that. She's been snapping at me ever since y'all got here this afternoon."

"Maybe you caught her at a bad time."

"A bad time?" I asked.

He nodded.

"Oh, I get it," I said. "One of *those* bad times."

"It happens. Every month if you're lucky."

"It's been six years," I said. "I forgot just how bad it can get."

There was a crash and then a thud across the room. And screaming. And a crescendo in the collective voice of the crowd. Everyone backed off, stunned and motionless. In the crescent-shaped clearing, a stocky guy with broad shoulders and black hair had pinned this other man against the wall with a forearm to the throat. The stocky guy was Bob Sanchez.

I rushed toward them, pushing people aside. The old MP crowd-control training kicked in, that muscle memory grooved into my brain by a thousand repetitions in the gym and later in the dives of Brandenburg back when we tried to keep the lid on a half million GIs, pumped and ready for those never-to-come orders to go in and kick the Ayatollah's ass.

I clamped down on Sanchez's shoulders. I planted my left leg across the back of his knees, and yanked hard enough to pull him down to the floor. I lurched at the other guy, the one who had been pinned against the wall. I positioned my feet for leverage, put one hand on his shoulder and one on his belt, and tossed him to the side.

Sanchez was the more dangerous of the two, so I jumped behind him just as he was rising from the floor. I wrapped one arm around his neck. With my other hand I grabbed his elbow and pulled his arm behind his back in a half-Nelson. His muscles were hard like a weightlifter's.

"Let me go! Dammit, let go of me!"

"Just calm down. I'll let you go just as soon as you cool off."

"Get that son of a beech out of my sight!"

I glanced toward the guy Sanchez had pinned against the wall. He was standing hunched over in the middle of the floor rubbing his cheek, the one that had been pressed against the wall, and keeping a cautious eye on us. I jerked my head to the side to try to signal him to get the hell out of the room.

"You don' know what you're talking about!" Sanchez hollered at the other guy as he walked away. "By God, you better stop runnin' your mouth!"

"Hey!" I tightened my grip on his arm. "Take it easy, Bob. This is a nice party."

He was breathing through his mouth, hard and fast. A minute later, I felt the tension ease and the panting subside. The other guy was nowhere to be seen.

"Let it go," I said. "You're making what they call in polite society a scene. It's bad form. And there are reporters here."

"He was saying Jason was a drug pusher. I loved Jason like a son."

"Can I let go now?"

He nodded.

I released my grip, crouched, and took two steps back, keeping a constant eye on his shoulders for any sudden swings. He pulled at his lapels, shook his head, and slowly turned around. He puffed his chest out and took short breaths through his nose and gave everybody the back-off signals of the challenged alpha male. With his broad face, dark complexion, drooping mustache, and yellow-tinted wire rims, he looked like a scowling Panama Jack without the hat. He took the measure of me with his dark and deep-set eyes before nodding, only once and very quickly.

"You and me, are we okay?" I asked, pointing at my chest and then at him.

"I apologize for my outburst. Please make my apologies to our host." He turned and walked through a parted crowd to the door, as stiff and erect as if on parade-field revue.

I walked back to the other side of the room, and, I swear, some guy reached out and patted me on the back. By the time I reached the bar the show was over and the crowd was as loud as ever. I was pretty warm and could feel the sweat running down the side of my face so I unbuttoned my two top buttons and loosened my sleeves. As the bartender handed me a Budweiser in a bottle, Jennifer in the orange dress and Laura, her redheaded companion, came across the room and cozied up next to me.

"Oh, I am *so* impressed!" Jennifer said. "What I've heard about you must be true."

"Why don't you just tell me what you've heard," I said, "and I'll tell you how much of it to believe."

Laura laughed and kept gazing at my chest and shoulders. "I can't believe you took on Roberto Sanchez."

"Is he supposed to be bad news or something?"

They glanced at each other and smiled.

"I heard he's killed people down in Mexico or wherever he's from," Jennifer said.

From across the room, I caught Sandy looking at us. The last three years of our marriage, Sandy started telling me how it was a redneck trait to get into fights for any reason. Of course, when I was working in her daddy's bank up in Memphis settling a difference with a fistfight was . . . well, the subject just never came up. But looking back on it, things would have been a lot more civil around that Godforsaken place had somebody kicked some ass somewhere along the line.

When I'm up in Memphis nowadays to visit Peyton, Sandy tries to steer me away from a certain pair of the MBA-type rat finks I knew from that bank. I owe both of them an ass whipping. And, by God, if I ever run into them on the street up there, I'll settle those scores in as public a fashion as I can. I've been told many times that I've got the sort of attitude that doesn't get me on the A list at dinner parties, in east Memphis or anywhere else where they actually have dinner parties.

I consider that one hell of a side benefit.

I started telling Jennifer and Laura some of the stories from cases I've handled. The way they were reacting, I got to thinking maybe I had been wrong about these two. Maybe they were ready to talk to a guy whose idea of taking a risk means something a little more dangerous than picking a stock when he should pick a bond. And I was getting a real kick out of Sandy's attempts to hide the fact that she was looking at us.

I had just started telling them about this case in New Orleans where this old woman used her voodoo powers to help her son control the city's cocaine trade, when Jennifer spotted two guys walking in the front door. The guys appeared to be the expected pair from the charter boat, sunburned and red eyed and wearing long-billed caps. Jennifer and Laura made their exits within seconds and left me standing there, halfway into my story. I guess my stuff wasn't as interesting as hearing how much money those two guys have made from their casinos after all.

Oh, well. No surprise.

I stepped out to the deck to get some fresh air and get away from the noise. It was fairly crowded with smokers. But the breeze coming in was cool and steady and strong enough to clear the air, leaving only a scent of cigar smoke. The muted sounds of the laughter and loud talk inside the house resonated through the plateglass.

"Jack! Come over and sit with us." It was Randall. "I heard about the ruckus. I apologize."

"No harm done."

He and this other guy were sitting around a rattan table with fat, long cigars and brandy snifters. There was no light outside except for that which came through the windows and the plate-glass door. I declined the offer of a cigar and sat in the one empty chair. The Budweiser I had been nursing was barely above room temperature. Randall introduced me to Doc, a charter boat captain who operated out of the marina on the bay side of the island. He was pushing Social Security age and looked like Ernest Hemingway with a ponytail.

"Doc here is from one of the island's old families," Randall said. "Y'all were here before the bridge. Right, Doc?"

Doc nodded as he blew out a gray line of smoke. "My mama's daddy, he used to deliver the mail to the island by rowboat. Daddy's family, they been here since 1910. Used to let their cattle range free all over the island. Didn't need fences before they built the bridge."

"I've been telling Doc about your case here on the island," Randall said. "He was big friends with Jason Summers."

"I don't know how friendly we were. We shared the same accountant and the same bookie. That's about it."

"Did the same guy do both jobs?" I asked.

Doc smiled and took a puff of his cigar. "The CPA is this kid who moved up here from Mexico a few years ago. Kid named John Villa. Jason introduced me to him. He's young, but he's some kinda sharp. He was the brains behind Jason's business, I guarantee you."

"Doc," Randall said, "is this Villa a Mexican-American?"

"Don't start all that hyphenated crap with me!" Doc said, his voice rising.

Randall smiled and winked at me. "So is he, or not?"

"He's from downtown, friggin' Mexico, by God! He came up to Auburn on a tennis scholarship and studied accounting. If he's done become a citizen, then that makes him an American. Period. You want me to start calling you Alabaman-American? You know that grates on me."

"I assume the bookie you mentioned was Bobby Earl Fair," I said.

"Bobby Earl, he's the only game in town," Doc said. "But Jason, he was in a bigger league than I'll ever be. That guy'd put as much on one game as I'd bet on the whole card."

"You think Jason could have gotten in too deep with his bookie?" I asked.

"Not with Bobby Earl. You don't do that." Doc took a long draw off his cigar. "Besides, Jason won as much as he lost, maybe more."

"I hear Bobby Earl's a bad dude," I said.

Doc shrugged and stared at the brandy as he swirled it around the snifter he held between his thumb and forefinger. "He's mostly just a hothead. Did some time at Parchman for aggravated assault. That's where he teamed up with this white supremacist group. They're the ones who set him up in Mobile after Vince died."

"What group are you talking about?" I asked.

"Hell, I don't know. White Resistance, White Revolution, something like that. Way Bobby Earl tells it, when you're in the joint, you either join up with 'em or the blacks—or, like Randall says, the African-Americans, they'll run right over your ass. Some of that White Resistance group got out of the pen and set up this organization that's done took over the football betting around here."

"Sounds like some kind of alumni association," Randall said.

"Do you think this White Resistance could have had anything to do with the killings at Jason's beach house?" I asked.

"I still think them crazy-assed Green Guardians did it."

"Aw, come on, Doc," Randall said, "most of that bunch don't look like they could harm a fly."

"Yeah, well neither did the Manson Gang," Doc said. "You ever take a good look at that Zandro character?"

"What do you think, Jack?" Randall asked.

"I'm sure the police will eventually find the killer."

"Killers," Doc said.

"Well it's a crying shame," Randall said. "I knew Jason, about like everybody else around here did. In fact, that's where we got these cigars. He had this import/export business and did a lot of dealings with Central America."

"Ha!" Doc blurted. "That's for sure. He had all kinda dealings."

"I don't believe those stories about him being a dealer," Randall said. "How many drug smugglers have you ever heard of who go out of their way to meet everybody in town?"

"Don't get me wrong," Doc said, "I liked Jason a lot. God knows, I'm the last mother's son on this island to pass judgment on anybody else. Besides, whatever else Jason might have been importing, at least he managed to bring in some Cuban cigars. This is probably the only country in the world where they're illegal. And that makes them mighty pricey. You sure you don't want one?"

I shook my head no. "Did Jason spend a lot of time here?"

"He lived on the island year round," Randall said. "Have you seen his beach house?"

"Only from the road."

"It was party central. I mean every day and night from Memorial Day to Labor Day. He'd bring in clients from Mexico, El Salvador, Costa Rica, every country down there. Jason used to charter my boat to take them out to the snapper banks. He'd go out fishing with them sometimes, and sometimes this guy named Sanchez would come down and go out with them."

"Are you talking about Bob Sanchez?" I asked.

"Yeah," Doc said. "He was Jason's lawyer. I hear he's here tonight."

Randall laughed and cut his eyes toward me and took a long drag on his cigar. "Doc," Randall said, "tell Jack about Sanchez and the death squads."

"Death squads?" I asked.

"Roberto Sanchez used to be a colonel in Nicaragua," Doc said.

"A specialist in terrorism, although I never have figured out whether that means he was the one who tracked the terrorists down or the one who was settin' off the bombs. From what I hear he could do it either way, depending on what Somoza wanted. Supposedly he cut his teeth with the death squads. His specialty was pushing people out of helicopters."

"The story's been floating around for years," Randall said. "I don't know how much of it I believe."

"Do you want me to tell this story or not?"

"Long as you tell the truth."

Doc laughed and sipped his brandy. "Son, the number one rule down here is you never let the truth get in the way of a good story. Besides, I think all that shit about Sanchez is true. Think about it. Sanchez was in the army down there. He'll tell you that outright."

"That doesn't mean he was in any death squad," Randall said.

Doc shrugged as if to say, Who cares?, and took a drag on his cigar. "Way I hear it, Sanchez is associated with some law firm in Mexico City and that's where he gets all those Mexican clients. Jason was an importer and dealt with some of the same people. That's how they got to know each other."

The muffled sounds from behind the glass blared as the door opened. "Randall, I hate to interrupt y'all," Susan said, "but our TV celebrity has arrived."

"You mean Carlton Rice is here?" Doc asked. Randall laughed and swallowed some brandy the wrong way and started coughing.

"Real funny," Susan said. "It's Darren Wright. Why don't y'all come meet him?"

"I guess I better go welcome him," Randall said as he stood. I stood also and walked with them back into the house. My beer had gotten warm from exposure to the breeze.

The presence of Darren Wright filled the room the same way the presence of a movie star would. The image we had seen on TV made flesh and walking among us. Consciously or subconsciously, every eye drifted his way. Darren had freshened up since I saw him earlier in the day at the convenience store, at least he had washed his hair, but his eyes were glassy and his face flushed. He had drawn a crowd and was shaking hands like it was the county fair and he was running for governor.

I followed Randall and Susan toward Darren because he had—no surprise—taken up a position right in front of the bar. And by that time my beer was downright hot. I was trying to ease past him when he recognized me from earlier in the day.

"Howya doin'," he said. "Where's that pretty young lady you had with you this afternoon?"

"She's back there with some PlayStation game," I said.

"Darren Wright," he said as he stuck out his hand. "Fox News."

"Jack Delmas." I pointed to the bar behind him. "Thirsty."

"Bartender, whatever my friend here needs. And put it on my tab."

The circle in front of Wright laughed, a little more than the joke deserved, and he pointed toward Randall and Susan and winked at them in acknowledgment of their hospitality. Nice gesture; I've seen celebrities who never think about who's picking up their tab. Randall made the appropriate wince to let everybody know he was indeed dropping a wad on this little soiree.

I got in behind this woman who was getting the bartender to give her a complete inventory of what he had before she made up her mind. No surprise, she settled on a daiquiri. As the bartender started scooping the ice into the blender, I eavesdropped on Darren as he spoke to the crowd.

"We still don't have the crime-lab reports," he said.

"Do you think the local police can handle this case?" someone asked.

"No."

Everybody laughed.

"That's not saying anything bad about the local police. How often are they called on to handle something like this? I'd guess never."

"You got that right," said a voice in the group. "We've never had a murder here."

"That's my point," Darren said. "The same thing happened in the Jon-Benet Ramsey case a few years ago. In fact, there are a lot of parallels between the media coverage of this case and the Jon-Benet case. Both happened in quiet, affluent communities that were not prepared for the eyes of the world to be focused on them. Nothing wrong with that. But when I say on the air that the local police aren't equipped to handle the situation, they take it personally."

Laughter again.

"Well, you better hope that Jimbo McInnis doesn't take it too personally," a voice called out from the second tier of the audience. This time the laughter was a roar.

"I've seen Deputy McInnis," Darren said. "Your point is well taken."

I finally got my Heineken and leaned against the wall and surveyed the room. I had learned that the party was a housewarming since Randall and Susan had only recently built the house. But they were both old Mobile, both longtime fixtures of Dauphin Island society, so the crowd was too much for the place despite the five thousand square feet and the thirty-by-forty-foot great room we were in. The ceiling fans were twirling full blast to help out the air conditioner and keeping up fairly well. There wasn't enough room to walk more than five or six feet in a straight line in any direction without maneuvering around a group. The two bars, one at each end, were turning out drinks at a steady pace and the tips jars at each were stuffed to the rim.

"How's it going?" It was Varner. He had eased up beside me unnoticed while I was observing the surroundings. "You listening to all this stuff our TV friend has been saying?"

"Not much."

"He's saying that Kellie Lee Simmons was rumored to be carrying on with some other well-known men besides Scooter Haney."

"That's no surprise," I said. "You want a drink?"

He shook his head no. "I'm flying tomorrow. Look, about Peyton staying over here tonight . . ."

"Let's don't start that again."

"What I was thinking is that instead of us leaving early tomorrow, we could take off at, say, four in the afternoon. That way Peyton could stay with the other kids tonight and you could pick her up in the morning and have most of the day to go to the beach or whatever."

"Was this Sandy's idea?"

"I haven't mentioned it to her. She's not feeling too good."

"If she's out of Midol, it'd pay you to go get some."

He chuckled and smiled at me. "So how about it?"

"What time could I pick Peyton up in the morning?"

"You name it."

Varner was trying hard, and I sensed it wouldn't be smart to turn this deal down. I'd hear about it for the next ten years or maybe longer. I said okay and he eased away.

"What we know so far," Darren Wright was saying, "is that robbery has been ruled out as a motive."

Give me a break, I thought. How long was he going to talk about it? Here we are at a cocktail party, and he sounds like he's got a camera rolling. I wondered if he talked that way at home.

"The thing you've got to realize is that Kellie Lee Simmons is the real story here. You've got a former Miss Global Alabama who's been the subject of rumors concerning some high-profile, high-power types. You'd all recognize their names. You take Kellie Lee out of the mix and you've got just another murder."

I debated about whether I should put that assessment into my report to Carolyn.

I probably should have; it was the truth.

EIGHT

The ferry was only half full as it neared the dock on its return from the Fort Morgan side of Mobile Bay. It would be unloaded, re-loaded, and headed back to the eastern shore in twenty minutes. Its sweet diesel exhaust drifted ahead to the pier where we had been standing and a clear, melodious, tri-toned note blared from its horn just before the captain put the engine in reverse to slow the big boat enough for it to drift softly to the landing.

"This will be fun," I said.

"It's stupid," Peyton said. "I don't want to ride on a boat."

"Look. It's about to touch the pier."

"What if it sinks?"

The line of waiting cars backed up along Bienville Boulevard began cranking their engines, but it would be a few minutes before the cars from the Fort Morgan side cleared out. Peyton and I were on bikes that I had found stored in the garage under the beach house. I had fixed some snacks and cooled some canned drinks and put them into a little Igloo cooler that fit into the rack over the rear wheel of my bike. It was the last few hours of our visit and we were going to have a picnic whether we wanted to or not.

It had rained earlier that morning, and the sun was still hidden by a gray, hazy bank of poorly defined clouds. The breezes were cool, puddles still stood along the side of the road, and the air still smelled of rain. The wooden deck of the house across the street was dark from the earlier soaking and water dripped off the pine trees in the median of Bienville Boulevard.

"Why can't I stay at Harper's house and play video games?"

"Because it's a pretty day and you need to get outdoors."

"It's raining, Daddy."

"It's not raining now. Just think, you'll get to ride out on the ocean. You can tell all your friends at school about riding on that big boat."

"I want to play video games."

"How would you like a strawberry drink?"

I was getting worried about that video-game business. Since I see Peyton only once every two months or so, I catch myself worrying that every little thing she does that I don't approve of will be carried in an unbroken line to its extreme. I know Sandy is a loving mother, I'll give her that. So when I see all this stuff like the video-game overdose and the ordering out for pizza every day, I have to tell myself that when I see Sandy and Peyton together these days it's when they're down on the coast or going to New Orleans. That's when they're on a fun trip, a vacation, when the normal routine goes out the window. I tell myself it's not like that every day. But I don't get to see what every day is like. So the old demons go to work in my head and raise all kinds of fears. By the time we got on the ferry with our bikes, I was imagining that Peyton was just one step removed from being in a Dungeons & Dragons cult.

We put the bikes in the rack on the lower deck and climbed the steps to the little raised passenger deck beside the wheelhouse. We sat on the bench and she drew close to me when the captain showered down on the diesel and the boat shuddered as it backed away from the dock.

"Where are we going?" she asked.

"We're going to ride our bikes and have a picnic and play Frisbee."

"Can we hunt for seashells?"

"Sure."

"This boat is scary."

I reached around her shoulders and pulled her closer to me. I looked over the cars on the deck below us and noticed this Plymouth Barracuda, a 1969 model, with a sparkling, showroom quality coat of emerald green paint. It had wire rim spinner hubcaps and lightly tinted windows all around. The two front windows were rolled all the way down. There was one person in the car, the guy sitting behind the wheel, and he was looking at us.

He was a white guy with a full head of black curly hair that was cut close on the sides but with a set of sideburns just a little too long to be in style. It reminded me of the way we wore them years ago when I was in college. He was a rangy guy with long arms. There was a tattoo on the forearm that was hanging out his window. He wore a black golf shirt and had a pair of black plastic sunshades propped on top of his head. He stared at us way longer than a comfortable time, long enough to let me know he was looking at me.

"Is that a big fish?" Peyton asked.

I kept one eye on the guy in the Barracuda as I glanced in the direction she was pointing. "I don't see it."

"Keep looking," she said.

When it broke the surface again, I thought at first it was a dolphin. But it was way too big, and it was black rather than gray. I reached into my backpack for my field glasses and scanned the area where it had surfaced.

"Are you looking at the whales?" It was a young man standing beside Peyton on the bench. He had a deep bronze tan and dishwater blond hair worn in a ponytail. He wore a Dauphin Island Sea Lab knit shirt, a pair of khaki swim trunks, and some scuffed deck shoes with white rubber soles worn smooth. The shirt had the name Danny embroidered just above the pocket. "We've been following them at the lab for a couple of days now."

The whales were off the starboard bow at the two o'clock position, a pod of a dozen or so. They are a rare sight anywhere, but doubly rare in the Gulf of Mexico. Most people, even the shrimpers and the roughnecks on the offshore rigs, never see whales, pygmy or otherwise. And even if they do, they think they're seeing big dolphins.

"In the southern waters we've got the killer whales, and the Bryde's whales, and occasionally the false killers," Danny said. "We don't have big ones like they have in the Pacific."

"I've seen whales twice before," I said. "Both times on long shrimping trips when I was a kid. But that was way out in the gulf. I've never seen any this close in." I handed the binoculars to Peyton and draped the cord around her neck.

"These are pygmy killer whales," he said. "And it's very rare for them to come in from the deep water."

Danny started telling Peyton about the whales and directing her attention to the biggest one, the one out in front of the pod. The other passengers had spotted the whales by this time and many of them got out of their cars and went to the railings or climbed the steps to the upper deck. The whales had encountered a vast school of menhaden fish and were cavorting in a feast of leaps and dives and flips. Peyton laughed and squealed, so excited she could hardly keep from jumping up and down.

The crowd oohed and ahhed as crowds do at fireworks shows. I glanced down at the cars below us; they were all empty. Every soul on the ferry was leaning on the rail on the starboard side taking in the show. One of the passengers at the rail was a well-built man about my size with a full head of neatly trimmed salt-and-pepper hair. I caught him staring at me, so I held my return gaze until he glanced away. With all these people looking at me, I was beginning to wonder if my fly was open or if somebody had taped a KICK ME sign on my back.

The ferry was closing in on the pod as they swam a course that would take them across our bow, and the passengers congregated along the front railing to see them up close. A juggler at the back of the ferry could have been tossing live cats around and not a soul would have noticed. Peyton was barely tall enough to see over the rail and she pushed up on her tiptoes far enough to hook her elbows over the top and pull herself up. She was completely enthralled by the whales, which were by that time close enough to where we could see the fluted, flat tails lifting slowly out of the gray water and then pushing back down with unhurried, effortless power. This downward push forced their dorsal fins upward until they peaked and fell back below the surface. Steady cycles, like the humping of the Loch Ness monster.

"I hear you been askin' questions about me."

I turned and was face to face with the guy who had been sitting in the Barracuda. "Do I know you?" I said.

"You know who I am."

The guy had hard, flat eyes, dark as coal. He smelled of cheap aftershave and cigarette smoke. His teeth were dingy and the bottom ones were crooked.

"I've never seen you before in my life," I said.

"You got a problem around here, you keep it to yourself. I better not be hearing no more about you tryin' to dig up some dirt on me."

"You've got a smart mouth," I said.

He glared at me as his eyes narrowed to slits, and started breathing through his nose. "Why don't you just go on back to where you come from?"

I couldn't figure out just where I ought to know this guy from, but I had other things to think about just then. I thought about trying to back him down by getting in his face and seeing what he'd do about it. If he made a move, I knew I could take him. He was leading with his chin, a sure sign of somebody who doesn't know the first thing about fighting. It wouldn't take much to put him on the deck.

"Daddy!" Peyton shouted. "Come over here and look at these whales!"

The guy turned his head toward her. I didn't like the way he looked at her. Don't know why, it just didn't feel right. "Yeah, you better go look at them big fish." He turned and walked down the steps, looking back at me over his shoulder.

The whales paid no attention to the voices of the crowd on the ferry, or their pointing, or their shouting, or their taking of hundreds of photographs. They were oblivious to the approaching ferry, oblivious to the cawing of the hundreds of grateful gulls feasting on the shad and menhaden they were stirring up. In the fashion of movie stars or house cats, they had decided that this was the time they would deign to let the mortals have their fun and express their admiration and, once having served that purpose, to just go away. I took two zoom shots of the pod and handed the camera to Peyton and showed her where the button was.

"They've been swimming around here for the past few days and the word has spread," the young man said. "We got people driving down from Mobile to take the ferry on the chance they'll see them. It won't last too much longer. We think the leader whale is disoriented, probably sick. He'll either get his bearings and head back out to deep water, or he'll beach himself."

"What happens to the rest of them if the leader beaches himself?" I asked.

"If we can isolate which one it is and remove him, we can pull the rest of them back out into deep water and maybe they can regroup and go back out into the gulf. Worst case, they all beach themselves and we can't isolate the leader fast enough to save the rest of them. Mass beachings don't happen often, but they do happen."

The whales were within a hundred yards now. The ferry was pounding the waves at an angle that created big splashes and filled the air with the clean, salty aroma of the gulf. A white spray came over the side and some of the tiny drops blew all the way to the upper deck. I could taste the salt on my upper lip.

The pod had changed its course and was now swimming directly at the side of the ferry, lunging toward a spot fifteen feet back from the bow, a spot where this pot-bellied guy was leaning over the rail smoking a cigarette. He had thin, black hair, heavily sprayed and combed across his skull, not covering all that much of it. He wore a black Jeff Gordon T-shirt, red and yellow plaid shorts, and white canvas deck shoes with a pair of black, mid-calf socks.

I counted six whales, all the same size, all about the length of a long-wheel-bed pickup truck. They came at us in a shifting formation with the two in front playing a game, racing each other for the lead position. It was neck and neck with the lead changing each time one of them poked its head out of the water. They drew close enough for us to see their little smiles, their little teeth.

In unison, as if on signal, all six rose, propelled skyward with synchronized pushes of their wide tails, vaulting above the water in an arc and coming down head first, hitting the water at an angle to send them deep enough to pass under the ferry. They hit the water and sent a spray straight at the guy by the rail, soaking him like a garden hose at full blast, extinguishing the cigarette and matting the strands of puffed hair into slick black strings.

The crowd erupted into laughter and most of them clapped and whistled in appreciation of the show. Peyton was squealing and pointing and just beside herself in the unrestrained glee that only a child can attain. The passengers scrambled across the deck to see the whales emerge on the other side of the boat. All the passengers but one. The guy in the Barracuda was in the driver's seat, smoking a cigarette and watching me through his black sunshades.

Peyton spotted the skinny brown rabbit the instant it popped out from the stand of sea oats. She took off after it as if she had been shot out of a cannon, following its sharp turns, weaving through the tufts of sea oats and lantana that dotted the low dunes. She followed each of the rabbit's twists and feints and angles as if she zeroed in on them by radar. She hit full speed in two steps and ran like a sprinter. Sure strides and pumping arms. Head down. Crouched to keep the center of gravity close to the ground. She negotiated the sharp banks and the zigzags as crisply as if she were rolling on rails.

God, when did all that happen?

It probably happened in a single transforming day. A day up in Memphis when she lost the halting, bobbing, jarring childhood trot, that heads-up variation of skipping that little girls have when on a playground, and took on the grace and liquid movement of the natural runner.

What was I doing that day? What dusty records vault was I in? What country song was playing on the CD player of my pickup the day my daughter passed from baby into pre-pubescence on some playground four hundred miles north of me as I sat with a zoom-lens camera, waiting to get the goods on some middle-aged crazy desk jockey whose wife wanted to build up the file before filing the divorce papers?

Peyton and I threw a Frisbee to each other on a hard-packed field that I thought at first to be a soccer field, but, on closer examination, turned out to be an old airfield. We raced each other on the bikes and chased rabbits and flew this cheap, balsa-wood kite I got from the Ship and Shore. Peyton and I walked the shoreline, barefoot with our shoes tied together and hung around our necks, running past the surge of the incoming waves along the soaked and packed sand and scattering the killdeers foraging in the tidal pools. I strung together a dozen seashells and made a necklace for her.

"Isn't this better than PlayStation?" I asked as I began packing up the ice chest and gathering up the trash.

"A lot better."

"Maybe those whales will still be there when we ride back across on the ferry."

She fingered the shells on her necklace and held them out, away from her chest, as she examined and probed with her fingers their outer ridges, and their sharp, serrated edges, and their smooth concave undersides. Those little fingers, so stubby just three months earlier, were now lengthening into the thin, graceful hands of her mother. My hands are broad and bigger than my size would indicate they should be, with thick wrists and thick fingers, which gave me a great advantage when it came to gripping a baseball bat, but rendered me useless as a guitar player.

At least she had my hair. That's one of my two good features, I've got thick blond hair. My other good feature, my nose, you can't really appreciate anymore, not since it got broken for the third time in a bar in Gautier when I failed to recognize the ex-husband of a woman who hired me to dig up some dirt on him during their divorce. The son of a bitch had shaved and cut off the ponytail. He blindsided me right as I was popping the top on the can of Dixie.

Peyton was growing into the best facial features of her mother, not quite there yet and still hidden from anyone who had not spent as much time studying her mother's face as I had, which is to say no one else in the world other than Sandy's father, T. W. "Buddy" Donovan, III, president emeritus of the second largest bank in Memphis, and her mother, Sarah Nell (SAY-ra Nell), a former queen of the Cotton Carnival.

Sarah Nell, to this good day, is pissed at me because I showed what she considered a complete lack of common decency by marrying Sandy. I think, though I'm not sure, that Sarah Nell has finally realized that I can't do anything about the fact that I was born outside the cotton aristocracy that orbits around Memphis. But, by God, I grew up fully aware of this deficiency, so she still thinks it was perfectly horrible and low class of me to somehow trick her daughter into marriage.

By way of contrast, Varner the X-ray reader inherited a few thousand acres of prime cotton land over in Cross County in the Arkansas delta. So deep down, he's really a cotton planter; this radiologist business is sort of a respectable sideline. I'm telling you, the guy doesn't have any weak spots as far as Sandy and her parents are concerned.

Peyton was stretching out, growing taller, losing the awkwardness and losing the baby fat, stepping into the earliest stages of graceful womanhood. Like I say, you may not be able to see it just yet. But, believe me, it's there and getting more noticeable every time I see her. And it broke my heart to think what other changes would be there the next time I saw her.

"You know what?" she said as we mounted our bicycles.

"What, darling."

"Today started out not fun, but later on it got to be fun."

"It certainly did."

"I'll race you."

And she took off and got the jump on me before the words were out of her mouth, just the kind of thing her mother would do, pedaling furiously across the bumpy remains of the tarmac of the old landing strip, her legs pumping so fast they were almost a blur.

An hour later, I dropped Peyton off at Susan and Randall's place so Sandy could get her ready for the flight back to Memphis. When I got to the beach house where I was staying, the phone started ringing while I was slipping the key into the front door. I got to it at the same time the answering machine kicked in. The caller had already started leaving her message.

"Mr. Delmas, I need your help." It was a soft girl's voice, just a touch of tremor. "I can't leave my number. I'll have to call back."

"Hello?" I said as I picked up while the machine was still recording. "This is Jack Delmas."

There was silence at the other end.

"Can I help you?" I asked.

She had started crying. Softly. Shallow, shaky breaths. A lot of sniffling.

"Hello?" I said. "Hello?"

I was about to give up when she finally spoke. "I'm in trouble. I've got to talk to somebody."

"Who is this?" I knew the voice from somewhere.

"We sort of met the other day at the store," she said. "You had your little girl with you."

"Are you the person who almost ran over me?"

"I told you I was sorry."

"How did you know where to call me?" I asked.

"This friend of mine over at the Neptune knew where you were staying."

I swear, I must have missed the front-page story the *Mobile Register* had obviously run on me and what all I was doing on the island.

"Wait a minute," I said, "before you say anything else, are you on a cell phone?"

"No, sir. I'm calling from a pay phone."

"Okay," I said. "Go ahead."

Three short blasts from a ship's horn sounded in the background. Sounded like the approach of the ferry. "I think the Green Guardians are about to do something crazy."

"How crazy?"

"I'm scared, Mr. Delmas." She had started sounding as if she were Peyton's age.

"We've got to call the police," I said.

I heard several cars starting their engines and the faint, flute-like calls of seagulls.

"Are you still there?" I asked.

"I thought you *were* the police," she said.

"I'm a private detective. You need to go to the Dauphin Island Police or the sheriff's office."

"Are you sure you're not with the police?"

In the background, the ferry sounded its final whistle as it docked. I knew exactly where she was, the only pay phone at the landing. "Heather," I said, "I want you to call the sheriff's office right now and tell them to come get you."

"How'd you know my name?"

"Call them now," I said. "Just do it, okay?"

"But all those sheriff's deputies, they hate the Guardians! They won't help me!"

Over the phone, I could hear the cars driving onto the ferry and Heather softly blowing her nose into a handkerchief. She was getting more distraught, and it was showing in her voice.

"Look, Heather, you need to call the sheriff. If you can't get him, call this deputy who patrols down here. The deputy's name is Jimbo."

"Oh, right!" she said, "Jimbo *really* hates me. He won't help."

"I don't know him all that well," I said. "But I know for a fact that he doesn't hate you. You call him, or I'm going to call him and tell him to go get you."

I could hear her sobbing. She didn't say anything else before she hung up.

I didn't walk out to the plane with them. We said our good-byes at the parking lot just beyond the fence at the little airstrip. I sat to watch the takeoff on the steps of the eight-by-eight-foot tin hut that serves as the control tower. Looks like a deer stand. It was one of the few days the manager was there. He was inside, checking the little radar screen; there wasn't enough space in there for both of us.

Sandy had been feeling better. She thanked me for taking care of Peyton and freeing up the past two weeks and for not acting like a horse's ass around Varner. I resisted the impulse to remind her that I was not the one who was taking the extra-strength Midol the night before.

Here she was thanking *me* for not being a horse's ass!

Like that's what she expected or something.

I tried to let it roll off my back, to fight the natural tendency to work it over in my mind until I get good and mad the way I usually do, the way I had done the past eight or nine years.

It was tough saying good-bye to Peyton. She thought I was getting on the plane with them. But I promised her I'd come up to Memphis a week sooner than I had planned and made up a story about how I was supposed to stay and take care of Sweetie, this huge dog that my mother and father had taken in after the death of its owner, an old family friend. Sweetie is a scary, territorial beast that Peyton had fallen in love with. She decided it was all right that I was going to stay behind since Sweetie needed me.

The Cessna taxied into takeoff position. Peyton waved to me, her little face framed by the round window on the side of the plane. The terminal manager stepped out of the tiny control tower and stood beside me.

"They friends of yours?" he asked.

I nodded. "What's the weather look like between here and Memphis?"

"Perfect. Not even any wind. That guy's flown in here before. Mighty good pilot."

That figured. Was there anything he wouldn't be good at? Of course at that minute I wasn't really upset to hear he was a good flyboy.

"You know the exact time of arrival?" I asked.

"It's a little over an hour, maybe an hour and a half. I ain't made the log entries yet. Way I look at it, what's the use in keeping up with all that paperwork when it ain't gonna make one bit of difference about when they get on the ground."

I thought they had to keep better records than that, but the Dauphin Island airstrip is not exactly the Atlanta airport. I waved at Peyton as Varner built up the power on the twin engines.

"Y'all picked a bad time to visit," he said. "We don't usually have all these TV camera crews running around. They been flying camera crews in and out of here, sometimes two or three a day. You not with the TV folks, are you?"

"No."

"Well, I reckon they'll be hanging around here until they catch whoever done it. That's terrible what happened to those kids."

The propellers had become invisible, whipped into transparent circles distinct only at the edges, little halos on either side of the cabin. The plane eased forward and began a slow roll to the end of the runway, kicking up a haze behind it as it blew away the light dusting of sand that had been blown across the tarmac the night before, clearing the concrete like a leaf blower.

"I knew one of them kids," the manager said. "That Jason Summers. Now there was your good pilot. He used to fly groups in and outta here all the time, sometimes a coupla trips a month. Had him one of them big Beechcrafts. It's still up there in the hangar in Mobile."

Varner's plane roared to a high pitch and took off down the runway. It built up speed quickly, like a sprinter out of the blocks, the big engines not even breaking into a sweat with the light load of only three passengers. The wheels were off the concrete before they reached the halfway point. There was no wind, and without much lift the climb was slow. He got up to a couple of thousand feet and began a long wide bank to the north.

The naked sun hit the plane and it gleamed white against the pale blue sky It shrank to a bright pinpoint above the horizon, then a dark speck, and then it disappeared. A perfect little family going back to the big house and the trimmed lawns and the tennis courts and the swim parties. And in that instant when the speck disappeared, I had an epiphany, a sudden clearing of dust and cobwebs and ghosts that had been walking around in my head for the past six years. At that moment the sky became a seamless blue curtain that came down on that scene of my life. And written across that curtain was the simple message that Sandy didn't hate me, she might even still love me, she just couldn't live with me. And Peyton was still, and would always be, my little girl.

Why had it taken me six years to see that? When that plane

faded away in the distance, Sandy Donovan Delmas, in a final and irreversible trip, without hate or rancor, went back home to Memphis, the Memphis she never really left, the Memphis where she should have been all along.

"You like cigars?" the manager asked.

"Huh?"

"Cigars. I got me some good Cubans, still got a few left. That Jason, the kid what got murdered? He used to bring me some when he'd go down to Mexico. I'd do him some favors ever' once in a while and he always brought me some of these Fuentes. I'm gonna miss that. Once you get used to these Cubans, the ones they sell around here just don't taste right."

I rode around in the Windstar after I left the airport. Put the windows down and drove across the bridge to the mainland and opened it up along Dauphin Island Parkway. It had been a good visit, long enough to where I didn't have to be "on" the whole time, long enough for me to get beyond that feeling I had to make up for lost time that always overwhelms me the first two or three days.

I had taken Peyton sailing twice on *Clockwork Orange,* Trish Bullard's Flying Scot. Peyton had an instinctive feel for handling the tiller and, after the first hour, no fear of capsizing when the boat hiked in stiff winds. We'd nearly lay it on its side, and all she'd do was squeal and laugh like she was on a roller coaster. We rode bikes, flew kites, went to Slippery Sam's twice, and went crabbing at the end of my pier. And she got to know her cousins, Billy and Lisa, and shared secrets with them and told scary stories and built forts inside the house by draping sheets over the tables and chairs.

Any minute now Peyton would be back in east Memphis—the Memphis of Sandy, and Buddy, and Sarah Nell, and Varner. As Kathy says, most people would think it's a pretty good life. And I'll admit that it is; it's just not for me.

The private school that Sandy had enrolled Peyton in comes

complete with drab uniforms and windshield decals bearing a single capital letter. That letter is the first letter of the name of the school, it being considered gauche to spell it out for the whole world to see, somewhat akin to writing on a bathroom wall. The people who really count know what that big, overpriced "S" stands for.

The Seeley Academy has riding lessons, soccer lessons, swim lessons, tennis lessons, and ballet lessons. I run into kids from such overly structured, high-pressure environments all the time. Some of them escape into the Internet underworld. Some of them I track down on the streets of New Orleans, Houston, Atlanta, or wherever they run away to. Their mothers and fathers pay good money for me to track them down and pay even better money to the psychologist who takes over once I return them home. I've tried to explain all this to Sandy. But all her friends at the club say that it's akin to child abuse *not* to send your kid to one of these schools. And guess who she listens to.

I watch the situation all the time, every time I'm around Peyton. And I'll admit that she's having a good time at school, so maybe this place isn't as bad as it could be. But on the other hand, she really seemed to be getting such a kick out of crabbing with me the other day. We took twine and tied it to the nasty old chicken necks we were using as bait, weighted the bait down with scrap metal we found around the boatyard, and dropped the weighted bait into the water at the end of the pier in front of my camp house over in Bay St. Louis. After the chicken necks sat on the bottom for a while, we pulled them up slowly and slipped a long-handled net under the blue crabs that had latched on. We dropped the crabs into a galvanized foot tub.

All told, we caught twenty-one crabs, and Peyton was giddy with excitement for the two hours we were out there on the pier. Maybe she was so happy because it's one of the few things in the past couple of years she's been able to do without having to take a lesson on how to do it.

I got back to the beach house an hour after I saw them off at the airstrip. As I reached in my pocket for the key to the front door, I spotted a package that someone had leaned against the wicker couch on the porch. It was a yellow, padded envelope, the kind you use to mail books. There was no name on it, no markings of any kind. It had some weight to it, not uniformly spread throughout the package, but bunched in a small bulge at the bottom. I squeezed the bulge; it was soft, squishy, like a wad of bubble plastic padding had been left inside. But it was heavier than that. At the other end of the envelope was a hard cylinder, about the size of a flashlight battery. For the entire length of the envelope there was something flat and stiff, like heavy-grade cardboard and about the size of an 8½ × 11 sheet of paper. I slit the spine of the top flap with my pocketknife and spread the envelope open, holding it so the sunlight shined down into it.

What I saw almost stopped my heart. I swear it felt like an eye twitch in my chest. I sucked in a loud breath and flinched so hard I fumbled the package once, twice, three times, and batted at it, trying to keep it up in the air. Out of reflex, I lunged for it and barely got my hand between it and the floor. I scooped at it and flipped it straight up and caught it with both hands.

I gently laid it on the floor and sat cross-legged beside it, shivering and sweating and panting. I forced myself to take deep breaths, trying to let my heart rate slow down and my hands stop shaking.

NINE

Now, when did you know you were holding a letter bomb, Mr. Delmas?"

"It just didn't feel right," I said. "I slit the seal and looked inside and saw the contact points shining in the sunlight. I knew what it was as soon as I saw it."

Carlton Rice, the high sheriff himself, was questioning me. Jimbo, the deputy I had earlier met, sat at the breakfast table just inside the French doors leading to the rear deck. He'd jot down a few notes on his dog-eared reporter's pad when the urge hit him. He sipped the can of Coca-Cola he had helped himself to out of my refrigerator and petted the bomb-sniffing German shepherd lying at his feet. The dog had made a pass through the place ten minutes earlier and turned up nothing.

"I was trained to spot bombs when I was in the MPs," I said. "This was the basic model. Plastic explosive with an electronically triggered detonator wired to a D-sized battery. They split the wire leading from the battery to the detonator, stripped off the insulation and wrapped the loose ends of the wire in tin foil. Then they stuck a sheet of poster board between the two loose ends to keep them from touching. If I had lifted the poster board out of the envelope and the two ends had made contact, you'd have a crew out here right now with wire brushes scraping me off the walls."

"So that's how it works," Rice said.

I debated whether I should tell this guy about the phone call I had received. The girl who had called me said Zandro was about to do something stupid. Could this amateurish letter bomb be what she was talking about? Any other time, I would have told the cops all about it. But if I did, I was pretty sure this clown would be searching out a TV camera within the hour. Besides, Zandro and the Green Guardians didn't have any reason to mess with me, at least none I could think of.

"Sheriff," I said, "what are you planning to do with this report you're writing?"

"Start an investigation. Now, you're saying the bomb didn't come in the mail?"

"The people who own this place have put a permanent hold on all the mail deliveries."

He wrote something on his note pad.

"Sheriff," I said, "I don't want this report made public."

Jimbo chuckled and looked out at the water and started scratching the dog's neck just below its jaw.

"This stuff's a public record," Rice said. "I don't have much choice."

"Of course you do," I said. "This is an ongoing case."

I was going to have to come down pretty hard on this business about giving out that report. He was nearly drooling over the prospect of showing off that baby to the TV cameras. I sure didn't need any army of reporters camped out on my doorstep, because I was damn sure going to get serious about my investigation. That letter bomb had turned the case into a hell of a lot more than any background check.

"I'm sure Alabama law doesn't require you to tell the whole world about a case that's still under investigation," I said.

"You a lawyer, Mr. Delmas?"

"Hey, Carlton," Jimbo said. "Don't you think we ought to put that note in a Ziploc?"

"Can we hurry this up?" I said. "I've got to make a phone call."

"Now tell me again where you found this note," the sheriff said.

"I'm not saying anything else until you give me your word you're not releasing any of this to the press."

Rice frowned and looked over to Jimbo for some support. Jimbo shrugged and sipped his Coke.

"I'll take the case to the Alabama Bureau if I have to," I said.

"This is a Mobile County case."

"But I'll bet the ABI would be glad to take my statement."

He tried once more to get Jimbo to weigh in on his side, but Jimbo just yawned and leaned forward and started scratching the dog's head. "Oh, all right," the sheriff said, "I won't go public with it."

"For how long?"

"How should I know?" he said.

Carlton Rice was a good-looking silver-haired man with a deepwater tan and a chiseled jaw. But he wasn't tough, not one bit. Didn't have the eyes of a lawman, that glare that longtime cops develop, that glare that can go right through even strong-willed men. There was no way I could count on him to keep this stuff out of the newspapers no matter what he said.

"Maybe I'd better confer with my lawyer before I talk any more about this," I said.

"Why do you think you need a lawyer?"

"I won't if you agree to keep this quiet," I said.

The note Jimbo had mentioned was lying on the floor when I walked in after finding the bomb. The bomber had slipped it in under the door. It was one of those cut-and-paste jobs like a ransom note from a black-and-white movie. But it had been photocopied; less touching involved, I suppose.

If you're reading this, the bomb didn't kill you. Tell that bitch you're working for to back off. Remember that we know where your daughter lives.

Those last words had hit me like a bucket of ice water. I had been trying to call Memphis every two or three minutes since I read it.

"I've got to make a call," I said as I picked up the phone.

"Just a few more questions," Rice said.

I punched in the number again and got Sandy's answering machine, as I had already done at least five times during the past hour.

"By the way, Jimbo," I said, "does Zandro have black hair? Cut kinda close on the sides?"

He shook his head no. "He's got long hair and it's almost red. Wears it in a ponytail most of the time. You might have seen him if you been riding around."

"I don't think so," I said, "but you ought to give the sheriff over in Pascagoula a call. They think Zandro made a death threat against Rebecca Jordan's mother. Somebody left her a note. You might want to check that out."

He was about to say something when Sandy picked up the phone, and I held up my hand to shut him up. Jimbo picked up the note with a pair of tweezers and slipped it into a plastic sandwich bag.

"Where's Peyton?" I said.

"Good to hear from you, too," Sandy said.

"I'm sorry, Sandy. I'm—is Peyton there?"

"She fell asleep on the way home from the airport. Varner's carrying her in right now. You must have worn her out at that picnic you two had this morning."

"Something's come up," I said. "You're going to need to keep her at home for a few days."

The phone was silent so long I thought the line had gone dead.

"Are you there?" I asked.

"My God, Jack. What have you done this time?"

"Look, somebody left me a threatening note. They want me to get off this case."

"So, what's that got to do with Peyton?"

"They kind of threatened . . ."

"Threatened Peyton?"

"Well, the guy said he knows where she lives."

I could feel the frost through the phone line. "Well, that's just friggin' great." She spoke slowly, her voice low and menacing. "It's not enough for you to risk getting yourself killed on one of your stupid cases. Now you're dragging your daughter down into that same cesspool."

"Now wait a minute, Sandy."

"No. *You* wait a minute! I've told you a million times that you can't be hanging around with all the trash you hang around with and—"

"Sandy—"

"And not expect some of it to spill over into your personal life."

"Sandy!"

"And sure enough! Now you've got some sleazeball threatening Peyton!"

"Dammit, Sandy! Shut up!"

"I'm not going to shut—"

"If you'd kept your damn mouth shut, none of this would be happening!"

"Oh, sure! Blame it on—"

"I've told you a thousand times not to talk about my cases. But I get over here and the whole island knows who I am, who hired me, what I'm looking for! Hell, they know where I'm staying, probably know which brand of deodorant I use. And they wouldn't know one bit of this if you hadn't run your mouth to Susan Chapman and God knows who else!"

The phone went silent again, and in a few seconds I heard her sniffle and draw in a breath in three shallow, shaky gulps. God, I hate it when she starts crying.

"Sandy, I'm sorry I said that."

"I'm scared," she said, her voice now small and high pitched.

"I'll find the guy."

"You're not staying there, are you? Surely you're not staying on the case!"

I had forgotten about the sheriff and Jimbo. They were sitting at the breakfast table staring at me. Jimbo was still sipping that same can of Coke.

"I've got to. I can't just sit around and hope this guy decides to back off. He thinks I know too much right now. He tried to kill me this morning."

"WHAT?"

"Oh, yeah," I said, "there's one more thing I need to tell you about."

The rest of our conversation didn't go too well.

TEN

After I put the Windstar into the garage and padlocked it shut, I walked to the cabin next door. Ever since I first arrived on the island there had been a steady stream of kids in and out of that place. Maybe one of them had been sober enough to see somebody put the package on my front porch.

Two college-age girls were sunbathing on chaise lounges on the sand in front of the cabin. One had a towel across her face. The other one sat up and watched me as I walked toward the steps. I gave her a little smile and a wave.

The cabin was eight feet off the ground. All the doors and some windows were open and from inside came the sound of a television broadcast of a football game. I was halfway up the front steps when a guy in baggy shorts and a Hawaiian-print shirt stepped out the door. He was wearing a Panama hat with a red, flowered band and a pair of Oakley sunglasses. He was a little thick around the waist and a had a sparkle of gray in his curly black hair. He had the walk and the relaxed grin of mild inebriation and was holding what appeared to be a blended margarita in a clear, neon green plastic cup.

"How ya doin'?" he said.

I introduced myself and told him I was staying in the cabin next door. "You live here?" I asked.

"I'm Curtis Semmes." He held out his hand. "My friends call me Easy."

"Easy?"

"Yeah. Ain't that a kick? I don't even know for sure where the name came from. Some say it's Easy Money. Some say Easy Street. Some say it comes from the Big Easy. All I know is it beats the hell out of Curtis. You want a margarita?"

"I'll take a Coke if you got one."

"Got anything you want. C'mon."

Inside the cabin a bunch of guys were sitting around a TV set in this big, open room watching an exhibition game. The back wall of the room was floor-to-ceiling plateglass with an unimpeded view of the Gulf.

Even though I grew up on the coast, I feel like a tourist when I see the clear water on the gulf side of the barrier islands. The water inside the islands is usually cloudy from the sediment deposited by the rivers that feed into the protected waters of Mobile Bay and the Mississippi Sound. This sediment is nutrient rich, and the bay and the sound, with their often cloudy waters, are incredibly fertile and bounteous habitats for oysters, shrimp, flounders, and crabs. But crystal-clear water is what the tourists want, the aqua, the green, and the deep azure of the waters outside the islands. And every once in a while, just like any tourist, I want it too. It was a view I could really enjoy if I could get that bomb out of my mind.

Of the five guys watching the game, none appeared to be over thirty. They were spread around the room, two on a couch, two lying on the floor, one in an inflatable chair.

"What's the score?" Easy asked no one in particular.

"Saints are ahead by thirteen."

He smiled at me. "Maybe this is the year."

"I didn't introduce myself," I said. "I'm Jack Delmas."

"You say you're over at the Mayson Marine cabin? You must be the private eye."

"Apparently not too private."

"Ain't no secrets around here."

He opened the refrigerator. There was a blender, filled halfway with icy lime green slush, set on the top shelf. Every other inch of shelf space was taken up by beer cans and soft drinks, must have been five cases of beer, all cans.

"Earlier today did you notice anybody stop by next door?" I asked. "Any visitors, delivery men, anybody like that?"

"I been too busy rubbing suntan lotion on those two sweet things out on those cots. Is a Pepsi okay?" He jammed one into a foam rubber can cooler and handed it to me. Then he poured some more green liquid into his glass. "They been down there most of the day. Let's go see if they saw anything."

The brunette was Missy; the blonde, Chloe. Missy was starting law school at Samford in a few weeks. Chloe was a Fairhope girl headed back in a week to the University of Georgia for her junior year. Easy sat at the foot of Chloe's cot and pointed for me to sit at Missy's feet.

"I want y'all to meet a friend of mine," Easy said to the two sun-bathers. "This is Jack Delchamps."

"Delmas," I said.

"He's a private eye."

"I've never met a private eye before," Chloe said. "I thought y'all carried guns."

"Not all the time," I said.

"Are you here on a case?"

"You mean you haven't heard?" Easy asked.

Chloe shook her head. She had blue eyes, a little-girl voice, and a constant smile.

"You must be investigating the murders," Missy said.

Missy had high cheeks and dark, intelligent eyes. Her voice was pleasant, but strong. She had a take-charge air about her.

"No, I'm not. I'm just trying to find out who dropped off a package at the cabin next door," I said. "Did either of you notice anybody over there today?"

"The sheriff and Jimbo were over there a little while ago," Missy said.

"How about before noon?"

"There've been a lot of cars in and out of that little street all day," Missy said. "People are always walking through these lots to get to the beach. You think somebody stole this package from your front porch?"

"No. I just can't find out who left one there."

"Would you hand me one of those bottled waters out of that ice chest?" Chloe said.

"Show starts in one hour," Easy said. "You want to stay for the show, Jack?"

"What show?"

"*Hard Copy*," Missy said. "They filmed a story last week and we're in it. It's going to be on TV tonight."

"I've got to go shower," Chloe said.

There was a cheer from the football watchers inside the house. "Anybody want a margarita?" Easy stood and stepped toward the house while Missy began packing up her lotions and towels and shook some sand off a paperback book that had been on the ground beside her.

"I better be going," I said.

"Why don't you come back and watch the show?" Missy said. "It'll be a hoot."

"Did you know any of the people who got killed?" I asked.

"Oh, sure. I knew all of them. Everybody around here did."

"What did you think of Rebecca Jordan?"

"I thought you weren't investigating the murders."

I stood and adjusted my shirt. "I'm just curious."

"I loved Rebecca. It's so sad. She was so in love with Jason, that's the one who owned the house where they got killed."

"What was Jason like?"

"He was okay. I mean, sometimes he could get on your nerves. But he wasn't a bad guy."

"You say he got on your nerves?"

"Yeah, he was the kind that would plan out everything. You

know, he'd say 'Let's go to the dog track,' and kinda expected everybody to want to go. It was like he was the social chairman or something." She reached down to the sand for her flip-flops. "I better start getting ready. Easy's been into those margaritas since lunch. I don't trust him to set the VCR."

"Is Easy your date?"

"He's kinda like everybody's date. This is his place. It's part of the inheritance. He just likes to have parties, I mean, like every day. You should have been here for the Fourth of July. Jason had about a dozen visitors he had flown in from Mexico and about ten cases of Corona beer they had brought with them. It was way beyond wild." She threw her beach towel across her shoulder. "You come back tonight and I'll give you some of the details."

ELEVEN

It was nearly time for the *Hard Copy* episode to start, and two of the three kids who were going to be interviewed on this week's show were seated on the couch sipping wine coolers and signing autographs. Jeffrey, the kid who had first seen the bodies through the window, was using a tube of red lipstick to autograph the cleavage of a big-busted girl in a bikini who was kneeling in front of him. She was lightly sunburned and lightly drunk.

"What did you tell 'em about finding the bodies?" Easy asked.

"Same thing I've told y'all about a million times," the kid said.

"You tell him about blowing lunch when you saw the blood?"

"I'll bet they don't show the blood," somebody said.

"God, I hope not," Chloe said. "I'd hate for Jeffrey to throw up all over the couch."

"Real funny," Jeffrey said.

"Is the VCR ready?" Chloe asked.

"Hell, I dunno," Easy said. He was stretched out on a fully extended recliner, the Panama hat he had been wearing all day cocked forward to where it nearly covered his drooping eyes, the neon green glass of near-melted margarita resting on his chest, where he steadied it with both hands. "Missy," he said, " 'sit ready?"

"Of course it is." She winked at me. "After all, this is my debut."

"Okay," Easy said as he pushed his elbows into the arms of the chair in an effort to sit up. "Here 'tis. Turn up the sound."

I estimated Easy to be in his mid-thirties, but he had a ruddy face and the start of a set of jowls, so he looked older. Missy told me that Easy went to the University of Alabama from the family plantation in Greene County just outside Eutaw. The first week his freshman year he started drinking one night at an SAE party, and just never stopped. He was one of those guys you find at colleges across the South, the lifetime frat man. They work on but never finish half a dozen different undergraduate degrees over the course of a decade or so until the money or their liver gives out. Easy had a trust fund that doled out enough to keep him in booze, an apartment within walking distance of Bryant-Denny Stadium, the beach house we were in, and tuition as long as he wanted it.

"You want to sit down?" Chloe asked. She scooted to the side of the padded armchair to make room for me to sit. She had on a Tri Delta T-shirt and a pair of cutoffs so short I could see the curves of her bottom. Though she was college age, she looked to be fifteen years old at the most, with a cute little face and a pretty smile.

"I appreciate it, darling," I said. "But I've got to go to the kitchen."

As I stepped away, one of the boys sitting on the floor hopped into the open spot she had created. I was looking back at her and bumped into a young man who had been standing with his back turned to me and talking with Missy. He was trim and handsome, with dark hair and a dark complexion. She introduced him as John.

"You might want to talk with John," she said. "He knew Jason Summers real well."

"Summers must have been a popular guy," I said.

"John's a CPA. He did Jason's books for him."

John looked down at his feet. "I just did his taxes for him."

"Jack's a private investigator," Missy said.

I might have just imagined it, but he seemed to tense up. He excused himself as soon as he could and eased to the other side of the room.

"You think that guy knew Rebecca, too?" I asked.

"He knew her, but I don't know how well. John did a lot of accounting work for Jason, so he must have run into her some," she said. "He was being modest when he said he just did the taxes. Poor Jason didn't even know how to balance a checkbook. Neither did Rebecca."

I looked across the room just in time to catch a glimpse of John walking out the front door.

The show came on and was greeted with that universal kid's call to party, that "Whoooooo!" yell you hear from cheerleaders, rock-concert fans, and every time kids, especially girls, start getting rowdy. They called Missy over to the couch since she was one of the stars. I watched a little of it and caught her ten-second inter-view. It was stuffy in the room and getting louder so I didn't hang around for the full segment. In the kitchen, Darren Wright, the reporter, sat at a small round table in the middle of the floor, swirling a drink in a highball glass.

"An appreciative audience in there," he said. "Nothing like it."

"I'm Jack Delmas."

"You're the detective. Met you last night at the Randalls' house." He reached into the plastic bucket sitting on the counter by the sink and pulled out two cubes of refrigerator ice. "So how's the investigation going?"

"I was going to ask you the same thing."

He smiled and raised the gin to his lips. It was so strong I could smell that juniper scent even six feet away. "So I guess we now play the game of standoff that investigators play," he said. "Try to see what the other guy knows without telling any secrets of your own. Well, what the hell. You see, we're both investigators, only you're a private one and I'm as public as you can get. Every day, I tell all I know to millions of people I never see. So I might as well tell you face to face."

He signaled for me to join him in the chair across from him. Another round of noise swelled in the next room. "At least I don't have to work for that god-awful *Hard Copy*. I've heard journalists referred to as whores, and I may be. But, by God, at least I work the penthouses and don't walk the damned streets."

I put some ice into a Styrofoam cup and filled it with tap water. "You got any theories on what happened?"

"I've got three," he said, "the same ones everybody around here has. One, it was a contract hit on Kellie Lee Simmons and the other three victims were just in the wrong place at the wrong time. That's the theory that's drawing all of us down here. Glamour queen with a sordid past, good old boy multi-millionaire known to have a bad temper, threatened palimony suit. That's good stuff in the news game."

"You believe that's the way it went down?" I asked.

"I didn't at first. But watch the news tomorrow night. I've got a report that's going to knock everybody's socks off. If they think the media coverage has been heavy so far, just wait until tomorrow."

"I don't guess you'd want to give me a hint."

He wagged his finger from side to side and smiled. "Remember what I said about investigators. I can't be telling all I know, not yet. Now, theory number two." Two fingers went up. "The Summers kid was running drugs in from Central America and the murders were a botched robbery or a rival drug dealer eliminating competition."

"Any evidence of that?"

"Not a shred. And theory number three" he held up a third finger— "the Green Guardians did it."

"Tell me what you know about the Green Guardians."

"They're a dangerous group, my friend." This guy had the sense of drama that is characteristic of an adventure freak. It might have come from years of chasing across the world for news stories, but I suspected he was that way before he took the job. "I remember Zandro from his tree-spiking days in California. He was fresh out of a two-year stretch at San Quinten on an assault charge when he got hooked up with the Guardians. It was a perfect fit for him— drugs, communal sex, and the chance to commit random acts of violence and actually have some people consider him a hero for it."

The show must have started up again after a commercial; there was a new round of cheers and applause. Darren sneered in that direction, curling his upper lip as if somebody had passed gas.

"What could those kids in that beach house have done to get crossed up that bad with some environmental maniacs?" I asked.

"Wouldn't have to do much," he said. "I tell you, Zandro is truly crazy. They kicked him out of the California group because he was too radical. He and some of the more extreme Guardians have this belief that the way to save the world is to somehow remove all human beings from it. They think that the souls of certain present-day humans, those who have reached this higher spiritual level—in other words, them—will survive and be implanted into the same species of man that used to inhabit the lands of Atlantis and Lemuria. They believe this species is already here on Earth, but nobody can distinguish them on sight from ordinary humans. The end result is that there'll be a new race that look like humans, but they'll lack the capacity to acquire, or desire, any worldly goods. Genetically programmed that way. In other words, they'll live about like a bird or a deer or a rabbit does."

"Sounds crazy," I said. "But still fairly harmless."

"When I said they would remove humans from the earth, I wasn't talking about some evolutionary process. They plan to unleash forces that will destroy mankind."

"Forces?"

"Viruses," he said. "Viruses that will kill only humans."

"Hoo, boy."

"So Zandro's got this mission, and it's made him paranoid. If he had some delusion that those kids were a threat to that mission, he'd kill them without a second thought. He's also got this God complex. If somebody crosses him, who knows?"

"Let me ask your opinion," I said. "If this Zandro thought someone had betrayed him in an environmental battle . . ."

"Battle?"

"An organized protest in a seaside community to block the drilling of an offshore gas well."

"Oh my God. Offshore drilling is one of Zandro's major hot buttons."

"If he felt that he had been double-crossed in such a protest, would he kill the person or persons who had done it?"

"I can't see Kellie Lee Simmons or Rod Eubanks in a battle to stop any kind of drilling, offshore or otherwise."

"I'm just asking."

"You asked my opinion. In my opinion, he'd do it in a heartbeat. Right now there are rumors that he's planning to blow up some of the rigs you can see off the beach here. He became an absolute maniac in that campaign to ban offshore drilling in California. If the Guardians had lost in court, there's no doubt in my mind he would have tried to explode any offshore rig they put out there."

"It's just that the Guardians I've seen don't look all that dangerous," I said. "In fact, one of them looked pretty damn good."

"You've got to be talking about the strawberry blonde with the great legs."

"Does she look like a killer to you?" I said.

"To an old guy like me, yes. She nearly kills me every time I look at her and wish it was twenty years ago."

"She would have been in kindergarten about that time."

He shook his head and sighed and took a big sip of gin. "I don't know what her story is. I suspect rich girl trying to protest something. She's just got that look. And you're right, most of them don't look like killers. Aside from Zandro, none of them do. But you never know."

"Do you think she's in danger being in that compound?" I asked.

"Of course she is. The man's nuts. But I doubt that she'll stay there for long. Not all the Green Guardians are in the hard-core inner circle with Zandro. Some of them, maybe most of them, are rich kids who think they can save the globe with their daddy's money. They're the kind Zandro shakes down for as much as he can before they get tired of the game. The girl you're talking about looks like one of those."

He frowned and looked into his tumbler of gin and tonic as he absently stirred it with his finger, studying it as if suspended in that clear, colorless, magical liquid were all the answers to all the questions that had driven him around the world for the past twenty-five years. He was TV handsome, the chiseled jaw, the high cheeks, the long, oval face. A facial structure so perfect that even two decades plus on the road didn't show. None of the bars, none of the strange beds, none of the memories of the women whose faces he couldn't quite recall and whose names he never knew.

"Do you ever think about it, Darren? All this stuff you see, do you think about it?"

He pulled his finger out of the drink and licked the gin off of it. "I didn't for the first ten years. I didn't start any of those wars. I didn't pull out the rifle and open fire on any crowd of shoppers. They were all stories to me, nothing more."

"How about now?"

He took a deep breath and blew it out hard. "That's the reason I'm at this party tonight, my friend. If I keep moving, I don't have time to think about such weighty topics. Besides, I've seen enough death to want to stay around people who affirm life. Look in the next room. Listen to them. No introspection, no doubts about the meaning of life in there. Not a one."

The girl in the bikini with Jeffrey's name scrawled across her chest walked in and opened the refrigerator. Her blue eyes were a little red from a day of sun and drinking beer and they appeared to be slightly out of focus. She popped the top on a can of Bud Light and smiled at us and hiccupped. She poured the contents of the can into a tall, clear glass.

"Nope," Darren said as he looked her up and down. "Not a single damned one."

"Aren't you Darren Wright?" she said. "Aren't you the news guy?"

Darren glanced at me and his eyes lit up as he raised his eyebrows. "I am indeed, my dear. Please come join us."

I stood and gave her my chair. She plopped down heavily and splashed a little of her beer out of her glass. She was real close to spilling out of that bikini top.

"We were just wondering how the show in there was going," Darren said.

"It just ended," she said.

"Were you one of the ones they interviewed?"

She shook her head no as she took a sip of beer.

Darren leaned close to her face and stared deep into her eyes. "Have you ever wanted to be on TV?"

"Well," she said, "I guess so. . . ."

"You've certainly got the, uh, face for it. What's this you've got written on you?" He stuck his face dangerously close to those big boobs and she giggled and pushed them even closer.

It didn't look as if Darren was going to give me any further explanation of his other theories on the murders or share any other thoughts on the meaning of life that he may have stumbled over in the past twenty-five years. I slipped away without listening to the rest of his evaluation of the girl's chances for TV stardom. I had a hunch she would soon be hearing that her chances were excellent.

Kids from the front room were drifting into the kitchen to refresh their drinks and get some more chips and peanuts and whatever else they could find. Somebody had popped a Motown cassette into the stereo and turned it up to redneck party level, enough to rattle any windows that might need re-caulking, and the group sang with high, loud voices the words to a bunch of Four Tops songs that were considered golden oldies even when I was in college.

I stepped to the door and looked into the next room. There was the sweet, smoky smell of pot filtering in from the rear deck and the citrus scent of frozen lime concentrate as somebody prepared the blender for yet another round of margaritas. It was a blend of music, and smells, and the heat of bodies dancing in a crowded room, up on coffee tables and chairs and couches, bumping against one another, side to side and back to back, that carried me back to a time that would have seemed just a few hours earlier like it was long, long ago had I thought about it. But somehow, looking out over the party crowd before me, there was a suspended moment when I was once again in some off-campus dump that passed for an apartment, waiting for Sandy to come back into the room after stepping out to freshen her makeup.

I spotted Missy dancing in the crowd, but I couldn't tell if she was dancing with anyone in particular or just by herself. She saw me and danced toward me; when she reached me she took me by the hand and pulled me into the middle of the group. I'm not much of a dancer, but the quarters were so close I didn't have to be.

Missy had the moves of the natural-born dancer. Everything I did had been taught to me step after slow painful step by Sandy back when we were dating. For a few minutes I forgot about the letter bomb. I even forgot the sight of that airplane receding into the sky on its way to Memphis. The song ended and Missy turned in a half circle, backed up against me, and pulled my arms around her like she was wrapping herself in a blanket.

"Are you having a good time?" she asked.

"Yeah. But everybody here is just *so* young."

"Not that young," she said.

"Like Chloe over there," I said. "She looks like she's a child."

"Didn't I tell you? Chloe's a captain for Delta Airlines."

"Oh, sure," I said. "Her father might be. They don't let teenagers fly jets."

"I'm serious."

"So you're telling me she's thirty-something years old, at least."

Missy called Chloe over and told her about my skepticism.

Chloe went into one of the bedrooms and returned with a laminated card, which she held out to me.

"See?" she said. "I fly those big jets."

The card had the company logo across the top and her picture in one corner. The FAA signage was all there. Her rank was Captain and her home base was Atlanta. For a split second I felt like I was a hundred years old, until I realized that what I thought I was seeing just couldn't be for real.

"What are you type-rated to fly?" I asked. "I didn't see it on your license."

"Jets."

"What kind?"

They started laughing. "I have no idea. All I know is that they're real big."

"Where'd you get this card?" I asked.

"Jason made it for me."

"Jason Summers?"

Chloe nodded as she stared at the card for a few seconds. It triggered something in her mind, probably dredged up a sense of loss, because her smile dimmed and her voice got lower. "He could make any kind of ID you needed. You name it, he could do it."

"You've never tried to use that thing, have you?"

"Oh, of course not. But, Missy, you remember what Donnie did with that ID he got from Jason?"

They started giggling. "That dumb-ass," Missy said.

"What kind of ID was it?" I asked.

"Jason gave this guy we know an Alabama State Trooper ID, and the fool showed it to this real state trooper one time when he got pulled over for speeding."

The music started back up and this kid Chloe had been dancing with came over and took her hand. He led her away without saying a word to any of us. She waved good-bye as she was being pulled backward to where all the dancers were.

"It's been a while since I've been to a party like this," I said. "I had almost forgotten what caveman manners are like."

"These guys never seem to get past high school." She squeezed my hands and laid her head back against my chest. "I'm about ready for a change."

I have lived long enough to pick up on a good number of the signals that the female of the species sends out. Not all of them, of course. If that were the case, I wouldn't be standing in the equivalent of a college beer bust while my ex-wife and daughter were up in Memphis. It was real clear that Missy was moving into that next stage, past the college-party circuit where getting "tow up" drunk was not an unfortunate by-product of the party, but the whole idea in going.

If that's what she wanted, I wasn't real sure I was the right man for the job just then. But there didn't seem to be any other candidates around other than Easy, who was probably not such a good choice either since by that time he was nearly comatose on the recliner. To his credit, he still had the margarita resting on his chest, still holding it steady even in his sleep, and the little smile still rested lightly on his lips.

And then there was Darren; now he could introduce her into several new levels. But he was in the kitchen arranging an impromptu screening for his latest star. So I was, by default, the one Missy had settled on. At least for tonight.

Of course she couldn't know that she wasn't exactly picking a strong and steady hand. She was dealing with a guy who was fully aware that he'd never see forty again, but who would never be as old as all those MBAs fifteen years his junior who keep coming out of the business schools in their gray flannel suits and their gray flannel souls.

"You want to step outside?" she asked. "It's stuffy in here."

"Are you here with anybody?"

"Could be," she said. "That's up to you."

Across the room, a guy walked in the front door. He wore baggy gray pants with a drawstring, leather sandals, and a loose-fitting Hawaiian-print shirt. From the back all I could see was the curly black hair on the top of his head, but when he turned around I recognized him immediately. He was that cocky son of a bitch who had confronted me on the ferry.

"That guy who just walked in," I said. "Who's that?"

"Bobby Earl somebody," she said. "I figured he'd be here sooner or later. He knows where every party on the island is every time. Of course, now that Jason's dead, this is about the only place where there's something going on every night."

"He's the gambler, isn't he?"

"That's what I've heard."

Bobby Earl greeted two of the dancers, using this four-step ceremony that took the place of a handshake, the first step of which involved touching the tips of each other's thumbs. I had seen it used earlier in the evening. Probably some ghetto grip that came out of the projects in Mobile or Birmingham. He took a swig from the Styrofoam cup that a tiny brunette girl in a bikini bottom and an oversized T-shirt held to his lips.

"He seems to be pretty popular around here," I said.

"He's kind of a redneck, but I guess he's all right. At least until he gets drunk."

"You know what kind of car he drives?"

"Sure, everybody on the island does. It's one of those old Plymouth Barracudas."

"When you were lying out today," I said, "did you see that Barracuda?"

"Of course," she said. "He comes by at least once a day, especially during football season."

TWELVE

The FBI isn't in on this case yet," the sheriff said as he slammed his desk drawer shut. "I'd like to keep it that way, Mr. Delmas. I'm gettin' my butt kicked around enough already without pulling those federal prima donnas into it."

"That sounds like you think I've got something to say about whether the feds come down here," I said. "The only reason they're not already is because that bomb didn't come in the U.S. mail."

The sheriff kept checking out his watch. Perspiration had soaked through his light blue uniform and his face was heated to a pinkish red, as if he had been jogging out in the sun. The window air conditioner rattled the glass panes, and the little office smelled of pipe tobacco.

"I'm not trying to cause any trouble," I said. "I'm just trying to find out what you've come up with on my case."

"I've got Jimbo on it." He tossed a manila envelope into the open briefcase on the desk in front of him and unclipped the handheld VHF from his belt. "Hey, Jimbo," he shouted into the mike, "call in. Over."

Jimbo called in, said he was at the fishing pier headed our way.

"Okay, Mr. Delmas. I gotta run. Gotta be in Mobile in an hour. When Jimbo gets here, he'll bring you up to speed." He slammed the top shut on the briefcase and pulled it off the desk. "I got enough to worry about right now without taking on any new cases. Jimbo tells me you're doing background checks on the four who got killed. Maybe you ought to go back home and try to get your information on the Internet."

"I've done as much of that as I can," I lied. It's gotten to where I'm feeling a little awkward admitting that I don't know a URL from Shinola.

"Well, that's about all there is to tell," he said. "Of course you could watch the news and find out all you'd ever want to know about the murder victims."

"The trash they're putting out on the TV news is the reason I'm here."

He pulled at the neck of his T-shirt and tugged at the already loosened knot of his necktie. "I can't assign anybody to watch out for you. I got all my men working these murders. You need to go ahead and wrap up your investigation and get on back to Mississippi."

"That might have been possible yesterday. But it's not now."

"You're putting your daughter in jeopardy, Mr. Delmas. Not to mention your wife."

"You think if I back off, this guy will go away?"

He frowned and rubbed his chin. "Yeah, I sure do."

"Sheriff, he didn't plan to just scare me. He had every intention of killing me. If I hadn't known something about letter bombs, he would have done just that. Whoever did it, he thinks I know too much. I'm not going to spend the rest of my life having to check for bombs every time I go to crank up my truck or open my mail."

The single-tone chime rang to signal the opening of the front door of the office.

"Hello, honey! I'm home!"

"That's Jimbo," the sheriff said. "He can tell you everything you need to know about that letter bomb."

"How about the note the bomber left?"

"Whatever." He glanced at his watch and winced. "I gotta run. If you're gonna stay here on the island, you watch your step."

He passed Jimbo on his way out the door. Jimbo was holding a white paper sack. I could smell the fried shrimp from the po'boy.

"What'd you say to run Carlton off?" Jimbo asked.

"He was acting like he was late for something."

"Oh, yeah." He chuckled and glanced at the wall clock. "Press conference up in Mobile. You had lunch yet?"

He pulled the keys off his belt and opened the door to the office next to the sheriff's. He hit the switch to the ceiling fan and set the po'boy on the corner of the desk and unbuckled his gun-belt. The wall behind his desk was covered with pictures, 8½ × 11s in cheap black frames, the kind of frames you can buy at the dollar store. They were photos, some black and white, some color, showing Jimbo in a football uniform. In the center of the photos was a plaque as big as a TV screen, the head of a bulldog in the center of a maroon field with MSU in 4-inch block letters across the bottom, right below the bulldog's spike collar.

"Now I remember who you are," I said. "You played defensive end for the Bulldogs, right? You were up at Mississippi State about the same time my brother was playing up at Southern Miss. You remember Neal Delmas?"

Jimbo took a bite of his po'boy and stared up at the fan. "Played tackle, didn't he? Tall guy? Yeah, I remember him. He was a pass blocker. He was a couple of years ahead of me. As I recall, he was real good at grabbin' a handful of your jersey and holding on to it just long enough so the referee didn't see it. Knew just how far he could bend the rules."

"He's a lawyer now."

"Somehow that doesn't surprise me," he said. "So how about you? Did you play?

"Baseball," I said, "over at Ole Miss. I was a few years ahead of Neal."

He pushed with his feet and rolled his chair over to a half-refrigerator in the corner next to the water cooler. He pulled out a can of Coke and held it up to offer it to me. I shook my head no.

"I almost went to Ole Miss," he said. "But my high school honey said she was going to State, so I signed with them. Damn, I was in love with that girl. Woulda married her in a Mobile minute."

"So what happened?"

"She dropped me like a bad habit and transferred down to Jones Junior College during the first two weeks of our freshman year. That's the biggest favor anybody's ever done for ol' Jimbo. God, if I'd a married her I'd have five kids by now and be some kinda deacon or somethin' in the New Life Church out at Buckatunna." He took another few bites of the po'boy, finished it off, and mashed down a few crumbs of fried batter so they'd stick to his finger and then licked them off.

"Y'all know anything more about that package somebody left on my doorstep?"

"You want the official party line?"

"Sure," I said. "Why not?"

"Let me see if I can remember the way I'm supposed to say it." He cleared his throat. "We sent the device off to the state crime lab for analysis. There are no suspects at this time."

"Is that it?"

"That's it." He licked the crumbs off his lips and wadded up the white butcher paper the po'boy had been wrapped in, then reached into his top drawer and pulled out a grip builder and started squeezing it, flexing the long muscles that rippled from his elbow to his wrist.

"I get the feeling the sheriff would just as soon I'd leave town," I said.

"It ain't his call. Nothing around here's his call. He's just gettin' on TV a lot. The whole show's being run by the D.A. and the state bureau."

"You think you could give them some help if they asked you for it?"

He dropped the gripper back into the top drawer and laced his fingers behind his head. He swung his leg up and banged his heel on the top of the desk. "I'm just a country boy from up around Waynesboro. Majored in football up at State. I ain't the smartest kid in the class, but, dammit, I know Dauphin Island. I know which rocks to look under. I got my ideas about what happened, but they ain't interested. So they been down here for two weeks now puttin' on a show for the TV cameras and the newspapers, and all they come up with so far is what I knew the minute I kicked that door in."

"You think you know who did it?"

"I ain't saying that. But I already knew about Scooter and Kellie Lee. I knew all about Jason Summers and his frequent-flyer club down to Mexico. Knew about his gambling, knew about Bobby Earl Fair hanging around down there. Hell, I even knew about the Green Guardians and that Rebecca girl. Poke a stick up any one of those wasp nests, and you'll find something. But like I said, they know what they're doin'. So, by God, they can handle it theirselves."

Jimbo finished off the Coke and belched. He tossed it into the trash can and pulled down on his underwear through his cargo shorts and ran his thumbs along the inside of the waistband to unstick them from the sweat-bonded seal that had formed.

"You do what you want," he said. "But if it 'uz me, I'd move out."

"I'm staying," I said.

"Well, go find yourself a different room, drive a different car. Start wearing dresses or something. But if I was you, I'd for sure ride that bike around for the next few days instead of driving that van I've seen you driving. I ain't never heard of anybody plantin' a bomb in no bicycle."

THIRTEEN

The *Fox 10 Action News at Noon* blared out its synthesized theme in upbeat ⁴/₄ time through the speakers of the TV mounted behind the upstairs bar of the Pelican Pub. The show started with taped head shots of the noontime news crew, shots that showed them moving just enough for me to tell I wasn't looking at still photos, flashing those frozen smiles they can hold seemingly forever.

The intros were designed to portray the anchors as regular guys and gals to the folks from Grand Bay and Pascagoula and Bayou La Batre, the folks who see them buying groceries at the Delchamps or eating nachos at the bar at happy hour at some watering hole out by the airport. If these anchors are good or lucky, one day they'll be gone—with neither warning nor explanation to the viewers—when the right spot opens up in Atlanta or Indianapolis. After all, we're just fly-over country down here. But, by God, the national spotlight was on Dauphin Island right now. In fact, I had the feeling I was the only guy on the island who had not been interviewed on TV.

I missed the opening line of what the anchor was saying because the instant she started talking, the bartender set the gumbo down right under my nose. It sent up a full blast of that aroma of oil mixed with flour and heated over a low flame until it becomes a dark gravy, what we call the roux. It's the base of the gumbo, the stuff you dump the chopped onions and bell peppers and garlic into before you add a few quarts of water. The gumbo before me had a dough-colored roux rather than the dark brown type they prefer in New Orleans. They serve this same light roux gumbo up at Wintzell's in Mobile in little white bowls, always with softened rice and a big oyster poking through the surface amid tiny, red, floating circles of hot sauce.

The place was clean, with windows all around looking out over the bay on the inside of the island. The bartender was a big-boned woman, late thirties, wearing a black T-shirt with the Harley-Davidson logo and, in white letters, the kind you press on with an electric iron, *Bay Area Bikers* written in a circle around the logo. She was friendly enough but not the chatty type. Any lead on a conversation would have to come from me. Looked like the kind of place I could sit and study my options for as long as I needed to.

"The investigation into the Dauphin Island murders took a dramatic twist today." The male anchor, the successor to Rod Eubanks, looked appropriately somber as he read from the teleprompter. Even managed a halfway believable frown at the end.

"That's right, Kevin," the female co-anchor said. "In a late-breaking story from Fox News, veteran correspondent Darren Wright has learned that audiotapes of a telephone conversation between millionaire Mobile businessman Scooter Haney and murder victim Kellie Lee Simmons show that Haney threatened Miss Simmons just one week before she was killed along with three others in a beach house on Dauphin Island. We switch now to the network for the latest in this surprising development."

Darren Wright was standing in front of Jason's beach house, squinting into full sunlight and holding a microphone. He was wearing a white knit shirt and the breeze off the gulf hit his hair at just the right angle to make it appear even fuller than normal, as if he was in some studio posing for glamour shots with a fan blowing on his face. I wondered if it was possible that he planned things like that, or if it was just part of the deal the good Lord gave Darren when he got all the rest of those good genes.

"Taped telephone conversations allegedly show that millionaire Alabama businessman Scooter Haney threatened the life of his alleged girlfriend Kellie Lee Simmons just days before Miss Simmons and three other persons were shot to death. Fox has obtained copies of the tapes in which Haney allegedly shouted, 'I'll kill you,' after learning that Simmons was planning to file a palimony suit seeking substantial damages based on Haney's alleged promise to divorce his wife of four years and marry Simmons."

"Whoo-eee!" a man across the bar said. "I wouldn't never say nothin' like that over a phone, 'specially not one of them cell phones. Hell, the whole world can hear you on one of them things."

"SHHHH!" A group at the table in the far corner glared the man into silence. One was wearing a cap bearing the ABC logo. Another was wearing a *Dateline* T-shirt with a silk-screened picture of Jane Pauley and Stone Phillips. They all had stopped eating and were watching Darren as if he were announcing an invasion from Jupiter.

"You need some crackers?" the bartender asked.

One guy at the table behind the group, sitting alone and chewing on peeled shrimp, appeared to be staring at me rather than the TV. Hard to tell since he was wearing dark green aviator's shades. He had on a light blue T-shirt, the kind with a breast pocket, that had a drawing of a sailfish breaking the surface fighting the hook in its mouth. The guy had a deepwater tan and a white scar down the side of his left forearm, a nose that had been moved around a time or two, and dark hair that was going gray. Maybe he was looking up at the TV and not at me. Maybe I was just reading too much into every situation.

"Damn!" one of the news crew said. "Where did that ol' fart Darren Wright come up with that?"

"We gotta find this Scooter Haney," another one said.

"We gotta call New York," a third one said.

One of the group pulled a phone off his belt and punched in a number so fast it looked like he was drumming his fingers on the little Touch-tone pad. They all pushed back from the table and drained their beers as one of them waved a Visa card at the bartender to signal for the check. They were gone out the door twenty seconds later, running like a firehouse crew when a bell sounds. One of them, a tall kid with a ponytail and a few wispy hairs on his chin, bumped into Easy, who was strolling in the front door. Easy didn't know and damn sure didn't care about this latest whiff of red meat that had been sniffed by the pack journalists.

In another fifteen minutes, Darren Wright would be sitting in the trailer at the far end of the island, his day over now that he had set off the stampede he knew was coming, popping the top on the first of his daily ration of beers and smiling that perfect smile, thinking he had just hit a journalistic grand slam. And that's what really counts to Darren. In a month, the world wouldn't know or care about those four kids in that beach house. No big deal. Next month it'll be something else somewhere else, so why get worked up about it? And about the public's right to know? The public knows what he tells them, nothing more.

There are a dozen wars going on around the world today. Darren and his colleagues could pick any one of them and, within a week, have the Democrats and the Republicans jawing at each other about whether to send in air strikes. Never mind that nobody but a handful of geography teachers would have heard of the place before the story aired, and nobody but that same handful would know about the place six months later. So what's the point?

But, hey, to come up with some story that gets the entire nation worked up and to broadcast it on the Fox report while CBS, NBC, and those supermarket rags are sitting around with their thumbs up their butts, *that's* the real game. And, damn, Darren was good at it.

"Is somebody giving away free drinks or something?" Easy said as he sat beside me. "Why the stampede?"

I shrugged and ate a spoonful of gumbo. Didn't feel like explaining it. "Good party the other night."

"So I hear. Must have been a real good one for you. Missy's bugging the heck outta me to be sure you come over for the one I'm having later this week. I tried to catch you over at your place to tell you about it, but you're hard to catch."

"I'm not staying there much. I'm looking for a place to stay."

"Oh, yeah. I remember. You can crash at my place if you need to."

"Would you feel comfortable with that?"

"Why not? My place may look like chaos, but at least we all know each other. Just throw your stuff into any closet and stay as long as you want. Sleeping arrangements are up to you."

"I might do that."

"Whether you stay there or not, stop by the house tomorrow night. I'm having a shrimp boil. I'll bet Missy would love to see you. She all of a sudden has developed this thing for mature men."

"I'm afraid she's a little young for me."

"Don't fool yourself, my friend. Missy's not too young for any man alive. Believe me."

The front door opened and in walked Bobby Earl Fair himself.

"How's it going, Bobby Earl!" Easy shouted across the room.

Bobby Earl looked at us and frowned when he spotted me.

"You and Bobby Earl big buddies?" I asked.

"He's the man I'm here to see," Easy said. "This is his busy season."

I shook a few drops of Tabasco into my gumbo. The smell alone cleared my sinuses. "It must be. I've sure seen him around a lot."

"I gotta get my bet in on the Tide before the spread changes. Can you believe they're only laying eight points against Vandy?"

"Vandy always plays the Tide tough," I said. "Was this Bobby Earl guy the only bookie Jason used?"

"He's the only one down here. Jason was one of his good customers. In fact, the last time I saw Jason he was right over there at that table in the corner arguing with Bobby Earl. Texas A&M won that early Kick Off Classic by seven and Jason had bet a wad on Michigan. He was claiming the spread was seven and a half when he got the bet in, and Bobby Earl was saying he got it in too late. Said the spread had gone down to seven."

"You could hear them?" I asked.

"Everybody in the bar could hear them. Bobby Earl's bad to try to change the spread on you. I won't bet more'n fifty bucks or so with him, 'cause I don't really trust him. But Jason, he had put down a big bet that day."

"Was Bobby Earl really mad at him?"

"Aw, no more than usual. He doesn't have any business sense. He needs to learn that you pay off the winners with a smile and sympathize with the losers. Bobby Earl, he'll haggle with you over a nickel. But since our old bookie retired, he's all we got unless we want to drive up to Mobile. And even up there they got this new group of rednecks who've done taken over from the old crowd." He pushed away from the bar. "Why don't you come over tomorrow night? I'll make sure Missy behaves herself. That is, if you want me to."

I told him I'd try to make it. Easy stepped over to the table and sat across from Bobby Earl, who by this time was chewing up a toothpick and running a pencil up and down some figures written on a sheet of lined legal paper. The bartender saw my empty glass and headed my way with a pitcher of iced tea.

"I haven't seen you around here before," she said. "You a friend of Easy's?"

"Seems like everybody around here is."

"Just the ones who like to party."

"I'm Jack Delmas," I said as I held out my hand.

While she shook my hand I could see on her face that the memory search was going on, could almost hear that computer clicking. "Are you the private detective?"

I sighed and nodded my head, and started eating the gumbo. Still needed a little hot sauce.

"Man, that is so cool. I'd love to do that kinda work. You think you know who killed all those people over at Jason's?"

"Did you know him?"

"On this island, everybody knows everybody."

"So I hear," I said. "Were you in here the day Jason and Bobby Earl over there got into an argument over a football game?"

She hushed me by putting her finger to her lips and glanced over at Bobby Earl and Easy as she leaned in closer. "Bobby Earl don't like for folks to talk about him. Truth is, they started out that day arguing about football, but the real fight was about some Cuban cigars. I never did figure out what the problem was."

"Was it a bad fight?"

"No worse than normal," she said. "Jason used to come in here two or three times a week. Sometimes to meet with Bobby Earl, sometimes to bring some of his customers from Mexico."

"He brought Mexicans in here?"

"Yeah. They were like business . . . uh, what's the word?"

"Clients?"

"Yeah, clients."

"And how many would he bring in here?"

"Six or eight at a time. They really got into seafood. I guess they get tired of all that taco kind of stuff. They'd sit against that wall so they could look out over the water."

"Did you know a girl named Rebecca Jordan?"

"Well, sure. She was with Jason sometimes. Always seemed real nice to me. That gumbo gonna be enough for you?"

I finished the last spoonful and pushed the bowl to the side. "So you didn't know her very well?"

She shook her head. "I didn't. But I can tell you who did. Rebecca was friends with this girl they call Moon. She's an artist, draws all this really weird stuff. But she makes a bunch of money selling it at art shows and stuff. She works over at the Neptune a couple of nights a week."

"Doing what?"

"Cocktail waitress."

"If she's making all this money selling paintings, what's she doing working at a bar?"

She scrunched her nose. Didn't know what to make of the question. "I guess she's just really into rock and roll."

I paid and stood to walk out. Bobby Earl and Easy were hunched over the table going over the spread sheets. As I walked down the flight of stairs outside, I caught Bobby Earl watching me through the window.

FOURTEEN

M r. Delmas!" It was a female voice behind me, louder than a whisper but nowhere near a shout, calling for me as I reached for the door of the van. "Hey! Over here!"

Across the parking lot, seated in her BMW, Heather was calling through her rolled-down window, glancing all around to see if anybody was watching. Since she obviously didn't want anybody to see her talking with me, I checked out the windows surrounding the top floor of the Pelican Pub, where I had just eaten my lunch. No one was looking down at us, nor was anyone coming out the door, so I turned to walk to where she was parked. But before I took two steps, she started her car and lurched across the lot, stopping beside me with the motor running.

"Would you follow me," she asked, "please?"

"Is there something wrong?"

"Please?"

She took off and stopped at the edge of the road, looking at me in her rearview mirror. She reached her hand out the window and waved for me to come on.

I followed her as she drove west along quiet streets where the shrimpers and commercial fishermen live, narrow, pine-shaded lanes where vinyl-sided Jim Walter houses sit close to the pavement. Shrimp nets, bright green from recent dippings and set out to dry, hung like moss from the limbs of oak and pecan trees. On the front porches were stacks of crab traps, chicken-wire boxes with little one-way chutes where the crabs go in but can't get back out. Briny air from the gulf side of the island sighed through the pine needles overhead and a hateful deerfly dive-bombed my arm and stung me before I could slap it dead. Felt like I got popped with a rolled-up towel. I turned on the air conditioner and rolled up the windows after that.

Heather made one more turn through the pines. When I saw the clearing up ahead, I recognized the narrow land bridge between the airport and the island, a dead-end street that is the only way in or out of there. Both street and airstrip were built no telling how many years earlier on dredge spoils dumped into the marsh for the sole purpose of creating an unobstructed runway without taking up too much of the island's precious real estate or taking down any trees. Neither tree nor shrub has been allowed to grow since the place was formed. It looks like a concrete football field that somehow got set down on top of a treeless marsh.

In other words, a flat patch of rock visible from all sides with nowhere to hide.

I'm not by nature an overly cautious person. Never will be; can't live that way. I would have walked over to Heather's car when we were back at the Pelican parking lot and never given it a second thought. But during the five minutes it took us to drive to the airstrip I had time to study the situation. Why the secrecy? And why was she leading me down a road with only one way out, a road that's usually deserted? The girl might look like an angel. But she was still a Green Guardian.

We got to the airstrip and, sure enough, no one was there. No cars in the lot, no planes tethered to the eye bolts set into the concrete near the one-man control tower. We parked outside the chain-link fence that separated us from the tarmac. Heather got out of the Beemer and waited for me, but I wasn't moving. As she walked toward me, I reached under the seat and laid the Glock on the floorboard beside me. I shifted into reverse and backed the van around to where the nose pointed at the road. And I left the engine running.

She ran toward me, waving her arms like she was afraid I was about to take off and leave her. She wore a pair of tight, white shorts and a sky blue T-shirt clinging to her so tightly that I could see the outline of her bra. If she was carrying a gun, I damn sure couldn't tell where it was.

"Stop!" she shouted. "Don't leave me!"

She reached the van and yanked on the locked passenger door with such force that she nearly fell down when the handle slipped from her grip. I signaled for her to come around to my window. As she walked around the front of the van, I scanned the bank of pines back where we had come from. Nothing there. She tapped on my window five times in rapid order and I rolled it down.

"Let me see both your hands," I said. "Hold them up."

"What?"

"Put your hands right here!" I slapped the base of the open window. "Don't mess with me on this!"

The confusion showed in her eyes, but she gripped the door frame without another word.

I turned off the engine. "I assume there's some good reason we're out here on a deserted airstrip where anybody within a mile can see us."

She nodded as she looked around. Her eyebrows were raised so high they seemed to touch her hairline.

"I didn't think about that," she said. "I was just looking for some place away from anybody else."

The orange windsock at the end of the runway hung limp, and except for an occasional distant boat horn and the low hum of cars and trucks on the big bridge and the cawing of some faraway gulls, there was silence. Heather started breathing faster as she looked back toward the trees, her hands still squeezing the door where my arm had been.

"What did you want to talk about?" I asked.

"So you think somebody might be watching us?"

"Who are you afraid of?"

"Who do you think?"

I laid my hand on top of hers. It gave her a start, but an instant later I felt the tightness ease. "Have you called the police yet?" I asked.

She shook her head.

"So I guess you must not be too worried." I turned the key and started the engine. "Why don't you come see me at the beach house I'm staying—"

"They're going to blow up one of the gas wells! Maybe tonight!"

I turned the engine back off.

"He said it's a good time to do it. The TV and the newspapers are all here, so he said it's a good time."

"He?" I asked. "You talking about Zandro?"

"Mr. Delmas, if one of those gas rigs explodes, it could kill a lot of people."

"Do you want that on your conscience?" I asked. "Do you want to have to live with that for the rest of your life?"

Tears welled up in her eyes and her voice got shaky. "I *can't* live with it! It's got me so worried I've been having headaches. I thought at first that it was all just talk. But, I swear, I think he's serious."

"So why haven't you gone to the sheriff or the police or some-body?"

"I'm telling you."

"I'm not the sheriff. I don't have a team of armed deputies I can send in to stop them."

"But couldn't you tell the cops?" She wiped her eyes with her finger.

"I haven't seen or heard anything except what you've told me. The cops are not about to go harass somebody and maybe get sued unless they've got a statement from an eyewitness. That means somebody who heard Zandro say he was planning to blow up one of the rigs."

"He never actually said it."

By this time she had started chewing on her top lip. There was no way she could keep on staying at the Guardian compound. Hell, if Zandro so much as blew his nose, she'd start spilling her guts. And that could get serious for her, and quick.

I started the van, put it into gear, and took my foot off the brake. It crept forward and she started trotting along beside it, her hands still on the window frame.

"You can't just leave me here!"

"I'm giving you until nightfall to either go to the cops or go back to Nashville."

She lost her grip and stopped running. "But I *can't!*" she cried. "I just can't!"

FIFTEEN

I didn't know how much plainer I could tell Heather to get in that car and get her young ass back up to Belle Meade. But short of kidnapping her and driving her to Nashville myself, I didn't know what else to do.

Even though I doubted that Zandro was going to try to blow up any gas rig, I called Jimbo's answering machine and gave him a heads up about Heather's story. Didn't leave my name, but didn't try to hide my voice, either. I had to say something, just in case, but I damn sure wasn't going to set off some false alarm if I could help it.

I had been thinking things over, and had cooled down some since my big scare, and I had about decided that as much as I wanted to stay on the island until I tracked down whoever had tried to kill me with that letter bomb, there was no way I could do it by myself. And until those beach-house killings were solved, there was nobody who could help me.

So the smart thing to do would be to get a little more information for my client about the way her daughter lived, since that's what I was being paid for, and then to go home and let the cops figure out who tried to kill me and why.

I'm getting better. At least nowadays I can usually pick out the smart thing to do. Now if I could only start actually doing it on a regular basis.

I figured I could talk to this girl they call Moon and see what she could tell me about Rebecca, and that ought to wrap up my work on the island. Then a stop or two in Mobile, maybe one more visit with Sanchez, and then a talk with this John Villa about the import business Jason had and what Rebecca may have had to do with it, and then I could go back and give Carolyn a report.

It was four hours before sunset and the only two guys in the Neptune were playing the Alabama Redemption Video machine over against the near wall. Above the machines was a framed photograph of Bear Bryant in his black-and-white hound's-tooth checked hat, his craggy face half in shadow from the shade of the famous hat's brim. It was a daytime shot and in the background you could see the stadium full of fans decked out in their Alabama red. The speakers behind the bandstand at the far wall had been hooked to the stereo and "I'm a Joker" by the Steve Miller band was playing, loud but not uncomfortably so.

There was a mop bucket in the center of the dance floor. A big, tattooed guy with a Marine haircut wearing a T-shirt with the sleeves cut off was replacing a broken windowpane in the front door, expertly spreading the putty along the frame and getting very little of it on the new pane. The front part of the Neptune had windows all around. The bar itself was a horseshoe configuration and backed up against the front wall. Moon was behind it, seated on a stool.

"What'll you have?" she asked.

"I need to ask you a few questions if you don't mind."

Her eyes widened and she cut a glance toward the guy fixing the window. She had a pretty, round, open face, completely devoid of guile. Her long blond hair and slim figure made her look like a high school girl. Except for the rows of three emerald studs on each earlobe and the tiny loops along the tops of her ears, she looked more like a sorority president than an artist. "Are you with the police or something? Did I do something wrong?"

"No, I'm not. And no, you didn't."

"I mean, I'm almost twenty-three. It's legal for me to work here."

"I'm not a cop, Moon."

The window-repair man stepped behind the bar and set the putty and spreader behind the bar on a bottom shelf. He tried to pretend he wasn't listening in on us. I ordered a Bud and he stepped back out and walked toward the mop bucket. He stirred the gray water around with the mop, releasing a pine scent, and slapped it down on the dance floor.

"Y'all keep a window-repair kit under the bar?"

"We break a lot of glass around here," she said. "What kind of questions do you want to ask me?"

"I'm trying to get background on Rebecca Jordan."

She tightened her lips and frowned as she began shaking her head. "You're a reporter, aren't you? Well, all I've got to say is that Rebecca was one of the sweetest persons I ever knew. If you're looking to dig up some—"

"Whoa! I'm not a reporter. And I'm not trying to dig up anything but the truth."

"Hey, Moon! How about another beer?" The guy at the Alabama Redemption machine was so deep into the game he never looked up. She slid back the top of the cooler and reached in for a fresh long-neck Bud.

"So who you digging up this truth for, anyway?"

"Her mother."

She studied me as she twisted off the top and walked the beer over to the guy. She came back, took her place on the stool, and I explained why I was the least private of any private investigator who ever set foot on Dauphin Island, Alabama. I told her that I was trying to tell Rebecca's mother whether any of the stuff the tabloids were saying was true. I gave her my most sincere head tilt and my most subtle nibble on my lower lip. She started talking in between calls for more beer.

Moon was on a fellowship, a three-year chance to hone her skills as a disciple of Walter Anderson and draw the herons, pelicans, and seascapes along the barrier islands of the northern Gulf Coast. No, Moon wasn't her real name, it was the name she used when she signed her paintings, a painter's pseudonym. She worked the Neptune two days a week for a little walking-around money and to take a break from painting. Rebecca had enrolled at a watercolor class that Moon was teaching up at the University of South Alabama and they became instant friends. She knew Rebecca before Jason came into the picture, and she saw the amazing transformation.

"So were you a friend of Jason's?" I asked.

"Yeah. Well, I guess I was. We didn't have a whole lot in common except for Rebecca. He was okay. But sometimes he got on my nerves."

"I hear he was an extrovert," I said.

She laughed. "He defined the term. I mean, don't get me wrong, he was a nice guy. But sometimes being around Jason was like being around a cruise director. He'd draw you out of your shell whether you wanted to come out or not. That's exactly what he did with Rebecca." She plunged a glass into the soapy water in the sink behind the bar. "Of course, Rebecca needed it. If anybody ever needed to build up her confidence it was Rebecca."

"You think they were serious about each other?" I asked. "You think they might have gotten married one day?"

She studied the question as she dried the glass. "I doubt it. I think Jason would have. But to tell you the truth, Rebecca had outgrown him. She had started begging off from a lot of his parties. She was tired of playing hostess. I think she would have broken it off with Jason, but he had one big thing going for him. Rebecca's stepfather just hated him."

I grabbed a handful of peanuts from one of the little bowls on the bar. "From what I hear, her stepfather is a little hard to get along with."

"The funny thing about it was that Jason was just like him, except he wasn't in the corporate world. Everybody thought Jason was a playboy. Truth is, he was a workaholic. Rebecca was beginning to realize that before she died."

"Did Rebecca hang out with Kellie Lee Simmons?"

"Kellie Lee was one of Jason's buddies. I doubt that Rebecca even knew her very well."

"Did Rebecca use drugs?" I asked.

"Didn't even drink."

"Was she promiscuous?"

"By her stepfather's standards, yes. She was sleeping with Jason. But he was the first. And the only."

"Her stepfather's standards?"

"It would have been okay with him if the guy she was screwing was an M.B.A. But an imports dealer who never wore a suit was not okay. Not by a long shot." Moon lifted the can of beer I had been sipping, wiggled it and saw it was empty, and put a new one in its place without either of us saying a word. "Rebecca really hated her stepfather. Used to call him Pe-tah. Her mother married him maybe a little too soon after her father died, and when she started having problems in high school, Pe-tah's response was that she needed to get over it and grow up. That's about the same way he handles the people who work for him, I would imagine. The man might be okay, I've never met him. But he wasn't what Rebecca needed at that time in her life."

"So that's why she stuck with Jason?" I asked. "Because he got under her stepfather's skin?"

"That's one reason. But there's another reason too. Rebecca just couldn't resist helping out somebody she thought needed some help."

"Wait a minute," I said. "I thought Jason was the one doing

all the helping. Are you telling me that he was depending on her?"

"Jason didn't need any help," she said. "I'm talking about Jason's mother."

"Rebecca was helping her?"

"All the time. And Mrs. Summers absolutely loved her. If you want to find out anything about Rebecca, you need to go talk to Mrs. Summers."

So it was right after Moon and I got through talking that I stepped out into the parking lot and got down on one knee to check under my van for any explosives that might have been planted there. That was when Jimbo drove up. I remember every word of what he said.

"Delmas!" he shouted. "I done told you to stop driving that van. You gonna get your ass killed, dammit!"

I remember it was as if his voice came down from a raised pulpit. I turned my head, still on one knee, and from that angle Jimbo once again looked to be ten feet tall.

"I think you might be right," I said.

"You and me, we need to talk," he said.

Wanted to talk some business with me, or so he said. And the next thing I knew we were in the Blackwater Saloon discussing the requirements to become a private investigator in Alabama. Then we headed to Shirley's Country Music Palace and, at that point, we were still talking business, at least to some extent. And I guess that impromptu interview later on with Bobby Earl Fair in that joint with no name could be considered business related. Maybe I should have asked our hostess for a receipt before we left.

I might be getting better at picking out the right thing to do, but I'm still having a mighty hard time when it comes to actually doing it. I damn sure didn't do it then.

SIXTEEN

When I woke up the next morning, the conversation I had with Moon while sitting on that barstool seemed as if it had taken place a month earlier. But it had in fact been only sixteen or seventeen hours. The only good thing about getting up the following day was that I was doing it in my own place and not the Mobile County jail. After the night Jimbo and I had just gone through, that by itself was a near miracle. As I propped my elbows on the breakfast bar and rested my head in my hands, I realized that I've gotten to the age where working late into the night is a lot tougher on me that it used to be.

Jimbo was still in the back bedroom recovering from all that business talk the night before, and I was on my third cup of dark-roast Luzianne after a head-clearing morning jog. I was thankful I had used at least some good sense and laid off the tequila. I felt that I needed to call Memphis so I picked up the portable phone and punched in Sandy's number. She answered on the third ring.

"Are you and Peyton all right?" I said.

"No, we are *not* all right," she said. "We're like prisoners in our own house. I don't suppose you've managed to find out who planted that bomb."

"I'll let you know when we do."

"I can't believe you'd put your own daughter in jeopardy over some silly case."

"Don't go down that road again, Sandy," I said. "I'm not the one who announced to the whole world that I was working a case here."

"I didn't announce it to the whole world. I just told Susan Chapman."

"Same difference," I said.

"You've got to find another line of work."

I had been up for an hour and was all packed up, which didn't take all that long since all I put in the hang-up was a jacket, two pairs of Dockers, and a couple of shirts. The swim trunks and T-shirts I wore 90 percent of the time I had stuffed into the tote bag. Felt fine except for the bone socket at the corner of my eye where that roofer's fist caught just enough of me to give me a bruise and make it ache when I pressed it with my finger. Made me hurt enough not to want to put up with any crap from Sandy, that's for sure. It was too late for an ice pack to do it any good.

Jimbo walked in from the back, still wearing his boxers and the MSU T-shirt from the night before. His hair was matted, stuck up on the side where he had slept on it without movement for the past eight hours. His face was puffy and his eyes filmed over with a pinkish hue.

"I thought you were moving out of that place," Sandy said.

"I'm leaving later today. I'll call and let you know where I'll be."

Jimbo knocked a coffee cup off the breakfast bar as he walked by. It hit the floor and shattered with a loud crash.

"Sounds like you've got company," Sandy said.

"Somebody needed a place to stay."

"Well, at least you waited until your daughter was out of town."

Damn, does she ever know how to flip my switches. She does that stuff on purpose. "I guess you and Varner stayed in separate rooms when you were down here."

"You want some coffee?" Jimbo shouted from the kitchen.

"You've got men over there, too?" she asked. "How many people needed a place to stay?"

"Don't worry about it," I said. "I don't think you're in any danger up there. But you ought to keep Peyton close to you for a while."

"You can bet on that. We're staying right here. We were driving to Daddy and Mama's yesterday and somebody followed us."

"You're psyching yourself out."

"You remember you told me how to spot a tail? Well, this man in a gray car stayed behind us for three or four blocks. At least three or four."

"That doesn't mean a thing, Sandy."

"He turned off, but guess what. He showed up again after disappearing for a few blocks. He was tailing us. I know he was."

"Was there anybody with him?"

"No, nobody. Oh, maybe you're right. Maybe I am psyching myself out."

But, then again, maybe she wasn't. "I've got this friend in Memphis," I said. "He's an investigator, but he's also a professional bodyguard. I'll give him a call and get him to keep an eye on y'all for the next few days."

"So you *do* think I was being tailed. I knew it!"

"I can't tell what's going on from a long-distance phone call. But I'd be willing to bet that whoever planted that bomb is still down here and has never even seen Memphis, Tennessee. I'll call the bodyguard. He's the best in the business."

She was silent for a while, the only sounds coming over the phone the TV audience laughter of some silly women's morning talk show. "Jack, do you think you could come up here?"

Well, well, well. I never thought I'd hear that.

"I would in a New York second," I said. "But I'm not as good a bodyguard as the man I'm going to send to you. And I think we'd be better off if I stayed down here until we caught this creep. We don't want to have to worry about him coming back if he decides I know too much."

"Just what is it that you know?"

"Not much. But he thinks I do."

The room was quiet except for the sound of the toilet running in the bathroom next to where I was sitting. Some Memphis car dealer on Sandy's TV was shouting about no money down and no interest until next year, but she wasn't making a sound. I began to wonder if she had walked to the refrigerator or something.

"Promise me you won't do anything stupid," she said.

"None of it ever seems stupid at the time I'm doing it."

She laughed. "God, you are out of control."

"As I recall, you used to like that."

"I don't want you to get hurt. Maybe you'd better just get off the island."

"Are you really concerned about me getting hurt?"

Jimbo was gulping water from a big Styrofoam cup when he stepped in from the kitchen. He pulled at his boxer shorts to put a little breathing space between them and his skin and walked barefoot out the front door.

"Of course I'm concerned," she said. "Peyton is, too."

"Sandy, please don't tell me that Peyton knows about that letter bomb."

"Of course she doesn't. But she's not stupid. She knows you carry a pistol, she's heard the stories about how you go after bad guys."

"She has?"

"Some of the kids at school talk about it. They hear it from their parents. They think it's really cool."

"Really cool, huh? Are you talking about the kids or the parents?"

"Grow up, Jack," she said. "Just walk away from this one. Okay?"

"I've got to find this guy. Do you want somebody running around out there who's made a threat to Peyton? Would you feel comfortable just sitting around and hoping he never decides to come after her?"

She sighed.

"You got anything besides de-caf in here?" Jimbo shouted, walking back in.

"Get back to your company," Sandy said.

"Let me talk with Peyton."

"She's still asleep."

"You talking to Darla?" Jimbo said as he walked back in.

"Darla?" Sandy asked. "You've got somebody there named Darla?"

"I've got to go," I said. "I'll let you know as soon as I find out something."

"Who is this Darla person?"

Darla. Dar-la. Hey, listen Sandy. Darrrrrr-lah!

I didn't say it like that.

But I might as well have. A woman with a name like Darla even sounds like she's got big ones. And that *always* pisses off Sandy. Oh, she'll recite the usual feminist liturgy about how men are only interested in a woman's boobs and how stupid that is, and how a secure woman doesn't care one way or the other. But despite all that talk, it really bothers her when some woman has a bigger set. Really bothers her. I mean, you name the woman, and if she gets a higher reading on the tape measure, Sandy's just got to start bad-mouthing her. Course Sandy can hold her own in most situations where there's no silicon involved, so there aren't many times when she gets overshadowed, so to speak. But the few times it does come up I get a real kick out of it.

And the great thing about this time was that I could tell she was getting jealous, could hear it in her voice even over a telephone line. And she was just assuming this Darla person had a big rack based on nothing more than her name. You may think I'm reading a lot into this, but I lived with the woman for five years. She was jealous, believe me.

"I heard somebody talking to her," Sandy said.

"There's nobody here named Darla," I said.

"So she's not a real person?"

"Oh, yeah. She's real all right. Look, I've got to go. Maybe you can meet Darla the next time you and Varner fly down."

I hung up after lining up the bodyguard and promising once again that I'd be careful. Hey, who knows? Maybe she really does give a flip whether I live or die. That was a step up from the other day; maybe the Midols had kicked in. Never did explain Darla to her. But I could tell that was really getting under her skin.

I wouldn't have toyed with Sandy like that a year earlier. I wouldn't have done it a week earlier. But I kept seeing that plane leaving and this feeling of release, like the pardon had come through, just mellowed me out. When I hung up, it was the first time in six years I had ended a conversation with her without seriously considering getting down on my knees and begging her to come back. God, it was as if the sky parted or something.

Jimbo was trying not to put any weight on his left foot. He had brought in a maroon Mississippi State gym bag, which he tossed to the floor beside the breakfast table. He poured himself a cup of coffee and another big glass of water and sat on a tiny chair at the table that groaned and threatened to break, then he closed his eyes and held the cup to his lips and let the steam of the coffee bathe his face.

"I'd let you have a fresh set of underwear," I said. "But I doubt that it would fit."

He reached into the gym bag and pulled out a bottle of B_{12} tablets and a squirt bottle of Visine eye drops. "Got it all right here. I keep this shack pack in the truck. Just never know when you might be spending the night somewhere other than your own bed." He popped the B_{12} tablet in his mouth. "Did somebody stomp on my foot last night?"

"I was too busy trying to keep us out of jail. I really didn't notice."

"Jail?" He frowned at me and drank down the glass of water in one breath. He eased the steamy cup of coffee to his lips and took a loud sip.

"I don't think either one of us hit one of the deputies," I said. "So we were looking at disturbing the peace, tops."

"Deputies?" He tilted his head back and held the Visine bottle above his left eye.

"You don't remember?" I asked.

"How did we get all that mud on my truck?"

"At what point did the lights go off, Jimbo?"

He put drops in the other eye and swept his hair straight back with his palm. "I remember seeing this guy at the pool table at Sollie's scratching bad on his break shot. Got under the cue ball and knocked it all the way off the table. And I remember you putting a quarter on the table to take on the winners."

"Sollie's?" I asked.

"Ain't that where we was?"

"I never knew the name of the place."

"Did we get pulled over or something later on?"

"You mean you don't remember insulting Bear Bryant's hat?"

He rubbed his eyes and started laughing. "I did that?"

"Said he must have been cruising in some queer joint when he found it."

He laughed real loud. Swallowed the wrong way on some coffee and got choked.

"God, I musta been *tow-up* drunk! You tellin' me I said something bad about the Bear's damned *hat*?"

"So I don't suppose you remember the fight."

He closed his eyes and shook his head. "Did we tear the place up?"

"You couldn't tear that place up with a sledge hammer."

I stood and walked into the kitchen. Jimbo leaned back and stretched and yawned real loud. The sun coming through the French doors was hurting my eyes; I knew it must be killing his. I dropped the roll-up shades all the way and ran the thermostat down to sixty. The air out of the ceiling vents smelled clean and salt-free and scattered the dust motes that had been drifting in the sunlight. I had my two suitcases packed and sitting against the wall beside the front door.

"Looks like you're moving out," he said.

"I was causing some problems for my client by staying here. Mayson Marine has got some Navy brass that needs it. I've got one more person I need to talk to before I wrap up this background check."

"Who you need to see?"

"Jason Summers's mother. Somebody told me she and Rebecca were pretty tight. I've really got enough to take to my client right now. She wanted to know if there was any truth to the tabloid stories, and I've got enough to tell her there isn't."

"You think it'd do you any good to see Jason's house?" he said.

"I've already seen it. That's where Rebecca died, but I don't know if it would tell me a whole lot about the way she lived."

"I'm talking about seeing it on the inside."

"I know all about Rebecca I need to know."

"Yeah, but you don't know everything you need to know about the guy who put that bomb on your porch." He took a big sip of coffee and swished it around in his mouth. "Besides, I want you to go over there with me and tell me how good an investigator I am."

SEVENTEEN

God, Jimbo," the young deputy said, "I'm about to go nuts in here. Why don't you see if you can get the sheriff to take me off this house-sitting detail for a few days."

"I'm the last person on the force you want to have going to bat for you right now," Jimbo said. "This here's my friend Jack. I told him he could come take a look at the place."

The deputy who was keeping watch over the house was a thick-bodied kid, deep tanned, with a baby face and a buzz cut. He wasn't wearing an earring, but there was a hole in his left ear lobe. Had a jam box set on a Pensacola FM rock station and had moved a kitchen chair over near the door where he could look out at the beach. He had a set of binoculars sitting on the floor beside the chair.

"Had some TV crew come up here this morning," he said. "Wanted to know when we were gonna let them come in and do some filming."

"I ain't heard nothing about that," Jimbo said. "When did you get here?"

" 'Bout seven this morning. Relieved Cassidy. That reminds me, he asked if I knew where you were."

"What the hell's Cassidy want with me?"

"He didn't exactly say. Did something happen last night I ain't heard about?"

I stepped into the big room and left them talking in the foyer. The room reminded me of a banquet hall. It had a vaulted ceiling and French doors across the front wall that opened up to the outside deck overlooking the beach. Toward the back of the big room was an archway, the only passage out of the room on that far side of the house.

"That kid in there said he had a visitor from the bank over here earlier this morning," Jimbo said. "Seems they're getting a little anxious about this house. Ain't no payments been made since Jason got killed."

"Why don't they go to see Bob Sanchez?" I asked. "I'd bet Jason had an insurance policy that'll pay off the balance of the mortgage. Sanchez could get the death certificate and whatever else they need to collect on the policy." ·

"The bank is saying Jason didn't own this place. Said his mama owned it."

"You think maybe she was involved with Jason's business?"

"I doubt it," he said. "She ain't the type. Probably put it in her name because of taxes or something like that."

"Well why doesn't the bank just call her?"

"They don't know where she lives. The address they have for her is right here."

"She shouldn't be all that hard to find," I said. "Maybe you could get a job with that bank. Sounds like they could use an investigator."

Through the window I saw a flock of pelicans floating like bath toys a hundred yards out from the beach, bobbing on the waves that were coming with a mounting rhythm as the eleven-o'clock high tide moved in. A wave runner going at full speed splashed from wave to wave and shot a thin, white arc of water behind it, and I could hear its motor roaring even through the glass.

"You see them dark stains on that couch?" Jimbo said. "That's where they found Rebecca Jordan. She was laid out right where she had been sitting. Got some of her blood up on the wall. See them splatter marks?"

"Were all four of the bodies found in this room?"

"All except for Rod Eubanks. He was at the foyer right there where we come in. Got shot in the back. I figure he was trying to run out the front door."

I looked back at the young deputy. He was looking out the front windows with the binoculars at a group of girls sunbathing on the beach.

"Headquarters looking for you?" I asked.

"We didn't get into any fight with a deputy last night, did we?"

"Not directly. At least we never actually hit one of them. But there were two in the place, whatever the name of it was. . . ."

"Sollie's."

"And there was a fight going on that we were in the middle of, and the deputies were trying to break it up."

He reached to his back pocket for the can of Skoal. "Cassidy's saying I hit a deputy. Hurt his shoulder somehow."

"That deputy who hurt his shoulder slipped and fell on the concrete. I saw that. Nobody hit him."

"Aw, what the hell. Cain't do nothin' about it now." He pointed to a spot at the side and slightly behind the couch. "I figure one of the shooters was standing right there."

"How many shooters were in here?"

"Could have been two. But probably three. Three weapons were used, but one of the shooters could have been firing with two guns. At least that's what the boys from Montgomery are saying."

To our right was a neat arrangement of twelve chairs, the metal with padded seats like you see in hotel convention halls. Three rows, four chairs per row. They were turned toward the far wall which was blank, without picture or ornament of any type. Behind these chairs was a movie projector sitting on a metal base with rollers. Up at the ceiling was a retractable movie screen. Behind this area set up for viewing films were two couches and two stuffed armchairs.

"You won't believe what kinda films and videos and stuff we found in here," he said.

"If they were films from Mexico, I can imagine."

"Naw, it wasn't nothing like that. It was like stuff from the Travel

Channel, but it was in Spanish. It showed all the tourist spots in Mobile, Pensacola, New Orleans. There were some other tapes showing how to make change and how to catch a bus, stuff like that."

"Those were in Spanish too?"

"They all were," he said. "And there were a bunch of pamphlets about condominiums over in Florida. Some of this time-share stuff."

The place had all the homey atmosphere of a bus station or an airport. At the end opposite the film-viewing area was a wide-screen TV and a CD unit with waist-high speakers mounted into a pressed-wood entertainment center taller than I am by a good two feet.

"What does this room remind you of?" Jimbo asked.

"Looks like a dance hall. Or maybe a dining hall in some castle."

"How about a classroom?" he said.

"That's exactly what it looks like," I said. "You don't think maybe Jason was selling time-share units or some kind of real estate to these Mexicans, do you? You know the drill on that stuff. Win a free vacation weekend and all you have to do is listen to one sales presentation."

Jimbo poked out his bottom lip and thought about that. "It shouldn't be too hard to find out if he was licensed to sell real estate."

"Somehow this doesn't look like the luxury beach house I pictured Jason using to entertain clients from Central America," I said. "It's like you said. Looks like somewhere you could be giving sales pitches to a group."

He nodded as he looked the room over as if for the first time. "The bedrooms are in the back part of the house through that archway," he said. "They're nice. Not exactly the Beau Rivage, but nice just the same. Six bedrooms. And the kitchen, it looks like the kind you'd find in a school or something. Got those big stainless steel refrigerators and the oven is big enough for a restaurant to use."

On the floor in front of the couches, and even on the couches themselves, were the chalked outlines of bodies in various states of repose. Printed signs with the logo of the Mobile County Sheriff's

Department warned us to avoid touching anything or walking in the marked-off areas.

"So what do you think?" I said. "You be the detective."

"First thing is, there was three gunmen. The crime lab said it coulda been two, but that's BS. The slugs in Jason here," he pointed to the near end of the couch, "they come from one gun. Rebecca got popped with a different gun. And Kellie Lee over there on that recliner, she got hit with a third one. No way it was two shooters. And look where the bodies were. They got popped so fast, none of them had time to react. Got shot graveyard dead right where they was sittin'."

"Except for Eubanks," I said.

Jimbo pulled off his sunshades and pinched the inside corners of his eyes with his right hand. "That proves my point. Rod Eubanks got shot by two different guns. That means the three killers each picked out one target and drilled them. Eubanks jumped up and started running and he got shot by two different shooters before he got to the door."

"Okay, there were three gunmen and not two. How'd they get in?"

"They got let in."

"So it was somebody Jason knew?" I asked.

"Didn't say that. Coulda been somebody any one of 'em knew. Not just Jason. I mean, this was party headquarters for the western end of the island. It ain't like they checked IDs at the door or something." He ran his tongue around the inside of his cheeks. "Hey, speaking of IDs, let me show you something. Wait right here."

He stepped through the archway toward the back of the house and left me standing there. The room was stuffy. The same air that was in there when the killings occurred had been sent through the air conditioner hundreds of times, never refreshed except for the few times someone walked in through the front door. A soured smell of dried-out blood mixed with the bitter odor of tobacco smoke embedded into the carpet, the furniture, and the drapes. The carpet was short matted with a thick pad that gave way every time I took a step. A solitary housefly, fat, black, and slow, buzzed against a windowpane, hoping to break through it, running up and down its clear surface.

"Look at this little number," Jimbo said as he came back into the room. "It's no wonder Jason was so popular with the college crowd." He held up what looked like a credit card machine, the kind they run your card through at the checkout counter.

"Jason took credit cards?"

"He made fake IDs. They got background markups in here that I can stick your picture in and laminate, make a card showing you to be a lieutenant in the French Foreign Legion if that's what you want to be. Mostly it's driver's licenses from Alabama and Mississippi. He's even got a couple of Social Security cards in here. You just fill in the name."

So, I thought, that's how he made Chloe's pilot's license. "Where would he get all that stuff?"

"Man, just go to the Internet and punch in the words 'Fake ID' and see what you come up with. Since they raised the drinking age for beer to twenty-one, fake IDs have become a growth industry. And there ain't no way in the world to control it."

I sifted through the box full of wallet-sized cards, the backgrounds on which you could affix your portrait and make yourself into any alter ego you wanted. There were backgrounds for driver's licenses, pilot's licenses, press cards, and student IDs for a dozen colleges. There were cards that could make you a policeman, a fireman, a paramedic, or a staff physician. You could be an agent for the FBI, the DEA, the INS, or the Boy Scouts. My favorite was the one for security squad for the Louisiana Superdome. I considered the possibilities if I could only lay my hands on one of those.

"You were asking me how to become a private eye," I said. "Looks like you can cut through a lot of red tape with this little baby."

He raised his eyebrows and studied the little lamination device he was holding. He smiled and moved it up and down a few times as if to test its heft, to get a feel for this newfound magical machine.

"What else did y'all find that was interesting?" I asked.

"Found every football magazine you can imagine. *Lindy's, Athalon, Street and Smith's,* you name it. Jason knew what he was doing on this football betting. He kept a book that had all his winnings and losings in it, at least the ones from last year. He naturally ripped Bobby Earl Fair a new one last year. I mean, if them entries was right, he just about singlehandedly busted Bobby Earl."

"Did you see anything from this year?" I asked.

"Naw. Musta started a new book. But I hear he had a wad bet on that Michigan State–Texas A&M game. They say if you gonna beat the bookies, the time to do it's the first of the season. Once they get a look at them teams for three or four weeks, you can forget about beating them." He rubbed the surface of his teeth with his forefinger. "About the only other thing we found was four or five dozen cigars."

"Man," I said, "he must have loved those Cuban cigars."

"I don't think he even smoked 'em. He gave 'em out as gifts." He ran his tongue across his top front teeth. "I gotta bad case of the cottonmouth. Let's go into the kitchen."

Jimbo got a sleeve of white Styrofoam cups out of the cabinet above the sink. He filled one with tap water and gulped down the whole glassful. "My mouth's got a coating on it like I done rinsed it out with Turtle Wax or something."

He hit the switch on the TV set on the counter by the sink. As he poured a second glass of water, the news came on. It started with a local report, a press conference called in the lobby of the Haney Building up in Mobile. Scooter Haney was standing behind the podium looking appropriately pissed. I missed the opening, but the first question was about the taped phone conversations being exposed as fraudulent.

"Damn right, I'm gonna sue," Scooter said. "I been slandered big time by the major news networks."

"How's your head?" I asked Jimbo.

"Not bad long as I wear these Ray·Bans. Tequila don't give me much of a headache. Main thing that hurtin' right now is my foot."

Jimbo, who had been listening to the TV as he polished off his second glass of tap water, turned to the screen. He reached out and turned up the volume with one hand as he reached to his back pocket for his can of Skoal with the other. I thought I heard a phone ringing on the screen.

"I can't just let these bald-faced lies go by without callin' BS on 'em," Scooter said. "I gotta protect my good name."

"Hah, hah!" Jimbo shouted. "That Scooter, he can say any damn thing with a straight face. That's why the sum'bitch gets so many women. Good name, my ass!"

"Hey, Jimbo!" the kid deputy in the other room yelled. "Somebody wants to talk to you on the phone."

"My good name. That's a good one." Jimbo stuffed a paper towel into his water cup. "Who is it?"

"Some girl. Didn't give her name."

He spit down the inside edge of the cup and walked into the next room. I watched the end of the report and turned off the TV. The air in the kitchen was stale with a light odor from the sink. I stepped through an arch into a breakfast room at the back corner of the house. It had windows on two sides and the shafts of sunlight came through at an angle that lit up the baseboards of the opposite wall and warmed up the room to where the sweat on my arms and around my neck clung to me like a film. Why didn't they air the place out?

Just inside the arch on the floor sat a cardboard box with scraps of copier paper, cut up into random shapes and sizes, and remnants of photostat copies. I picked up a handful of these paper scraps and thumbed through them. They were copies of newspapers from south Texas, mainly from San Antonio. Most of them were from the 1960s and 1970s. Somebody had cut out obituary notices, wedding announcements, and anniversary celebrations. Several stories had been lifted from the local news page, mostly stories of car wrecks, drownings, and other accidental deaths.

"You're not gonna believe who that was callin' me," Jimbo said. He stood in the archway, hands above his head, holding onto the molding and hanging from it, smiling like he'd just sunk a thirty-foot putt.

"It was that blonde from the Green Guardians compound," I said. "The one with the great set of legs."

Jimbo cocked his head and dropped the smile. He took off the sunshades and assumed this puzzled look. "How'd you know that?"

"Did she want to take you up on your offer to make her forget all those tree huggers she's been hanging with?"

"Seriously, how'd you know that? Was it some kind of private eye trick?"

"I told you and Carlton Rice both that she'd be calling, remember?"

"Way I feel this morning, I can barely remember my own name."

"What did she have to say?" I asked.

"She just wanted to talk to ol' Jimbo."

"You're lying."

"She called to tell me the same thing some anonymous caller told me on my answering machine yesterday afternoon. Something about those Green Guardians. You wouldn't know anything about that, would you?" He flashed back into a toothy smile. "I see you've found Jason's papers."

I rubbed the ones I was holding between my fingers. "What is all this stuff?"

"He had been cutting out old newspaper stories from twenty or thirty years ago. Some go back as far as the late 1950s. The Bureau took most of them up to Montgomery. He had clipped every Mexican birth announcement, obituary, wedding, you name it."

"Any idea why he was doing that?"

"Looking for relatives, I guess."

"Whose relatives are you talking about?" I asked. "All these stories are about Hispanics down around San Antonio."

"You mean you didn't know?" he said. "Jason's mama, she's a full-blooded Mexican."

EIGHTEEN

You're free to stay here as long as you want," Easy said, "I'll be heading up to Tuscaloosa tomorrow, but you just go back there and claim a bed. Throw your stuff into any closet you want to."

"I'll be out of your way in a day or two," I said. I said. "Maybe not even that long."

"I'd just as soon have somebody in here the next few days while I'm up at the game."

"They still got the Tide laying eight against Vandy?"

"I put two dimes on Bama yesterday, when the spread was still eight. It was when I saw you at the Pelican Pub. Everybody around here was jumping on that spread. I pick up the paper this morning and see where Coach Woody up at Vandy's done suspended two starters for some curfew problem and the line's jumped to ten. If Bobby Earl fooled around yesterday and didn't call out to Vegas and lay off some of that Bama action, he's gonna take a big-time hit Saturday. I don't know if the boy had enough sense to call in."

The story of the murders was cooling off; you could feel it the same way you feel mild fronts in late September easing in from the north. Nobody had seen Darren Wright since he broke the story about Scooter. A rumor was going around that he was going to be pulled to cover an assassination in some little pissant country. I guess I had heard the name of the place, but I sure couldn't remember what it was. It sounded like the kind of place that ought to be the answer to the $125,000 question on *Who Wants to Be a Millionaire*. The focus of those TV cameras that had been on the island the past few weeks had already started shifting to other stories in other places, and I got the feeling Carolyn wasn't going to get the chance to clear Rebecca's name before the whole thing became yesterday's news.

"You know how to boil shrimp?" Easy asked.

"I learned how to do that at my mama's knee."

"Well, you're about to earn your keep," he said. "I've got some folks coming over tonight for a shrimp boil and I need somebody who knows what he's doing. To tell you the truth, I think I overcook mine most of the time."

Out on the rear deck I set up the tripod and hooked up the cannister of gas. The aluminum pot used for the boiling was only slightly smaller than an oil drum. Easy had a good twenty pounds of shrimp, most of them thawed from his freezer, but a good many of them were fresh. He had also bought the cole slaw and potato salad at Greer's Food Tiger a few miles up Dauphin Island Parkway and the guests were supposed to bring whatever they wanted to drink.

There had been a thundershower an hour earlier, one of those late-afternoon storms that build up in the gulf until the clouds get so top heavy they've got to spill out a few tons of rain. There was a pleasant smell of wet sand and the wet wood of the deck, and the air wasn't as salty as usual. The sea oats bent over from the weight of the water and tiny gulls were shining bright and white against the dark gray sky of early evening.

I sliced three onions and six lemons and dropped them into the water when it came to a boil. I licked some of the lemon pulp off my finger and it puckered my mouth. The door opened and the music got louder as Missy walked through.

"Mind if I join you?" she said.

"Glad to have somebody to talk to," I said. "You here alone?"

"Yeah. I came with three guys and Chloe."

"How about opening that box of salt for me. My hands are kind of wet."

I poured some lemon juice over my fingers to cut the stickiness from handling raw shrimp. It stung when it hit a little cut I had picked up somehow. Missy poured in the salt until the water turned cloudy and then sat in the deck chair and rested her feet on top of the railing, raising those long, hard, tanned legs to the level of my waist. I dropped in four bags of shrimp boil and the red steam burned my nose and made me want to sneeze.

"You remember what you were telling me about Jason?" I asked.

"Kinda."

"You said he acted like he was the social chairman. You remember that?"

"That's exactly how he acted," she said. "He used to have all these visitors from Mexico who'd come up here and he ran them from place to place like they were on some guided tour."

"What about these Mexicans? Did they act like tourists?"

"They all had some money. All of them spoke English real well. I got to be friends with one of them. His name's John Villa. You remember him, he's the one you met at the party. That cute guy who was the CPA."

"I've heard he practically ran Jason's import business."

"I don't know about that," she said. "All I know is that he's real smart." She pulled an empty deck chair close to hers and patted it for me to sit. Missy smelled like coconut oil. She piled her hair on top of her head and snapped it into place with a pink plastic clip. "I was hoping you'd be here tonight." She lowered her eyes and watched her finger as she ran it along my forearm with such a light touch it made the hairs rise as if they were charged.

"Tell me, Missy, do you go to the movies often?"

"Do I what?"

"Have you seen that new Harrison Ford movie?"

"Oh, yeah," she said. "I just love Harrison Ford."

"Oh, you do? Did I ever tell you—"

"Son!" Jimbo shouted from behind us. "We gotta have us a talk for a minute or two. 'Scuse us, Missy."

"Hello, Jimbo," she said.

"When did you get here?" I asked.

"I figured this would be a likely spot to catch up with you."

"Okay," I said. "You caught me. Let's talk."

"I mean in private."

Missy lowered those perfect legs and popped out of her chair with the fluid movement of a healthy, firm, agile, twenty-something beach girl. She stood and stretched her arms over her head and stood on her toes, gently flexing her calves. This girl definitely had some good features. "I'll go get us something cold to drink and let you boys have some privacy. You need anything from the kitchen, Jimbo?"

He shook his head without looking at her and sat down in the chair she'd just vacated. He leaned in close to me.

"I sure hope this is something important you want to talk about," I said as I followed Missy's retreat into the kitchen. She was wearing something that was mighty close to a thong.

"She'll be here when you get back," he said.

"That's exactly what you said about Darla," I said. "Hey, wait a minute. Didn't I just hear you say something about getting back? Back from where?"

"We got us a little mission."

"Does this little mission involve Darla?"

"I'm serious, son."

"I am too," I said. "Last night I had Darla—hell, I don't even know her last name—but I had her rubbing up against me and the next thing I know Ernest Hemingway's honor code pops up and we're fighting our way out of some juke joint because you decide to insult Bear Bryant."

"You told me it was his hat."

"It doesn't matter! I don't know if you've noticed, but Missy in there seems to have taken a liking to me, and I damn sure ain't interested in trading that for the chance to go clean out any more beer joints."

"You want to find out who left that package bomb, or not?"

NINETEEN

The truck still smelled like the drink Jimbo had spilled in it the night before. The mud from our ride through the swamp had dried in rooster tails above all four wheel wells, and there were dead dragonflies sticking to the grille. Despite the heat, we didn't run the air conditioner and put the windows down, and that tequila smell wasn't doing Jimbo's stomach much good. That's the thing about tequila, you can taste the stuff for two days afterward.

"So Heather was right," I said. "The crazy son of a bitch is going to try to blow up one of the gas rigs."

"Looks like it. Called me from a pay phone, and I went and got her right then."

"So she's out of the compound?"

"You couldn't get her to go back in that place for no amount of money."

"Where are we going now?"

"We're going to make sure Zandro don't blow up no gas wells."

"We can't go out and intercept a boat full of dynamite on the gulf," I said. "If these people are half as crazy as you say, they'll blow themselves up and us with them."

"You want to just let them go blow up that drilling rig?"

"Don't y'all have a Sheriff's Water Patrol or something? For that matter, how about the Coast Guard? I don't know why you think I need to go out there. I'm a civilian."

He started the engine and goosed the accelerator. "So am I."

"What you talking about?"

"I'm on administrative leave as of this morning. Seems that some of the boys at the department took a dim view of our little pool game at Sollie's last night."

"You're suspended?"

"It'll just be for a few days." Jimbo stepped on the gas; the big tires spun in the sand and yelped when they hit the asphalt at the end of Easy's drive. "No big deal. It ain't the first time this has happened."

"Tell me once more where we're going."

"We're going to meet with Heather and this friend of mine. He'll fill you in on the details."

"So Heather's still here on the island?"

"Not for long." He turned on the air conditioner and set it as high as it would go, aiming one of the vents at his face. "By the way, I checked the Real Estate Commission yesterday to see if Jason was licensed to sell time shares and such. He wasn't."

"Well, it was just a thought."

"While I was at it, I did a few quick background checks on the four that got killed."

"What kind of checks?"

"Well, I already had some of their stuff from the case files. Social Security numbers, driver's licenses, addresses, where they went to school, that kind of stuff. I made some copies of some of the stuff." He reached over and popped open the glove compartment. He pulled out a tan envelope and dropped it in my lap. "Not a whole lot there, but you're welcome to it."

"You're going to be a private eye before you know it," I said. "Did you check them out with the National Crime Information Center?"

"That's the first thing I did. All four of 'em were all clean except for a few traffic violations on Kellie Lee and a disturbing the peace on Rod Eubanks."

"Nothing on Rebecca?"

He shook his head. "You can tell her mama there ain't no skeletons."

"Nothing on Jason?"

"Not a thing. But I got to thinking about Jason and that import business of his. I think I figured out what the boy was doing to make all that money. He was smuggling something into this country from down in Mexico."

"That's the first thing I thought of," I said. "But nobody's come up with one bit of evidence that links him or any of the other three to any drug trafficking."

"Ain't talking about drugs," he said. "I think the boy was sneaking in a whole bunch of Cuban cigars."

We pulled into the shell-covered parking lot of the marina behind the Sea House Restaurant on the bay side of the island. The sky had cleared from the afternoon's rain and the sun was low and casting long shadows. There was hardly any stirring of the heavy wet air; two V-formations of pelicans were flying along the shoreline, headed up the bay toward Mobile. The smell of fried shrimp from the vents of the restaurant hung in the air. We got out and Jimbo pointed at a boat tied off at the end of one of the piers, close to the gasoline pumps.

"You might have something with this cigar idea," I said. "It would fit. He flew in and out of Central America all the time. He has a lot of business contacts down there. Yeah, it all fits."

"It just hit me when I went into Ship and Shore last night to buy me a few cans of Skoal. Hell, they done got the price of tobacco jumped up so high with all them taxes nowadays, somebody could make a killing smuggling some in. They already got a black market started in Canada on cigarettes. For all I know, they've got one here. I got this friend who tells me there's one brand of Cuban cigars called Cohibas that sell for a thousand bucks a box in Europe. That's forty dollars apiece. And they're legal in Europe. You find somebody who can buy them for you wholesale down in Mexico, can you imagine what you could sell 'em for up here?"

Heather was on the rear deck of a thirty-foot houseboat, leaning on the railing and talking to this man with salt-and-pepper hair who was wearing jeans and a black, nylon windbreaker. When we were halfway down the pier, Heather and the man walked into the cabin.

"His name's Harry Bell," Jimbo said. "Me and him go way back."

"Is he a deputy?"

"I'll let him tell you who he's with. That is, if he wants to. Don't ask a whole lot of questions, you understand?"

We boarded and stepped down into the cabin. Heather was sitting with her legs crossed on a couch along the wall and kicking her foot back and forth. Harry Bell had turned a chair backward and straddled it, using its back to lean his arms on. They had flipped the air conditioner on, but it hadn't run long enough to relieve the stuffiness and overcome the stale air that had been building up all day in the closed cabin. Heather looked like she was about ready to jump straight up if somebody so much as said boo.

"Harry Bell," Jimbo said, "this is Jack Delmas. He's the one who got the bomb planted by his front door."

"Don't I know you?" I asked.

"I've seen you around the island," he said.

Bell had the same piney-woods accent that Jimbo had. Some guys lose some of it when they take jobs up north and stay there a while. But not this guy.

"You were at the Pelican Pub the other day when I was there." I snapped my fingers. "And you were the guy on the ferry that day. Why have you been tailing me?"

"We haven't exactly been tailin' you, Mr. Delmas."

"We? You wouldn't happen to have a partner in Memphis, would you? Maybe riding around in a gray car?"

"We've been tryin' to make sure that neither you nor anyone in your family gits hurt."

"Well how about you taking the guard off me down here and doubling up on the one in Memphis?"

"I cain't call in anybody else from the agency. They don't know that I'm involved in this case, and they don't know about Memphis. We're operating on our own time."

"Just what agency are you with?" I asked.

Jimbo had been standing just inside the door with his arms crossed. He suddenly seemed to find great interest in this spot on the floor a foot or two in front of his toes. Bell chewed lightly on the inside of his cheek and waited for that subject to disappear.

I turned and faced Heather. "Where do you fit into this?"

"We're trying to make arrangements to get this young lady home," Bell said.

"You're leaving the Green Guardians?"

"I left that place right after I talked with you." Her voice was so quiet I could barely hear her. "Zandro is a raving lunatic."

I rubbed my hand across my face, stepped over to the couch, and plopped down beside her. "All right, folks. Let's take it from the top and get me some answers, or I'm going back to this shrimp boil I was invited to."

Bell sat frowning at me, perfectly still except for blinking a few times. He took in a deep breath and held it, as if he was getting ready to lift something heavy. "All right. Here goes. I'm Special Agent Harold C. Bell operating out of New Orleans. For purposes of this briefing—"

"So, how about you Heather?" I said. "Are you special too?"

She smiled. "I guess not."

"Well, neither am I. How about you, Jimbo? Are you? Maybe we need one of those red plates that says we're special today."

"I don't get what you're saying," Bell said.

"This isn't a congressional hearing," I said. "Nobody's under oath, and this is not a briefing. You have our permission to speak plain English. We don't know what a special agent is and don't much care. Besides, you already said you're on your own time."

Harry smiled and pushed up from his chair. He stepped to the refrigerator and got a six-pack of Buds in a plastic ring that had two cans missing. "All right. Let's take another run at this thing." He pulled two cans out of the plastic ring, handed Jimbo one, kept one, and gave me the remaining two. "We been keepin' an eye on Zandro and his bunch ever since they set up shop on the island. We got ever' one of our agents in Florida, Mississippi, and Alabama watching them. So far they're clean."

"Well, not exactly," Heather said.

"Heather tells us there's some drug use in the cabin," Bell said.

"You wouldn't be using any of those old drugs, would you?" I said.

"Not the bad ones."

"They're all bad," I said. "Some are just worse than others." I popped the top on a beer and handed it to her. "So if the Guardians are clean, why is some super-secret federal agency keeping an eye on them?"

"We get just enough bad reports that we cain't afford not to." Bell sat back in the chair. "Heather gave us this latest report."

"Zandro says he's going to blow up one of those big natural gas rigs," she said. "Probably tonight."

"I owe you an apology," I said. "I should have taken you more seriously. I just didn't think Zandro would know how to do something like that."

"Believe it or not," Harry said, "he could. He's a trained pyrotechnics man."

"How good is he at letter bombs?" I asked.

"See?" Jimbo said. "I told you ol' Jack here's pretty quick."

"Yeah. It coulda been him who planted that letter bomb," Harry said. "But I doubt it. They got a complete set of Zandro's prints. The one clear print they could git off that envelope they found at your place wasn't his."

"They?" I asked.

"The Alabama Bureau of Investigation," Bell said. "I got my sources there."

"It might have been somebody else in the compound," I said.

"Not according to what Heather tells us."

"Nobody in there but Zandro knows anything about bombs," she said.

"How in the world did you get tied up with that bunch?" I asked.

"I thought they were like the Sierra Club or something. I didn't know they were serious about killing people."

"They could make a run at one of those gas rigs tonight," Harry said.

"Heather," I said, "what makes you think they're about to do something like that?"

"I saw the dynamite," she said. "They brought in two crates of dynamite yesterday."

I took a sip of beer and propped my feet on the coffee table. "Well I don't know about you guys, but I'm not about to move in on two sticks of dynamite, much less two crates. You better call in the ATF."

"They know about it," Harry said. "They've already set up sur-veillance."

"So if you think they plan to load that stuff onto their boat and go out to a rig, don't you think you better tell the Coast Guard too?"

"I cain't do that until Zandro makes a move," Harry said.

"And what if he does? What if the Guardians decide to take out the gas rig tonight?"

"If that happens, I call in the Coast Guard choppers. But unless it looks like Zandro's boarding his boat, I just sit here and wait. We'll be watching that boat around the clock from now through the Labor Day weekend. If they really plan to blow one of the rigs, they might want to do it when there's a big crowd on the island."

I leaned forward and propped my elbows on my knees. "I've been listening to y'all for fifteen minutes, and, believe me, it's been interesting. But I still don't have a clue as to what I'm doing here."

"Why don't you step out here with me, Heather?" Jimbo said. "It's done got a little stuffy in here." He took her little-girl hand in his, holding it as gently as he would a newborn chick, and they stepped out to the rear deck.

"Jimbo told me I ought to tell you this, and I think he's right. The person or persons who tried to kill you may be part of a hit squad that operates out of Mexico."

I leaned back on the couch. "Oh, Jesus. What great news."

"It's the same group that I'm sure killed those four people in that beach house. I've known about them for several years now, ever since the drug wars down in Colombia. They're called *Los Tres Fantasmas*, The Three Ghosts. High-priced talent."

"I've never heard about any Mexican mechanics around here."

"Things go according to plan, and you probably never will. *Los Fantasmas* are a folk legend in Mexico. Lots of folks down there believe it's just that, a legend. Don't believe they really exist."

"But you do," I said.

Bell gave me a hard stare as he nodded his head. "They're real. We don't talk about them, but they definitely exist. The press covering the murders here on the island hasn't picked up on them yet, and chances are they won't. Pretty soon all you'll have is four more folders in the cold case file. The sheriff's department will stay on the case, and maybe the ABI. At least for a year or so. But there's no way any local cops are going to be able to get to this bunch."

"But you're saying you guys could?" By this time I was figuring that Harry Bell was with either the FBI or the CIA.

"We haven't so far, and that's the whole problem. This group has come to the States once before. It was a personal matter involving the sister of one of them. And they only went as far as Eagle Pass, Texas. They know if they stay out of the United States and stay out of Europe, they can probably operate for years and retire as rich old farts in Cancun. But if they give us a public reason to really go after them, it's all over. So they stay out of our gun sights."

"If they didn't want to come to the U.S., what were they doing in Alabama?"

"Somebody with enough weight to have 'em on their payroll sent 'em here. But it'd have to be some big-time player. These guys did jobs for Pablo Escobar. I mean, they're big league."

I felt the floor move, a light rocking, from the wake of a shrimp trawler coming in to the fueling dock on the other side of the marina. I caught myself curling and uncurling the fingers of my right hand into a fist.

"I haven't heard anything so far that tells me why you think this all-star hit squad killed those folks," I said.

"Well, first of all, there were three killers."

"Hey, that settles it."

Bell smiled and nodded. "You're right. That alone don't mean squat. But there's two things common to each of the four bodies. All four were shot in the head right at the ear, except for Eubanks, who apparently had a split second to try to run away. And they put a slug into him at the same spot after he fell."

"Again," I said, "all that shows is that the killers were professionals."

"And after Jason, Kellie Lee, Rod, and Rebecca were already dead, somebody shot a .32-caliber bullet into their hearts. There was a contact wound and powder burns on each of 'em where somebody held the same gun hard against their chest and pulled the trigger. That's a signature move of Los Fantasmas."

"But even if this bunch killed them, that doesn't mean they're after me. Somebody tried to blow me away with a letter bomb. These guys sound like your classic shooters."

"Didn't you get a note with that bomb?"

I nodded. "Same kind you see in an old black-and-white B movie."

"In Colombia, we know of at least one case where they rigged up a car to explode when it started. Could be more. And after they did it, they sent a note, same kind. I can't say for sure they were the ones who tried to kill you. If we knew all that much about them, they'd be dead by now. All I'm saying is that they probably killed the four in the beach house. And after you start poking around, you get a package bomb on your doorstep. You ought to be told what you're up against."

I looked through the window to the rear deck. Jimbo and Heather were sitting on the transom, laughing like they were on a date.

"You think the Green Guardians could have hired them?" I asked.

"Maybe. The Guardians are getting a lot of money from some-where. Hell, who knows? It could have been them, could have been Bobby Earl's group, could have been a drug cartel that was using Jason as a mule, could have been anybody. What I'm saying is that *Los Fantasmas* pulled the triggers. And there's a good chance they put that letter bomb on your doorstep."

"Has Jimbo told the sheriff any of this?" I asked.

He shook his head no. "There's no reason for him to. If Jimbo said anything to Carlton Rice, the first thing that would happen would be a press conference. Then we'd all deny that we ever heard of any Mexican hit squad and Rice and Jimbo would both come off looking like crackpots. No federal agency is going to admit they ever heard of *Los Tres Fantasmas.*"

"Why not?"

"Nothing but pride, Jack. We haven't been able to catch 'em, and that embarrasses the hell out of the top brass. So we just act like they don't exist. And as long as we do that, there's not a chance the press can find out. Especially when almost all the hits are in Latin America."

"So why are you telling me about it?"

He took in a deep breath and blew it out, puffing his cheeks.

"Somebody tried to kill you and threatened to go after your little girl. I cain't sit back and let somebody get his ticket punched without at least giving him a heads up. And if a bunch of desk jockeys in Washington get a little red faced, tough luck."

"But, Harry, it's like you said. If somebody doesn't tell the ABI or the sheriff, they'll never find these guys."

A little bulge ran up and down his cheek as he pressed his tongue against the inside of his mouth. "Whether the killers are found or not, Jack, those four kids are dead. You and your daughter ain't."

I turned up my can of Bud and finished it off. "You say those guys are big leaguers. Okay. Somebody with some money and connections hired some top talent to take out the four in the beach house. But why would they go after me? I never knew any of the four, never had any business with them. No reason for them to come after me."

"I asked Jimbo to bring you here for two reasons," he said. "First, I wanted to tell you about the danger you were in."

"Just thought it was the right thing to do, huh?"

"That's exactly right, Bubba. If the agency wasn't gonna tell you, somebody had to."

"And the second reason?"

"Because you're making somebody real uncomfortable. And like you said, that somebody has got money and connections. So tell me, what do you know about those murders?"

"No more than you do," I said.

"I can't help you if you won't cooperate."

"I'm telling you," I said, "if I have any information worth killing me over, I sure as hell don't know what it is."

TWENTY

Outside the houseboat, a purple twilight was in its last stages and the sky was clear except for this thin, pink cloud high above the western horizon. The evening star glowed almost silver, brighter than usual. It was time for a full moon that night, and the sky over toward Pensacola had taken on an orange-red glow.

Heather and Jimbo were still talking and laughing out on the deck. There she was, carrying on with the same guy I could have sworn she said she hated not a full day earlier. I long ago quit wasting my time trying to figure out how that kind of stuff happens. Some guys have just got what it takes.

"We can get you out of the country for a while if that's what you need to feel comfortable," Harry Bell said.

"I don't know what Jimbo might have told you," I said, "but I'm just a small-time private eye. I do insurance-fraud work. There's absolutely no reason any world-class hit squad would even know who I am. Or, for that matter, give a damn."

"But there's a good chance they know exactly who you are," he said.

"They don't."

The tiny phone on his belt tweeted and he flipped it open and pulled out the antenna. I got up from the couch and stepped to the window. It was fully nighttime now and the air was so clear that I could see the flash and twinkle of the stars. The moon was coming up, big and dark red. Bell snapped the phone shut and pushed up from his chair.

"It's show time," he said. "Some guys over at the Guardian compound are down at their pier gettin' their boat ready to head out."

"Who was that on the phone?"

"The ATF. They've been anchored in this shrimp boat out from Zandro's place, keepin' an eye on the situation." He stepped to a closet and pulled out what appeared to be a set of oversized binoculars and two Ruger .223 models with shoulder straps. "They've called in one of their muscle boats. It's headed this way."

"So what are those rifles for?"

"They might need some backup." He grinned and sucked on his teeth. "You never know."

I followed Harry outside to the deck. "Time to rock and roll!" He tossed a rifle to Jimbo.

"Heather," Jimbo said, "you stay here and wait until we get back."

"By myself?"

He looked at me and jerked his head to the side to tell me to follow him.

"But what if they come here?" Heather said.

"They're out in the gulf on a boat. You'll be fine."

Harry, Jimbo, and I stepped off the houseboat and hustled along the pier toward the shore; the clacking of our footsteps echoed across the water. The tide was in with its strong salty smell, covering the barnacles at the base of the pilings and bulkheads, and the moon was high and bright and gave a luster to the water out on the sound. The night shrimpers had cranked up their diesels and one by one they made their way out to the channel, their green and red and white lights gliding evenly above the calm water of the island's lee side. The moonlight was strong enough for us to see the pelicans and gulls resting on the sandbars near the bridge and to see every contour of the grounded shrimp boat that some storm had pushed out of the channel some years earlier.

"Where are we going?" I asked.

"To my boat," Jimbo said.

"Jack, you don't need to be going out with us," Harry said.

"We need the extra set of eyes," Jimbo said. "If the idea is to keep them in sight, we need all the help we can get."

"What are the rifles for?" I asked.

"It's against agency policy to have civilians on board."

"Yeah," Jimbo said, "but you're here on your own, so I don't guess agency rules apply. Besides, this ain't no official mission, remember? He was in the MPs so he knows how to handle a weapon. Don't you, Jack?"

"Don't I get a vote in this?" I asked.

"Don't worry. We ain't gonna do nothin' except follow at a distance and make sure the ATF boat doesn't lose sight of the Guardians. We'll let the ATF handle everything."

"You got fuel?" Harry asked.

"I top off the tank after every trip."

Jimbo's boat was across the road, backed into one of the slips near the weigh-in station. I guess nobody noticed us running across the road carrying a pair of military rifles. If they did, they sure didn't stop us and say anything about it.

His boat was a twenty-one-foot Glastron, an older model with a white cuddy cabin over a high-sided, deep-V yellow hull. It had a straight inboard. The seats had been configured for fishing with a lot of open space and two swivel fighting chairs bolted to the floorboard at the stern. The white fiberglass decking up top glowed almost blue under this humming mercury vapor light set high on a solitary pole at water's edge. The light had attracted the usual swirl of night bugs.

We boarded and Jimbo opened the cabin and hooked up his VHF. While he turned on the blowers to clear the sweet-smelling gasoline vapors out from the space between the hull and the deck, Harry set the radio to the pre-arranged monitoring frequency and listened for the code only he knew which would tell us when the Green Guardians would be pulling out.

I picked up the oversized set of binoculars Harry had set on the passenger's seat beside the wheel. Turned out to be SPI night-vision goggles. We had some old infrareds back when I was in the MPs, and they worked to the extent that you could distinguish the form of a man from that of a cow or something. But these new things were amazing. I spotted a cat over by a Dumpster and examined it through the goggles. The yellow-green image was so sharp, I could even see this dark patch of fur on the cat's back.

A voice came over the VHF saying something about the big fish running. "They're in the water now," Harry said. "Let's go."

Jimbo turned off the blower and hit the starter switch. The deep-throated engine coughed and started, but barely turned enough RPMs to keep from going dead as it warmed up. This caused it to idle rough and make the deck vibrate under our feet. The pumps that pulled in the water to cool the engine sputtered as they primed themselves and then started gushing water in spurts, which splashed against the bulkhead behind us. I hopped up on the deck to cast off the bow lines and Harry handled the stern.

The channel leading out ran roughly parallel to the shoreline between the solid ground on the island and the shallows where the sandbars are. We followed it on a northwesterly course heading out toward the Intracoastal. When we cleared the point of land where the airstrip sat, we had a clear view of the shore for as far as we could see, and the Guardian compound is not all that far down the beach. Jimbo pulled the gear lever into neutral and we sat on idle. He pointed in the direction of Zandro's dock, and Harry searched the shoreline with the night-vision goggles for their boat.

"I think I see it." He handed the goggles to Jimbo.

"You mean that runabout towing a skiff?"

"Would you recognize Zandro's boat?" Harry asked.

"I would in the daytime." Jimbo kept the goggles trained on it. "It's a Boston Whaler with twin outboards, big ones. Hundred and fifty horsepower Mercuries. That looks like it, but I don't know why he'd be towing a skiff."

"Will this boat keep up with them?" I asked.

Jimbo shook his head. "Not even close. I've seen Zandro run that Whaler wide open before. We might be able to stay close enough to keep it in sight, but that's about it."

"The reason they're towing that skiff is so they can fill it up with dynamite and float it under one of the rigs so they can set it off by remote control," Harry said.

Back toward the bridge where the grounded shrimp boat was, in the opposite direction from where we were headed, two Lafitte skiffs meandered through the sandbars—I swear, a Lafitte skiff could float in a bathtub—and on both of them someone at the bow was holding a silver-globed propane lantern, the sure sign of somebody out gigging the flounders that lay flat on the sand bottom. It's a good idea to use a boat to go flounder gigging this time of year rather than wading. The stingrays move in close to shore starting in August and when they lie on the bottom, they look an awful lot like a flounder. And you don't want to make that mistake.

A few miles out the Intracoastal toward the west I saw the green bow light of a fast-moving boat. I tapped Jimbo on the shoulder and pointed at it.

"That's probably the ATF boat," Jimbo said.

"They need to slow down," Harry said. "We don't want to spook these guys."

"I hate to bother y'all," I said, "but could somebody explain what we hope to accomplish out here? And please tell me that we *don't* hope to confront a psycho with a boatload of dynamite."

"Officially, we're not doing one blessed thing. But if the ATF can stop 'em with explosives on board, we can help make a case against 'em in court," Harry said. "But they gotta let Zandro get far enough out to where we can cut him off from beatin' it back to the dock. So we'll keep an eye on him until then."

Jimbo pushed forward on the throttle to maybe twelve hundred RPMs, about twice idling speed, and we headed west toward the Boston Whaler. The Whaler was by this time easing toward the

Intracoastal, barely pulling a wake, the skiff behind it riding high with the bow pointed up. The course we were on would put us at their wake, cutting off their retreat, in about ten minutes. I was guessing that once we got there, we would start trailing them and lag behind to see where they were going.

But then they stopped.

And just as soon as they stopped, the boat that had been hauling ass up the Intracoastal, the one we had pegged as the ATF boat, pulled back on its throttle so abruptly that its following wake lifted it up a good three feet. Besides that, the sound of the engine gearing down rang out across the water so every boat within two miles knew that it was putting on the brakes. Under the bright moon, we could plainly see the series of four waves that the sudden stop had set off.

Then, of course, we didn't have any choice except to come to a stop ourselves.

The three boats sat in the calm water, like three points of a triangle, watching each other. Or at least we thought Zandro might be watching us, we didn't know that for sure. A million white sparkles danced along the wide trail of the moon's reflection and the only sound was the now-and-then whine of the cars on the bridge going onto the island. It was as if three teams had huddled, each trying to come up with their next play.

"Okay, Zandro," Jimbo said. "It's your move."

"I knew they were coming in too fast," Harry said. "And using a damn patrol boat. God, they might as well have turned on the blue lights and the siren."

Using the SPI night-vision goggles, I was scoping out the Boston Whaler and the three guys on board. All three of them were standing and looking toward the ATF boat ahead of them a mile or so and to their port bow. I could clearly see that one of the guys had a beard. I figured that must be Zandro.

"What do you think?" Harry said. "Looks like whichever way they go we've got 'em boxed in."

Jimbo grunted and shook his head. "He can blow past us and

there's not a thing we can do about it unless we want to play cow-boy and try to take him out with these Rugers. But we don't know that he's doing anything illegal yet. Besides, for us to hit any fast-moving boat at night, we'd have to be pretty close to it. Close enough to where we don't want to be setting off any dynamite."

"Maybe he doesn't realize we're back here," Harry said.

On the Guardian boat, the guy with the beard picked up a set of goggles and trained them on the ATF boat, which by this time was no doubt watching him back. I could make out his green-glowing image as plainly as if it were noontime. The beard, the parka, the shape of the field glasses he was holding. He started a slow, sweeping survey of the bay in all directions. Just before he aimed the field glasses at us, I yanked mine down to my side and looked away.

"He's watching us," I said.

"How do you know that?" Harry asked.

"Don't look at him!" I said. "I could see him scoping out the whole sound. He's got a set of these night-vision goggles."

"Sit down, Jimbo," he said, "they could probably recognize you."

Ten minutes passed and the three boats held their positions. I sat on the stern with this big trolling rig so I'd look like I was fish-ing in case Zandro was still looking. The wind was calm and the water flat. Now that we were away from the streetlights on shore, the stars were even more vivid and the moon was bright enough to read by.

Zandro was trapped, sort of. If he went forward toward the channel, he'd get stopped by the ATF patrol boat. If he tried to go back to his pier, we'd either stop him or get to the pier about the same time he did. Either way, if we caught them with a hundred pounds of dynamite, all three of the guys on that boat were look-ing at jail time. And I couldn't imagine Zandro going quietly into that situation, especially since he was already an ex-con.

"They do have one chance," Jimbo said. "They don't draw no more than two feet of water on that boat. So they might be able to cut across that shallow water over there where them two Lafitte skiffs are floundering. But if they gonna do that, they got to know exactly where the cuts are."

"What about this boat?" Harry asked. "Could we go across that shallow water in this?"

"No way. I gotta have at least three and a half feet."

I picked up the goggles and looked at what was going on over at Zandro's boat. One of the guys was stepping to the stern and reaching for the tow line holding the skiff. He reached down to the cleat to which the line was fastened, and it appeared as though he untied it.

"Get ready," I said, "they're about to cut that skiff loose."

"Call that ATF boat," Jimbo said.

"They're seeing the same thing we are," Harry said. "What am I supposed to tell 'em?"

"Tell 'em not to follow Zandro into those mudflats. Tell 'em if he makes a break for it, to go around—"

The Boston Whaler lurched forward. We saw it rising a split second before we heard the roar of the huge Mercury outboards. The bow stood almost straight up as they showered down on the gas. Looked like a submarine surfacing. The little skiff that they had set adrift bobbed in the wake.

"Oh, shit!" Harry said.

There was a second's pause before the guys on the ATF boat saw what was happening. Then they laid down on their throttle and the thunder of their motors echoed across the bay. The heavy boat shoved the water out of the way as it got out of the starting blocks. The blue lights began pulsing and the siren began rising.

The twin Blue Water Mercury 150s screamed as Zandro's boat got up on a plane. He was headed out to the Intracoastal. But he let off the throttle a notch and banked the Whaler hard to starboard until he negotiated a ninety-degree turn and lined up with the channel we were in. Then he put the hammer down once more and streaked toward us. With three hundred horses pushing an open fiberglass hull and no wind, the thing was going so fast it was hardly touching the water.

I threw the fishing rig to the floor and snatched up a rifle. Jimbo mashed on the throttle and the big inboard bellowed as we leaped forward. I fell backward and slammed against one of the swivel chairs at the stern, dropped the rifle, which clattered along the floorboard. Harry dug his fingers into the back of the passenger seat and leaned against the surge to keep from hitting the deck.

"Where you going?" Harry shouted.

"I ain't about to just sit still and let him ram us!"

Jimbo's motor strained to get the heavy, deep-V hull going, but it did move us along fast enough to where I had to struggle to crawl forward. I retrieved the rifle and scooted to the side facing the oncoming Whaler. I got to one knee and laid my arm across the top of the gunwale to steady the Ruger and draw a bead on them.

Jimbo was skirting the edge of the channel, not going straight at Zandro, but off to the side. Trying to get out of his way. The water was still calm, so our big boat was running smooth and steady. Steady enough to let me line up the oncoming Whaler in the crosshairs of my infrared scope. I took aim at where I knew the wheel was, and began following it, holding back on taking a shot until it got closer.

The blue lights behind Zandro had reached the mouth of the channel. The ATF boys had built up some pretty good speed by this time. But nothing close to what that Boston Whaler was running. I mean, that thing was flying.

Harry had crawled up beside me with his rifle. He raised it and aimed toward the Whaler. "Don't shoot yet!" he shouted over the roar of the engine. "The ATF boat's behind 'em."

"They're turning!" Jimbo shouted. Harry held his hand out so I'd hold my fire.

The Boston Whaler veered away from us, left the channel, and took out over the flats. It was shooting a magnificent rooster's tail behind it and the motors were running at red-line speed, wailing like a pair of Irish banshees. It was making sixty knots at least. The poor fishermen in the two Lafittes who had been canvassing the area for flounders were both standing in their boats, holding their gas lanterns and waving them side to side, stuck in their tracks and hoping this oncoming fool would see them and not run over them.

On the other side of the shallows was the Intracoastal. Freedom for the three Guardians. The only way we could go after them if they made it to the other side would be to double back up the channel, go the mile or so out to where they had been before the chase started, and then loop around and follow the Intracoastal and try to catch them. Fat chance. They'd have that dynamite hidden somewhere or dropped overboard by the time we saw them again, and the worst they'd be facing was a charge of failing to stop for the ATF's blue light.

"You think they know what they're doing?" I asked Jimbo.

"They know what they're *trying* to do. Let me put it that way. But they need to be farther over to the right, about where those skiffs are. The area they're heading to is too close to that grounded boat. It'd be a sandbar if it wasn't high tide." He picked up the night-vision goggles and raised them to his eyes. "Besides, that's where there's a couple of poles sticking up with signs on them warning folks about the low water."

I knew from the sound what happened next. Knew it even before I had time to realize what I was seeing. This sharp sound, a crack blended with just a bit of a thud, reverberated over the water. The Boston Whaler turned a cartwheel, all except for this big piece of the hull that whirled away high and to the side like some out-of-kilter boomerang. Their stern came up out of the water and the engines whined like an electric drill as the mangled boat sailed fifty feet through the air before slamming into the side of the grounded shrimp boat and breaking in half. The engines and the entire rear transom separated from the boat and splashed into the water on the other side of the shrimp boat and there they sputtered until they died.

"Looks like they found one of them poles I was telling you about," Jimbo said.

TWENTY-ONE

Harry Bell and I managed to keep our names out of the news stories that came out the next several days. But Jimbo, bless his heart, got caught. Right after the boatwreck the night before, we had eased Jimbo's Glastron as far into the shallows as we could in an attempt to see if any of the Guardians were still alive. But we didn't get twenty feet out of the channel before we heard and felt the bottom of the boat scraping against sand, so we backed out and jumped overboard and started wading toward the wreckage.

By the time we got there, the two fishermen in the Lafitte skiffs had already found a crate of dynamite, a remote-control steering device, and two dead Guardians. One of the dead ones was Zandro. They had pulled the third one, still alive, out of the water. It was the kid who had been with Heather that day I was at the compound. He was cut up pretty bad and had a broken left leg for sure and was hurting like hell. So we ferried him back to Jimbo's boat and called ahead for an ambulance to meet us at the weigh-in station.

When we got the kid into Jimbo's boat, we doctored him up the best we could with what was in the first aid kit and gave him a Dilaudid that Jimbo had gotten from God knows where to knock out the pain. Then Jimbo gave Harry and me a pair of life jackets and left us in the waist-deep water while he took the kid to the dock. We swam and waded to shore near the Pelican Pub. There

was a car waiting for Harry. He said a quick good-bye and got in
and they took off. I haven't seen him since then, and doubt that I
ever will. No telling what agency he was with.

As far as the sheriff's office and the Alabama Bureau of Investigation were concerned, the case ended that night. The press felt the
same way; they had milked it for all they could and it was time to
wrap things up. But there were some follow-up stories to be done,
and since Zandro and his bunch were being tagged as the killers,
the angle about Carolyn and Rebecca and their earlier troubles
with the Green Guardians was getting a lot more attention.

I had questions about Zandro being behind the killings. But
once investigators think they've got their man, it's almost impossible to get them to keep on looking. Especially if the guy they think
is guilty is dead and not around to defend himself.

Besides, maybe the Guardians really were guilty. They had
already made a death threat against Carolyn, and when Zandro
died, he was on his way to blow up an offshore drilling rig. So
there was no question they were capable of killing off an innocent
victim or two.

What was bothering me was something I knew that the local
cops didn't. I knew that the actual trigger men were hired talent
from Latin America. And I couldn't stop wondering how some nut
case like Zandro could call in *Los Tres Fantasmas.* I wouldn't think
Zandro could have called in a hit from Miami, much less Bogota
or Mexico City.

But I couldn't go to the cops with that. Bell had already said the
feds would act as if they never heard of *Los Fantasmas,* so what
could I tell the sheriff without sounding like some conspiracy theory crackpot? No, I was just going to talk to Jason's mother and get
her opinion of Rebecca Jordan. I didn't want to go back to Carolyn
empty-handed. And after that, I was going straight home to Bay
St. Louis.

Jimbo was going to drive me to meet Mrs. Summers. He knew
her from the investigation and he was trying to dodge the press.

He had been taken off department probation. Since he was the only link the sheriff's office had to the bust of the Green Guardians, Carlton Rice needed him in order to get in on the press conferences. So Rice forgave him for the misunderstanding we had with a couple of other deputies out at Sollie's a couple nights earlier. In fact, he forgave him retroactively and with back pay plus three days off.

"This woman we're going to see does speak English, doesn't she?" I asked.

"She speaks English better than I do," Jimbo said. "Her name is Anna Maria Summers."

"You think she'd know anything about Jason's business dealings?"

"Looking at her, I'd guess no. But she owns the house he was living in, so she might know something. Don't ask me too many questions. I ain't a private investigator yet, son."

Jimbo was once again selling himself short about this private investigation business. I always had the feeling he was a lot smarter than he let on.

"I've been thinking about what you said the other night about the Cuban cigars," I said. "I never have heard the first soul say that Jason ever handled any pottery, but he was passing out cigars like his wife had just had twins. There's a lot of demand for Cuban cigars. They're easy to handle. You can go to any wholesaler in Latin America and buy them legally. It wouldn't be a bad racket."

"There's just one problem," Jimbo said. "You gotta have some way to sell 'em here in this country. That's where I think Jason got in over his head."

"I'm not following you," I said.

"The politicians gonna save us from ourselves one more time, so they done got the price of cigars and cigarettes jacked up out of sight because of taxes. You can make a pot full of money off cigars, if you can avoid the taxes. You gotta have a distribution network that don't pay much attention to the tax man."

"Black market?"

"Black market is another way of saying drug ring. That, or mafia. Either group don't take kindly to outsiders stepping into their territory. First thing Al Capone did, he let all the little guys know they weren't welcome in the illegal booze business. That's what the tobacco bootleggers are going to start doing soon as the do-gooders get the price up high enough. And it's real close to being there now. You get the black-market price just right and a few of these independents operating out of their station wagons, they start showing up on the sides of country roads with their throats slit and their guts hanging out. It's the mob's little way of saying stay out of our territory."

"So you think Jason may have been a victim of competition?"

He shrugged. "Maybe so. Of course, he could have been in with them. That's almost as dangerous as workin' against 'em. That White Resistance group Bobby Earl's tied in with, they done branched out and started runnin' football bets. But what pays the bills for them is sellin' crystal meth. It's the redneck version of crack. One hit and you can drive a big rig from here to Shaky-Town and back, assumin' your heart holds out. They got a network of truckers who could handle all the Cuban cigars that bearded son of a bitch Castro could dream of turning out."

We were almost to the Fowl River Bridge when Jimbo wheeled the truck onto a driveway I wouldn't have noticed except for the sign. Set off from the road was the St. Rose of Lima Catholic Church, a white, wood-framed building and the cemetery beside it. Both are visible from the road, but only if you turn to look. It was still fairly early in the morning but already hot as a cheap hair dryer. The moss hung from the trees like old flags faded and torn by the winds off Mobile Bay. The smell of decayed vegetation from the marshes along the Fowl River blew in from the north and a single wave runner roared as it crossed under the bridge.

The yard of the church was well tended, but treeless and bright under the morning sun. There were three dusty cars parked at the rectory beside the church.

"She might already be here," Jimbo said. "If not, it won't be long. She comes every morning."

"You think she'll remember you?"

"Who knows? She was pretty upset the one time I was talking to her."

The cross above the doors was homemade, wooden and rough cut. There were clear panes of glass in the window casings. Nothing fancy, but real neat; somebody kept flowers planted and the hedges trimmed and there was a fresh coat of paint. There was no parking lot and the grass under the trees at the edge of the lawn was flattened from the cars on Sunday mornings. We stepped into the church and saw her kneeling up front to the side of the main altar. The walls were plain paneling, the kind people use in their dens. There were three red votive lights glimmering on the stand at the side of the sanctuary beneath a statue of the Virgin Mary, her hands spread at her side.

Anna Maria Summers was on a single kneeler facing the candles and the statue. Her hair was jet black, her skin smooth. She was a full-bosomed woman, short, with just a bit of extra weight but attractive. She crossed herself and stood and turned to walk up the center aisle. She sucked in a quick breath, startled by our presence, but took on a slight smile as she recalled Jimbo.

"Good morning, ma'am," he said. "I'm Deputy Sheriff McInnis."

"I remember you. I saw you on the television yesterday. They said you got those people who killed my Jason, those Green Guardian people."

"We think that's right, Mrs. Summers," he said. "But we need to know a few more things before we can be sure."

"And you think I can tell you these things? I know nothing about these Green Guardians. Why would they kill my son?"

"They might not have been trying to kill Jason," Jimbo said.

"They may have intended to kill one of the other young people who were in his beach house that day."

Her eyes showed she was puzzled.

"We'd like to get some information about Rebecca Jordan," he said.

"Are you saying they wanted to kill Rebecca? But she was a wonderful girl. She was always helping other people."

"What kind of help do you mean?" I asked.

"She loved to help the people who came here from Mexico."

"You mean the clients Jason would bring up here?"

"*Si.* Those clients."

"What kind of help are you talking about?" I asked.

"She would find the work for them."

"Find the work? Do you mean she would help them find business?"

"*Si.*"

Somehow I had pictured this tiny, stooped white-haired woman in a veil. But she looked more like Jason's older sister. She had the same facial shape, but was a shade or two darker than her son. Brown eyes as big as walnuts. Jimbo introduced me as an associate and that seemed to satisfy her. We sat on one of the front pews.

"Mrs. Summers," I said, "would you feel comfortable talking with Rebecca's mother? I think she'd like to hear some of this."

She cast her eyes downward and her voice grew quiet. "Yes. I will talk with her. I know how she feels." She looked toward the altar. "You see that statue of the Blessed Virgin? That was a gift to the church from Rebecca. Jason got it for her in Mexico."

"It's real pretty," Jimbo said.

"I can show you the fountain by the rectory. Jason gave it to the Monsignor. I can take you to the cemetery and show you more. He gave so many statues to the church."

The stuff she was talking about was basically garden statuary. Not exactly the high-profit items you'd be flying your own plane in and out of Mexico for.

"Sounds like Jason was a generous person," Jimbo said.

"He was a good boy. He is buried outside beside his father."

"Did you know any of the people he had business with in Mexico?" I asked.

Jimbo cocked one eye and gave me a questioning glance, but I just had to find out what the hell Jason had been doing. Might not have had a thing to do with Rebecca, and the case was basically closed now, but I had gotten too far into it not to want to know. Besides, I still wasn't all that sure that it was the Guardians who had planted that bomb at my door. So even if I'd never get the case re-opened, I sure wanted to get that cleared up.

"I would meet some of them. I would go to Jason's house sometimes to cook for his visitors. I enjoyed talking with them about home. When I married Jason's father, God rest his soul"—she made the sign of the cross—"I moved here where his family is."

"Was your husband from Mexico?"

"No, he was a shrimper from Bayou La Batre. I don't go home much. Jason said he would take me on one of his trips, but I am afraid of flying in these airplanes."

"How often did Jason go down?" I asked.

"He would go the first week of every month. He would stay for two days, maybe three. And he would come back with his business friends."

"Were you involved with the business, Mrs. Summers?"

She shook her head.

"I thought maybe you were the one with the contacts in Mexico. It doesn't seem that it would be easy to start up an import business without some contacts."

"A lawyer in Mobile who got Jason started. Jason would sometimes help the Monsignor when they needed an interpreter. Jason always said God gave him a mission to help the people of Mexico. He said they should have some of the nice things like the people have in this country. Sometimes the sailors from the big ships would go to the church in Mobile and sometimes they could not speak English, only Spanish. Jason would help. That's where he met this lawyer. At the church."

"What was the lawyer's name?"

"Roberto Sanchez. He is the man who hired my son to import all these things. They make a lot of money for the people in Mexico who make these beautiful statues."

"Are you saying that this Roberto Sanchez was in business with your son?" I asked.

"Yes. Jason worked for Señor Sanchez. Jason could also fly the plane. Señor Sanchez knew many people in Mexico."

"So Roberto Sanchez ran the business?"

"No, Jason ran it for him." She was getting confused. "If you need to know about this, you should ask John Villa. John Villa knows all about Jason's business."

TWENTY-TWO

Was Bob Sanchez in Jason's import business or not? And if so, what were they importing? If not statues, could it be cigars? The only thing I knew for sure was that nobody seemed to want to take credit for this business. But all signs pointed to either Bob Sanchez or John Villa, or both, as being the brains of the operation.

Jimbo drove me straight from the little church to Easy's so I could get my van. He must have understood why I couldn't give up the case just yet; he never brought it up. I needed to see Sanchez and it was still only ten in the morning. Jimbo had to leave me to take care of Heather and make sure she had what she needed until the FBI got there to take down her statement.

Sanchez wasn't in his office; his secretary said he was at the courthouse. It was ninety-four degrees according to the bank thermometer, but the parking space I had near Sanchez's office was as close as I was going to get to the courthouse, so I just walked over there. The courthouse is in that area near the river where there are one-hundred-and-fifty-year-old brick buildings lining narrow streets with wrought-iron grillwork along second-floor balconies set in close along the narrow streets. They have front doors with leaded glass that divides the light from the chandeliers in the foyers into glints of red and yellow and blue and purple. Streamers of gray Spanish moss hang from the gnarled limbs of live oaks in

Bienville Square, the heart of old Mobile, where the squirrels are so tame they will eat peanuts out of your hand. You can't see the bay from Bienville Square, but there is sometimes an aroma of brackish water, an occasional white gull among the pigeons, and always the deep-throated whistles of the ships over at the state docks. Mobile has the soul of a port city.

By the time I got to the courthouse, my undershirt was clinging to me from sweat and my feet felt like a pair of potatoes that had been wrapped in foil and put in some oven. Sanchez was in the lobby, the anteroom leading into the courtroom, talking in Spanish to a pair of thirty-something-year-old Mexicans. They were watching every word he was saying to them as intently as a robbery victim watches the muzzle of the pistol pointed at his face. One of them did what little talking Sanchez allowed, and that was only in response to his questions. As he spoke, Sanchez glowered at him, his heavy mustache making his frown even more pronounced.

I leaned on the opposite wall, waiting for a stopping point in their little conference. Sanchez noticed me and said something harsh to the Mexican spokesman, cutting him off in midsentence. The man said something in Spanish to his companion, and Sanchez turned and stepped across to me. He put his palm flat against the wall close to my shoulder and leaned toward me, a little closer than was comfortable, smiling like he was glad to see me.

"Illegals," he said. "They got picked up on the interstate heading for Florida. The administrator always calls me because the court is too cheap to hire an interpreter."

"I need to find out more about Jason's business."

"I've told you all I know," Sanchez said. "I can tell you no more, my frien'."

"I get the distinct feeling you may have overlooked something. For instance, why is it that Jason's mother says he worked for you?"

His jaws tightened. His eyes hardened and grew mean. "Like I told you before, my frien', I was Jason Summers's lawyer. I drew up contracts for him and gave him some advice on the law of imports and exports. If his mother told you that he worked for me, she was mistaken."

"Did you advise Jason that it is illegal to import Cuban cigars into this country?"

The edges of his lips curled into a slight smile, but his eyes were not smiling. "I'm sure Jason was aware of that. All countries have stupid laws."

"Did you know he didn't own the house that he was living in?" I asked.

Sanchez laughed. "Mr. Delmas, I had nothing to do with Jason Summers's business. I did not understand the other day exactly what you were wanting to know about Jason. But if you were looking for the persons who killed him, I suggest you investigate the gamblers or the drug dealers. Or any of the Green Guardians who may still be alive."

"Why did Jason put his house in his mother's name?"

"I don' know that he did."

"She's listed as the owner in the land records of Mobile County. But when I asked her about it, she said she wasn't aware that she had anything to do with it. And you know what? I believe her. Since you did his legal work, I assume you drew up those papers."

The muscles of his jaw were grinding so hard, I could almost hear his teeth scraping against other. The two Mexicans on the bench had begun an animated conversation and were getting louder with a lot of hand motions. A bailiff stepped through the doors of the courtroom and the two Mexicans fell silent.

"Okay, Bob," the bailiff said, "the judge is ready for you now."

"Jason's mother sometimes gets confused," Sanchez said. "He probably told her he was putting the house in her name and she doesn't remember. I'm sure it had something to do with taxes. Maybe liability. I don' know."

"Bob, I hate to rush you," the bailiff said, "but the judge is trying to wrap this up before lunch."

Sanchez gave the bailiff an impatient wave and walked away from me toward his two Mexican clients. He ordered them to stand with a movement of his head. As they walked toward the door, he glared at me with those hard eyes. Between Bob Sanchez and Anna Maria Summers, there was no question who would tell me the truth.

"One more thing, Bob," I said. "What other assets are hidden under the name Anna Maria Summers?"

He stopped and let his clients walk on into the courtroom ahead of him. "You seem to be good at digging up such things, my frien'." he said. "Maybe when you find out, you can come back and tell me."

TWENTY-THREE

I f I wanted to find out who was running that import business, I'd have to talk with John Villa. I took the rest of the afternoon doing some preparation before going to his office. I remembered that Jimbo had said they questioned Villa in the early stages of the investigation, so I called him and got Villa's Social Security number. I took that number and called this old MP buddy of mine who is now on the New Orleans police force, this bona fide Cajun who has become, of all things, somewhat of a computer nerd and an excellent skip tracer. He spent the rest of the afternoon on the Internet for me and came up with some surprises.

It turned out that the John Torres Villa with that Social Security number was born in America. Born in San Antonio thirty-one years ago. Trouble is, some one-year-old child with the same San Antonio address, also named John Torres Villa, died from meningitis that next year. And the John Villa who played tennis at Auburn was indeed from Mexico City, but so were several hundred others with that name. And yes, it was entirely possible that the John Villa who got an accounting degree from Auburn had assumed the identity of the John Torres Villa who died long ago.

Early the next morning, Jimbo and I were in the parking lot in front of Villa's office. It was nondescript, a corner suite in an office complex off Airport Road near the big shopping centers. The gold leaf on the glass front door read "J. T. Villa, CPA." The tens of thousands of cars on their way into downtown Mobile from the western side of the county kept up a steady drone punctuated by an occasional angry horn blast and a few screeches of the tires of tailgaters as they had some close calls. Reminded me of some bad old days up in Memphis when I drove to the office every morning.

"So when are you gonna be ready to give this case up?" Jimbo asked as we sat in his truck.

"As soon as I figure out who planted that bomb on my doorstep."

"Gee," he said, "I don't know. How about the Green Guardians? Seems they had the corner on all the explosives around here."

"Did you get a good look at the bomb on my doorstep?"

He shrugged. "Good enough, I guess."

"Son, that thing was so amateurish I don't think it would have gone off even if I had pulled the piece of cardboard out. The Guardians were more advanced than that."

"How about that Mexican group Harry was telling us about?"

"He said it would take some big-time connections to pull them in on a job here in the States. One, I doubt that the Guardians ever had connections like that. And, two, even if they did, they sure couldn't get Los Fantasmas to come back up here a couple of weeks later just to smoke somebody like me."

"So you're saying you don't think Zandro hired the Mexicans to come up for the hits at the beach house?"

"That's exactly what I'm saying. I mean, think about it. You think they'd spend the ton of money it'd take to get *Los Fantasmas* up here to out four kids because they had some minor beef with one of the kids' mother? And that's assuming some loser like Zandro had the weight to even know where to call those guys."

He stuck his arm out the window and stared in silence at the traffic on Airport Road. "Maybe not."

We gave Villa's receptionist a story about seeking his help in opening a new business. After a short telephone consultation, she sent us down the hall to his office. We knocked on his door and he called for us to come in.

"Please have a seat, gentlemen." We sat in the two armchairs across from his desk. He smiled but kept looking at me as if he were trying to place me. "What can I do for you today?"

"Jason Summers was taking a lot more than garden supplies into Dauphin Island from Mexico," I said. "How long had he been involved in smuggling?"

His smile dropped and the color poured from his face. If he had not been sitting, I'm sure he would have fallen down. Jimbo, with cop instincts, whipped out his badge and held it out as he leaned his big frame forward until he was halfway across the desk.

"We're here to get some information on Jason Summers," Jimbo said. "You kept his books for him and we want to see them."

Villa nodded weakly and stared straight ahead without focus.

"We believe your client Mr. Summers was in business with an attorney in Mobile by the name of Roberto Sanchez."

The name Sanchez jolted him back to life. His eyes grew wide and he began shaking his head. "No, no," he said. "Jason Summers had a sole proprietorship. He did not have any partners with him."

"Sanchez was his partner," I said. "But I suspect that you've cooked the books so that we'll never see Sanchez's name."

His big eyes were already round and boyish, but the fear in them made him look like a child.

"You don't have to worry about Sanchez," I said. "You cooperate with us, and we'll go on our way. You'll never hear from us again."

"But if you don't play ball with us," Jimbo said, "we'll padlock this place and have your ass back in Mexico City before the sun sets. We know your name ain't John Torres Villa, we know you stole that name off some dead kid. You give us what we want, you got a chance to stay here and keep this business. You might as well tell us what you've got, because we're gonna get it one way or the other."

"I was only doing Jason's books as a favor to him," Villa said. "I wasn't involved in anything illegal."

"You don't call smuggling illegal?" Jimbo asked.

"We know all about the smuggling operations," I said.

"I wasn't involved with that," Villa said.

"You did his books for him," Jimbo said. "You had to know what was going on. I suspect you were making a bunch of false entries and jacking the price of all those statues and fountains and all that other crap so you could account for all the cash he was bringing in from those cigars."

Villa got this puzzled look on his face and started shifting his eyes from Jimbo to me and then back to Jimbo. "I don't know what you're talking about," he said in a halting voice.

"Cut the crap, man," Jimbo said. "What I'm telling you is that nobody could be importing a million dollars worth of illegal Cuban cigars without his accountant knowing about it. Now what we want to know is where did Sanchez fit into the mix?"

"What is this you are saying about cigars?" Villa asked.

"The game's over," I said. "We're not interested in the cigars or who got the cigars; we just want to know how Sanchez fits into the whole scheme."

Villa sat back in his chair and stared at us with his mouth open. The confusion showed in his eyes. "If I give you a copy of Jason's file, will you promise not to tell where you got it?"

"Are we gonna be able to read these files and see what Sanchez was doing?" Jimbo said.

"I can only give you the file. I can't say anything more."

"Son," Jimbo said, "if you don't tell us what Jason Summers and Roberto Sanchez were up to, you'll be back in Mexico tomorrow."

"You can't tell anybody where you got this file," Villa said. "You've got to promise me that."

TWENTY-FOUR

Of course, neither Jimbo nor I could tell diddly squat from the records. We sat in Easy's beach house with a pot of coffee and some legal pads and stared at balance sheets and ledger entries until our eyes started crossing. None of that stuff ever made any sense to me when I took Introductory Accounting back at Olc Miss. And when I was working in the bank, I never had to fool with such things. We had an army of accountants to do it. I mean, what good is a balance sheet? Even if you lose three million dollars during the year, it shows that assets and liabilities are the same amount. I'm talking to the last penny. So where did the three million dollars go?

"What does 'double declining balance' mean?" I asked.

"You're asking *me*?"

"How about 'sinking fund'?"

"Why don't we just look at these bank deposit slips," Jimbo said. "I can understand that."

"I already looked," I said. "Jason made deposits twice a month. But they were never all that big."

"So where was all this big money he was supposed to be knocking down?"

"I doubt that these are real records. Probably just enough to satisfy some bank that he's really got a business. But look at this." I tossed him a few receipts from a wholesale jeweler in Birmingham.

"He was buying jewelry?" Jimbo said. "You mean he was spending a wad on diamonds and stuff?"

"I'm talking wholesale buying," I said. "He must have been selling the stuff."

"Maybe he was legit. I mean there's no law against buying wholesale jewelry and selling it to outlets in other countries."

"Did John Villa look like we had uncovered some perfectly legal business operation by one of his clients?"

"Well, anyway, Jason had his finger in so many things we'll never figure it out," Jimbo said. "Did you run across the name Roberto Sanchez yet?"

I shook my head no.

"So where do the cigars come in?" he asked.

"Damned if I know. Of course, I doubt that they'd keep a record of that."

"You seen any entertainment expense?"

"Yeah," I said. "He's got some receipts, but they're mainly from Mexico."

"What about this money he spent on the airplane?" Jimbo handed me a legal-sized envelope, unsealed. "It looks like he kept real good records on that plane."

I thumbed through the gas receipts, hangar receipts, landing fees, and other receipts for the money that Jason spent on the plane. I arranged them by the month and wrote down the dates when he bought gas. It was a steady pattern. He'd top off his tanks the first and the third week of every month. Other records showed he made regular bank deposits at roughly those same intervals.

"Here's what it looks like," I said. "Jason was flying to Mexico two or three days before he'd make deposits, and the deposits were always under ten thousand dollars."

"Was the money from cigars?"

"Where do they check out planes coming in here from Mexico?" I asked.

"Hell if I know," he said.

"There's never anybody at the Dauphin Island airstrip," I said. "Don't you imagine you'd fly into Mobile first and then hop on down to the island?"

"I never have thought about it."

"C'mon, son," I said, "we got to get to the airport."

We didn't have any trouble getting to the flight logs at the general aviation hangar. Jimbo used his badge, but I think we could have probably got to them anyway if we just asked real nice. The flight logs showed that I was right on target. Jason was flying in and out of Mexico just before he made his deposits. The records on what kind of merchandise he was carrying were too general to do us much good.

"You think anybody around here would remember anything about Jason?" Jimbo asked.

"I guarantee you they would," I said. "He never met a stranger and he was in here twice a month. Hell, he probably kept everybody around here stocked in Cuban cigars."

"I'm gonna go ask that lady who let us in here," he said. "You want to come?"

I shook my head no. "Use your boyish charm."

When Jimbo stepped into the next room, I picked up the flight record for Jason's trip on July the second, about two months earlier. He took off from the General Aviation airport in Mobile early, 7:15. It was a clear day, not a cloud over the gulf. He was scheduled for a three-hour flight, due to arrive in Mexico City at 9:23 A.M. Mountain Time. He declared a case of jewelry, the value listed at U.S. $78,000. The jewelry was classified as business inventory. The return flight was that night, set to arrive at 11:15 P.M. Neither flight showed any passenger on the manifest and neither showed any destinations other than Mexico City and Mobile. The maintenance logs were stamped approved and the pre-flight check showed everything to be in good working order. The weather on the return flight was also clear, but the winds were stronger. Jason had been cleared to cruise at an altitude of—

Hey, wait a minute.

I re-checked the manifest, starting at the top of the page. There it was, plain as day.

"Hey, Jimbo!" I shouted. "Get in here! Quick!"

TWENTY-FIVE

We raced along Airport Road in Jimbo's truck, headed back to J. T. Villa's office. Jimbo kept slapping himself on the thigh and saying, "Damn!"

"How in the *hell* could I have missed it?" he said. "I ain't never gonna be no private eye."

"You did just fine," I said. "Weren't you the person who found out that John Torres Villa was not who he claimed to be? Didn't you figure out that he was an illegal alien?"

"But I was so (slap) *sure* about it. I just (slap) *knew* that Cuban cigars was what Jason was smuggling in from Mexico. I'll never get the hang of this stuff. I'm gonna look into the bounty-hunter business."

"Quit beating yourself up," I said. "You ever hear the story about the factory worker over in Russia back when the Commies were in power? They figured this guy was stealing stuff out of the factory because every day when he'd leave work he'd be pushing a wheelbarrow full of straw. They never could figure it out. It got to where every day they'd search through that straw and every day they'd come up empty. This went on for weeks and they never did figure it out. You know what the guy was stealing?"

"Is this the kind of question they ask on the Private Eye Exam?"

"There ain't no exam, son," I said. "The answer is that the guy was stealing wheelbarrows."

I could see him working that one over as he weaved the big pickup through the traffic. "So what's the point?"

"We were all overlooking the obvious. I did it too. Maybe I'm wrong. But let's hit John Villa between the eyes with what we've found and see if we're right."

When we got to Villa's office there was nobody at the front desk. The computer screen on the desk was dark. We figured the receptionist was in the bathroom, so we sat in two armchairs and waited for her to get back. We heard some bumping around from down the hallway, sounded like somebody was dropping stuff into a metal trash can.

"Hello?" Jimbo called. "Anybody home?"

The bumping down the hall stopped. And three seconds later a bell rang from down the hall, the same kind of loud, sustained clanging you hear in school when it's time to change classes. We jumped out of our chairs and bolted toward Villa's office. The steel door leading to the rear parking lot was wide open. As we ran, Jimbo reached to his shoulder holster.

I took a quick look into the office. The drawers of the filing cabinet stood open, manila folders lay strewn across the floor. The desk drawer had been pulled out, its contents spilled on the carpet. The alarm kept ringing.

Outside I heard Jimbo shouting at somebody to stop. I raced to the rear door. Jimbo was standing at the side of a Blue Pontiac, his pistol pointed at the head of the driver, John Villa. The car was still in its parking slot. The white backup lights were on, but the driver was trapped.

"Get out!" Jimbo shouted. "Get the hell outta this car!"

Villa turned off the engine. Jimbo backed off two steps to give him room to get out but yelled at him to keep his hands in sight. Villa stepped out of the car. Jimbo ordered him to put his hands on the roof and spread his legs. I ran over and patted him down as

Jimbo held the gun on him. I nodded to let Jimbo know he was clean.

"You don't act like you're too glad to see us, John," Jimbo said.

Villa kept his eyes straight ahead. He was breathing so hard we could hear it. His right hand started shaking and he looked like he was about to puke.

"Calm down," I said. "We're not going to hurt you."

"How do you turn off that damned alarm?" Jimbo asked.

"Let's go inside," I said.

Villa turned his head toward us. His eyes were twice their normal size. He swallowed twice and licked his lips.

"It's all right, John," I said. "You're safe with us."

We walked him back inside and disengaged the alarm. We stepped into his office and sat him in one of the armchairs. He was jumpy, completely terrorized by Jimbo's size, not to mention the service revolver, so I sat with him while Jimbo went up front to lock the door.

"Okay, John," I said, "let me tell you what we know and what we need from you."

"I've already given you the file on Jason."

"Why are you so scared of Roberto Sanchez?"

He tried a smile. Didn't work. Tough to smile with your chin quivering. Jimbo stepped back into the room, and I gave him a hand sign to keep things calm.

"Let me start things off," I said. "Jason Summers was working for Bob Sanchez. They were smuggling illegal immigrants from Mexico into the United States."

"That's not right."

"We checked the flight records," I said. "He never showed any passengers. Even the Fourth of July when everybody on the island knew that Jason had flown in a big group from Mexico City. He had a dozen visitors at Easy's cabin for a Fourth of July party, but there was no listing of even one passenger when he landed in Mobile the day before. He picked them up in Mexico City and dropped them off at the Dauphin Island Airstrip before he flew into Mobile."

"That's impossible," Villa said. "Any flight coming into Dauphin Island from Mexico has to go through customs in Mobile. They've got radar, planes, satellites. They watch every square inch of the gulf. There's no way a plane could stop off at the island first without being spotted."

"Unless you've got inside help," I said.

Villa started to say something, but bit his lower lip instead.

"That's how it went down, isn't it? Jason and Sanchez paid off some insider to give them the green light."

He let out a big breath and slumped in his chair. I had nailed him, and he knew it.

"And that's how you got into this country," I said. "Jason Summers smuggled you in."

He rested his elbows on the arms of the chair and buried his face in his hands. "Will you give me protection?"

"Tell us what you know and we'll put Sanchez behind bars," Jimbo said.

Villa looked up and shook his head. "If the word gets out I've told you what was going on, I'll have more to worry about than Bob Sanchez."

Jimbo nodded. He assumed this gentle little smile, sort of like a favorite uncle. I thought for a second he was going to go put his arm around Villa's shoulders. "John, we're your only hope. Even if Sanchez never hears a word about us being here, you're dead meat without us. You're the only person around who can testify against Sanchez. How long do you figure it'll be before he comes and pumps a couple of slugs into your head?"

"I've already figured that out, man! Okay? I'm talking about the witness protection program."

"That's a federal program," Jimbo said. "But I'm sure I can get you in."

Villa's eyes darted from Jimbo to me and back. "I thought you two *were* the feds."

"I'm a Mobile County deputy sheriff," Jimbo said. "And Jack here, he's a private investigator."

"But I thought you were the FBI, or at least the INS."

"You think we misled you, you need to file charges," Jimbo said. "Maybe next time you need to take a closer look when somebody flashes a badge at you."

Villa stared at the floor and started chewing on a thumbnail. "Shit!"

"It doesn't matter what we are," I said. "If you don't help us nail Sanchez, it's all over for you anyway."

Villa stared at me as he worked with that thought. "I guess I don't have much choice."

"You got anything to drink in here?" Jimbo asked.

"You say you can get me in witness protection?"

"Let's don't jump the gun," I said. "If we work this right, you won't need any protection. Just tell us what you know."

"I need something to drink, too," he said.

Villa started his story in Mexico City with Sanchez's law firm. The law firm set up an employment service and started funneling Mexican citizens into the U.S. through the branch office they had set up in Mobile. They handled only well-educated, white-collar types. Many of the clients had been educated in the United States. Not the types likely to wade across the Rio Grande at night, or pile into the back of a U-Haul. When you used the firm, you knew you were safe.

The firm flew a client into the States and gave him a new identity. Social Security card, birth certificate, driver's license, you name it. For an extra fee Sanchez would set them up with jobs. There were a lot of computer technicians, geologists, and accountants—folks who made good salaries. The firm charged what amounted to half a year's salary, but never collected any money until the services were rendered. The clients paid Jason when they were delivered safely on American soil. This no-money-up-front policy enhanced the firm's reputation for legitimacy.

"Jason would set up bank accounts for the passengers as soon as they landed," John said. "They'd pay the fee in monthly payments."

"You mean this firm let them pay in installments?" Jimbo asked. "Are you serious?"

"These are professionals we're talking about," John said. "It's a sure bet they're going to pay. These aren't the types who are going to disappear into the barrio."

"So what was Jason's role in all of this?" I asked.

Villa explained that Jason was a well-meaning guy. He considered himself a Mexican, and thought he had a mission to help some of his countrymen to get set up in the U.S. He'd fly the clients out of Mexico City and drop them off at the Dauphin Island airstrip. This was where Rebecca came in. She would pick up the clients at the airstrip and take them to the beach house. Jason would continue the trip to Mobile by himself to check in and go through customs. He always carried enough merchandise on the flights to make it look like he was running a legitimate business.

At the beach house the clients got a few days of orientation to American culture. Jason took them to stores and restaurants and other places to show them how to handle themselves. It was a great cover, pretending they were business clients. Jason would create a whole new identity for them using the names of Hispanic children who had died years ago. He got the names out of old newspapers from South Texas. Rebecca was an employment counselor, so she found jobs for some of them in the Mobile area. But most of them just went straight to one of the big cities where they could blend in a little easier.

"So what happened to upset this arrangement?" I asked.

"Sanchez got greedy," Villa said. "Like I said, Jason would keep track of the people he brought into this country. When they started making money, he'd take in the payments. American dollars. He'd take the cash to Sanchez, take his cut, and go back to the island. But Sanchez started pocketing some of the money before

he laundered it. The amount getting back to Mexico kept falling off. I found this out after Jason got killed."

"How do you know the money was coming up short?"

"I used to work for the firm myself. I was in their accounting division. It's a very large firm." He unbuttoned his collar and pulled his tie loose. "I went to college at Auburn. I like it up here. After my student visa expired I started saving up enough to come back. I just got lucky and got a job with the firm. That's how I found out about the program."

"So how do you know Sanchez was ripping them off?" I asked.

"I've got a friend who's still with the firm back home. He told me."

"Maybe Jason was the one doing the stealing," Jimbo said.

Villa shook his head. "I did Jason's books. I know the operation. We kept it right to the penny. You don't want to get caught ripping off the firm."

"That don't sound like much to worry about," Jimbo said. "They sound like the Mexican version of Snelling and Snelling to me. You think they'd sue you or something?"

Villa frowned and started rubbing his fingers together. "They're smuggling illegal immigrants and they hired Roberto Sanchez, a man who used to run Somoza's death squads in Nicaragua. A man who wouldn't hesitate to kill a five-year-old child. They specialize in laundering money and they represent most of the Colombian drug cartels. Don't let the nice offices and the reputation fool you. The firm plays hardball."

"Have you ever heard of *Los Tres Fantasmas*?" I asked.

"Of course I have," he said. "Why do you think I want to get into the witness protection program?"

"Would this firm have the contacts to hire the *Fantasmas* for a job here in the States?"

Villa laughed. "They've probably got them on a retainer. Like I said, you don't want to get caught ripping them off. That's why I made sure Jason kept such good records."

"So tell us what Sanchez was doing," I said.

He told us that Jason was handing over a lot of cash to Sanchez. Sometimes he'd fly in eight illegals on a single trip. At twenty to thirty grand each, that added up to a quarter of a million bucks. In cash. You can't just stick that much cash into an envelope and mail it back to Mexico. And you can't transfer it through the banks because if you make a deposit of over ten thousand dollars into an American bank, they have to report it to the U.S. Treasury. So in order to get the money back into Mexico and stay quiet about it, Sanchez used one of the simplest forms of money laundering.

He would buy diamonds at a wholesale jeweler in Birmingham and pay in cash, American money. He'd then ship the diamonds, via Jason Summers, to this sham wholesale jeweler in Mexico City that the firm had created. There's no law against shipping business inventory, in this case diamonds, to Mexico. The law firm had lined up some retailers who would buy the rocks from the sham wholesaler at a 10 percent discount off the wholesale price Sanchez had paid in Birmingham. These Mexican merchants would, of course, use squeaky clean pesos to buy the diamonds from the sham wholesaler.

So if Sanchez bought a diamond, wholesale, for a thousand U.S. dollars in Alabama and shipped it to Mexico City, a retail merchant down there would buy the diamond from the firm's sham wholesaler for the equivalent in pesos of nine hundred dollars. Neither a dollar nor a peso ever went into any bank on either side of the border. And although diamonds crossed the border, not a cent in hard currency ever did, except the cash that Jason's illegals were carrying on them. The law firm had nine hundred squeaky clean pesos in its hand, the retailer in Mexico City got his stuff at an extra 10 percent discount off regular wholesale, and there was no way to trace any of it.

"This money laundering doesn't always come out to the penny," Villa said. "But it wouldn't be hard to see if the amount the firm was getting back into Mexico over a period of six or eight months was way too low. My friend tells me it had gotten way out of line."

TWENTY-SIX

Jimbo and I stood in the parking lot and watched John Villa drive off. What else could we do? We sure couldn't arrest him. We headed back to the island, south on Dauphin Island Parkway. Jimbo was booked on a turnaround flight to Nashville in a few hours to take Heather back to her parents, and he wouldn't return to Mobile until 2:15 in the morning. It was a clear, hot Friday afternoon, the first day of the Labor Day weekend, and the realization that this was the last blowout of the summer had hit the entire city of Mobile at the same time. I couldn't see the end of the line of cars ahead of us even though I was riding in the cab of Jimbo's jacked-up truck, high above anything else on the road. As we rode, neither one of us had much to say.

I was going to pack up the Windstar and drive back home to Bay St. Louis. There was no reason to hang around. Everything had run off the tracks. Even the report I had for Carolyn didn't look so good anymore. Despite any noble intentions, Rebecca had been a player in a scheme to smuggle illegal aliens into this country. No way to go to the press with a story like that and come out ahead.

Jimbo tried to talk me into staying a few more days. He had called Lila and Darla and they didn't have any plans for the next night, but I told him I'd take a rain check. I didn't feel much like partying.

Bob Sanchez was going to skate. We couldn't touch him. Nei-

"So you think they confronted Sanchez about this imbalance?" I asked.

"Of course they did."

"Let me guess," Jimbo said, "At that point, Sanchez pointed the finger at Jason."

Villa nodded as his eyes darted from Jimbo to me and back. "Sanchez was using this money to buy property under the name of Jason's mother. She doesn't have any idea, of course. She owns condominiums in Gulf Shores she doesn't even know about."

"How do you know that?" I asked.

"I found two of them when I was looking for some records in Pensacola under the name Summers. I dug a little deeper and found that Sanchez was the attorney who drew up the deeds. I figured it out from there."

"Did you tell Jason about it?" I asked.

Villa looked down at his hands. "No. I really figured he knew. But looking back, he probably didn't."

"So Sanchez had it set up so it'd look like Jason was the one socking away the cash," Jimbo said, "and when the firm realized they were being ripped off, they sent the hit team up here."

Villa nodded and kept looking down. Air whistled out of the ceiling vent as the air conditioning unit kicked on. He closed his eyes and began rubbing the back of his neck. "Does Sanchez know that you two are looking into Jason's records?"

Jimbo glanced at me and raised an eyebrow.

"Bob Sanchez doesn't know we're here, if that's what you mean," I said.

"But he knows you're looking," Villa said.

"Screw him," Jimbo said. "If he worries you, get out of town for a few days."

"My car's out in the parking lot, packed and ready to go," Villa said. "And if Sanchez thinks you've found him out, you two ought to think about getting out of town yourselves."

ther of us said it out loud, but it was a fact. Even if we saw John Torres Villa again, which was doubtful, we didn't have anything but his uncorroborated speculation and a bunch of records that didn't even mention Rebecca Jordan and only showed that Jason Summers was involved in an import jewelry business with a little lawn art thrown into the mix every once in a while. Nothing we had come up with would tie Sanchez even to the smuggling of white-collar Mexicans, much less to any beach house murders.

"I know Sanchez is one mean sum'bitch," Jimbo said. "But why do you figure he had all four of them folks killed? That don't make sense."

"He meant for Rebecca to die," I said, "because she knew what was going on. But as for Kellie Lee and Rod Eubanks, I guess it just wasn't their lucky day. Whoever happened to be in that beach house when Sanchez drove the firm's hit team over there was going to get popped."

"Yeah," he said. "I knew from the first day that somebody let the killers in."

"Not a doubt about that. There was no forced entry, no signs that the victims got spooked in any way. I mean, three of them never even moved, got shot right where they were sitting. They saw Sanchez out on the front porch with some visitors and figured they had come to party."

"And what about the bomb at your place?" Jimbo asked. "You think Sanchez put it there?"

I nodded. "I had screwed up and told him that I was looking into Jason's business a lot closer than the cops were. And he sure didn't want that. So he tried to scare me away from here. He was nothing more than a Somozan terrorist down in Nicaragua, so he knew how to make a letter bomb."

"So you think the *Fantasmas* are gone for good?" he asked.

"No doubt about it. They didn't come here on the orders of Roberto Sanchez. They got their orders from that law firm down in Mexico City. And they've taken care of that job."

As we got closer to the gulf, the trees thinned out and the soil at the shoulders of the road grew lighter in color, sand replacing the black dirt. Somebody in one of the RVs in the roadside park was starting the barbecue. That strong smell of chicken on the grill stayed with us for half a mile. The breeze picked up, and one sudden gust sent a shower of yellow hackberry leaves fluttering across the road. Autumn was coming.

"It's none of my business," I said, "but I think you ought to wait a while before you make any decisions about becoming a private investigator."

"You don't think I can handle it?"

"Of course you can."

"You ain't gonna hurt my feelings," he said. "Go ahead and tell me the truth."

"Okay. Here's the truth according to Jack Delmas. You'll make one hell of a fine private eye if that's what you want to do. But don't base that decision on what you've seen in this case. Most of what you'd be doing as a PI would be in a newspaper morgue or a courthouse record room. Or sitting outside some cheap motel room with a zoom-lens camera for nine hours at a stretch, peeing into a plastic cup because you can't take your eyes off the door for the five minutes it'd take to go to some nasty gas-station bathroom. And a lot of the time, maybe most of the time, your client is not the good guy and the person you're trying to dig up the dirt on is not the bad guy. You've got the brains to do it, no doubt. But you need to make mighty sure it's what you want to do."

"So how am I gonna find that out?"

"Since you're the guy who single-handedly tied the sheriff's office into the bust of the Green Guardians, your stock's pretty high right now. Go tell Carlton Rice you want to be an investigator. Try that out for a while. You'd get some great training at the county's expense. You can always jump into the PI business later."

"You really think I can handle it?"

"Son, you're a natural."

Jimbo grunted and stuffed a napkin into a white Styrofoam cup that had been rolling around on the floorboard. I'm sure he didn't want me to see it, but I caught this little smile forming at the corners of his mouth. I looked out my window and left him to his daydreams.

We left the mainland, and the air whipping into my open window became salty. I caught the occasional whiff of the decayed fish that wash up on the shores flanking the road on both sides. The marsh to the west flattened out into an unbroken expanse that at a distance looked for all the world like a wheat field, uniformly amber-yellow except at the center, where a tiny maverick cloud cast a dark, star-shaped shadow.

An hour later, I was packed up and headed back toward the mainland. I was right at the Sea House Restaurant not far from the bridge when an eighteen-wheeler from one of the seafood docks blew past me going way too fast, especially with all the cars that were on the road that day. The traffic leaving the island was thick with folks who had been out on the beach all day and were ready to get home to a hot shower.

The drive to Bay St. Louis wouldn't take much longer than two hours, so I'd be home way before the sun went down. I had a taste for some vegetables after eating seafood almost every meal for the past week, so I thought I'd go to Mama's when I got home. She usually has some peas and cornbread at supper.

This black Infiniti started riding my bumper. That really chaps me. I slowed to let him pass, but he stayed right on my tail. A Toyota pickup with oversized tires passed both of us. When I got onto the bridge, brake lights all the way to the crest glowed as the traffic slowed. In the van, I was sitting high enough to see what had happened up the road. The eighteen wheeler that had blown by me earlier sat straddled across the highway, blocking the whole bridge, even the emergency lanes. Its load must have shifted or something, because the fool had jackknifed.

I glanced in my side mirror. The Infiniti on my bumper had drifted toward the center stripe. It was close enough for me to see the face of the driver. He was a stocky man with both of his huge hands on the top of the steering wheel. A dark-haired man with a handlebar mustache.

The driver was Roberto Sanchez.

My pulse speeded up and so did my breathing. Sanchez wasn't there by coincidence, he had probably been following me since I left Easy's place. I had hoped that he was going to let the whole thing drop. Surely he had to know I couldn't prove a thing on him. But what if he had gone to Villa's office and found it cleaned out and empty? What would that have made him think?

I spotted a gap in the traffic a few cars ahead of me. I wheeled to the right, got into the emergency lane and stomped it. My tires squealed and spun on the white concrete, leaving parallel black strips of rubber and sending out a blue cloud of smoke. I lurched forward, fighting the wheel to keep it straight, and raced past the two cars in front of me. I streaked toward the gap, pushing the little motor harder than it had ever been pushed. Sanchez also turned into the emergency lane, but it had taken him a second or two to react, so I put some space between us.

I whipped back to the left and squeezed through another gap just before it closed. I held my breath, hoping I wouldn't scrape the front bumper of the car I was cutting off. The driver laid down on his horn as I U-turned in front of him into the southbound lane back toward the island. Sanchez didn't get to the gap in time. He got trapped in the emergency lane by the line of stopped traffic.

I hit the gas and the van jumped into passing gear as I raced back toward the island. I laid down on the accelerator and whipped past the marinas and fishing piers. By the time I reached the Circle K store, the Infiniti was nowhere to be seen. At the intersection, that three-way stop where the road dead-ends into Bienville Boulevard, I made a Hollywood stop as I hung a left fast enough to make the van lean and the tires sing.

I sped east toward the ferry. With the bridge blocked, it was the only way off the island. Even if the ferry wasn't in, there would be a crowd waiting for it. So even if Sanchez got untangled from that traffic jam back on the bridge, and even if he figured out where I was, there would still be too many witnesses around for him to try anything. And I'd have time to go into my suitcase and get my Glock.

The ferry was just pulling in to the dock when I got there. There were only two cars in the lane waiting to get on, and I pulled in behind them. When the last car disembarked, I drove with the rest of the waiting line onto the boat. I parked near the bow.

I stepped out of the van and walked to the back doors to get the gun. I dug it out of my shoulder bag, looking all around to make sure I wasn't noticed. I stuck it in my waistband and leaned against the back of the van for a few minutes to check out the cars boarding the ferry. I could see all the cars, even the ones out on the street, but the sun was at an angle to bounce a lot of glare at me off the windshields. Not a sign of any black Infinti. The last car to get on was a BMW.

I climbed back into the van and stuck the gun under the seat. I had made it onto the ferry and Sanchez was probably stuck in traffic on the bridge. I took a deep breath and let it out slowly. I let down the windows, leaned the seat back a notch, and tried to relax. As those old fight-or-flight juices worked their way out of my system it made me just a little queasy. I closed my eyes and began some controlled deep breathing to get back on keel. The ferry sounded its horn, the captain gunned the diesel, and we pulled away from the dock.

What in the world was I going to do about Bob Sanchez?

I didn't have any kind of a case against him to take to the police, so I couldn't exactly go hunt him down. John Villa had been right.

If Sanchez knew I was looking into his records, I might ought to get out of town. But I didn't have anywhere to go. At least nowhere he couldn't find me. And he was already searching.

A little girl squealed and a man standing at the stern rail shouted his wife's name. The whales were back, putting on their show fifty yards off the stern to the starboard side. Everybody got out of their cars and walked back to watch the pod as it broke the surface in graceful, looping cycles. I thought about going back to see them one last time, but I had too much on my mind.

Of course there was a chance Sanchez would realize that I couldn't touch him and just forget about me. Maybe since he had spooked me and made me run, he'd figure I would go back home and keep my mouth shut. Now that I had calmed down and was thinking straighter, it seemed more possible that he would do just that. Nothing at all. He wanted me out of town and I was leaving. Mission accomplished as far as he was concerned.

But I knew that was wishful thinking. I'd have to take Sanchez out somehow. I'd try the police first. Maybe even try Immigration. Maybe Harry Bell could help if I could ever find him. But even if I could get any of them to act, it'd take time. And Sanchez had already made it clear that he knew where Peyton was. In other words, he knew how to keep me from going to the police or anybody else.

Maybe I ought to pick up a few things in Bay St. Louis and drive straight to Memphis. I could call Sandy as soon as the ferry landed at Fort Morgan.

The wind coming through the window was cool, almost chilly, against the perspiration that had popped out on my arms and neck when I was driving like a demon to get away from Sanchez. The ferry turned at an angle that let the sunshine bathe the side of my face and the warmth soothed me. I let the seat all the way back and closed my eyes and listened to the steady drone of the diesel and the pleasant oohs and ahs of the crowd watching the whales. I could have just floated off to sleep.

The voices, the shouts and laughter over at the railing, out for a holiday. Laughing voices of little kids. Safe and happy and surrounded by family. When do you let them go? Do you ever? I never met Rebecca Jordan, but I knew her. A kind soul who wanted to help, a soft-hearted rebel. Probably took in every stray cat she ever saw. And Heather. Cut out of the same cloth. Just wanted to make the world a better place. Save the Earth.

But in their attempts to make the world better, one lived and one died. Why? Who the hell knows. Why is one family in Nashville spared, while in Pascagoula there's a mother whose only remaining hope is to salvage her dead daughter's good name?

No doubt about it, I was gassing up in Foley and driving straight to Memphis to be with Peyton. I could call the cops from up there and tell them all about Roberto Sanchez.

His fingers gripped my windpipe and I flinched. I snapped awake, my eyes popped open. I cut my eyes to the side and there was Sanchez. His big left hand was pinning my neck against the seat. I couldn't swallow, couldn't breathe.

The world was turning dark. I couldn't suck in air. Couldn't scream. I grabbed the hand at my throat, but his grip was like a steel clamp. His nails dug into my skin.

In his other hand he held an icepick. He pointed it at the side of my face, lining it up as I tried to jerk away, ready to push the damned thing straight through my eardrum into my brain. His eyes blazed and his jaw was clenched.

I used both hands to catch his wrist just as he pushed the ice pick. I jerked it to the side and felt a sharp prick of steel across my temple. He grunted and tried once more to jam the pick into my ear. I caught his thumb and wrenched it back and forth, trying to break it.

I held on with all my strength. I strained to twist my head away from that icepick. I dropped one hand to try to find the switch to raise the window.

I began to feel like I was floating because I had no blood going to my brain. The world had darkened to the last stages of twilight. I strained to take in tiny breaths, but I was going numb. The world had gone black by the time I found that damn window switch.

I mashed that switch so hard it pressed into the flesh of my thumb. The fingers Sanchez held on my throat began rising with the window. Sanchez wasn't tall enough to rise with it, so the window broke the grip he had on my throat. He jerked the hand away just before the window pinned it. I held tight to his other hand, the one holding the ice pick. I didn't know if an automatic window could amputate somebody's arm, but I was damn sure going to find out.

Sanchez got on his toes for one last shove of the icepick. I was belted in and could hardly move, so I had to make a split-second decision. Did I hold my ground, hold my finger on the switch, and hope the window would close fast enough to stop his hand from coming forward? Or did I lunge to the side to get my head out of the way and hope the ice pick didn't hit anything vital until I could get the belt undone?

A spurt of blood splattered across the outside of the window. The ice pick dropped flat against my left shoulder. Sanchez's mouth moved, but no words came out. His jaw was ripped open at the chin: the flesh as pink as fresh hamburger. Bright red blood gushed down the side of his neck and soaked the shoulder of his white shirt. The shock showed in his bulging eyes, like *what the hell just happened*? He dropped like a sandbag and fell straight down out of my sight.

"Move over, son!" Jimbo shouted. "Hurry up!"

My whole body was shaking. Real close to convulsing. I sucked in air one puff at a time. My throat burned even with little swallows, and I started coughing up phlegm.

"Come on, man! We gotta move! You can throw up later."

He jerked the door open, looking toward the crowd at the stern rail the whole time. The van was tall enough to shield us from the view of the ferry captain in the raised pilothouse on the starboard side. Jimbo pushed me aside and I rolled over to the passenger seat. He stuffed Sanchez into the van behind the steering wheel and shut the door. Sanchez was unconscious and limp, but still breathing. I heard the gurgle of fluids in his lungs as he struggled for short, sputtering breaths.

"Pull him on into the back," Jimbo said. "Lay him on the floorboard."

I wiped the mucous off my upper lip and the blood off my neck with my sleeve. My breath had come back, but my throat was hurting bad. "Where the hell did you come from?"

"We can talk later," Jimbo said. "Get him out of sight."

I gripped Sanchez at the waist of his pants and the collar of his shirt and dragged him off the driver's seat. In addition to the bullet that had torn off a good bit of his jaw, there was a hole in his shirt at the rib cage and a round, wet, darkening stain around it. I crawled over him to the backseat and pulled him through the space between the driver's and the passenger's seats.

Jimbo shut the door and strolled to the bow of the ferry as relaxed as if he were walking through Springdale Mall. He leaned forward against the rail, his back turned to everyone else on the boat. He pulled something out of his waistband—I couldn't see what—and, while looking back over his shoulder, dropped it over the side. He stuck his hands into his pockets and walked back to my van.

"I knew that throw-down piece would come in handy one day," he said as he got in. "Take these. They're the keys to Heather's BMW."

"How in the world did you get on this ferry?"

"I was just about to gas up Heather's car at the Circle K when I look up and here's this tourist in a van haulin' ass through my island. I saw that U.S.M. Golden Eagles sticker in the back window and knew it was yours. You really ought to take that sticker off if you ever expect to sell this thing."

"But how did you know Sanchez was coming after me?"

"Well, about the time I put the gas nozzle back in place, here comes another fool tearing down the road going the same direction, and this guy's driving a green Ford Escort. I could see that it was Roberto Sanchez. So I knew it was rock and roll time somewhere."

"He must have carjacked somebody back on the bridge," I said.

"What?"

"I'll tell you later. So you followed us. What happened then?"

"I saw the line of cars getting on the ferry," he said, "and you were right up at the front. And sure enough, there was the green Escort. So I figured I'd take a boat ride. I saw Sanchez walking toward your van, and I knew that wasn't good. So I unstrapped the throw-down piece I keep around my ankle and I fell in behind him. About the time I could get positioned, I saw him grab you and out came the ice pick. You know the rest of the story."

Sanchez coughed and let out a low moan.

"Check his pockets for the keys to that Escort," Jimbo said. "You drive it off the boat when we dock and park in that lot off to the side. Just lock the keys in it. They'll be looking for it, so wipe your prints off."

"What are you going to do with him?" I asked.

"After you get the Escort parked, run back on board and drive Heather's Beemer off."

"Are you going to drive him to the hospital?"

"You might want to go back and get in that Escort," Jimbo said. "We're getting pretty close to the dock."

"He's still alive, Jimbo," I said. "At least I think he is."

Jimbo stared straight ahead. "I might need to stop to put some gas in this thing. It'd be a shame to run out on the way to the hospital."

"Get serious. What are we going to do with him?"

"Roberto don't look like he's gonna make it," he said.

I looked back at Sanchez, balled up on the back floorboard. I couldn't tell if he was still breathing. Jimbo was right: He didn't look as if he would make it. The crowd of fellow passengers shouted in unison about something the whales were doing. I couldn't see where anybody had noticed what had just happened. A wave broke over the bow and a salty mist settled on the windshield.

"You've got to take him to the hospital," I said.

"The son of a bitch set up two kids to take a fall for him," Jimbo said. "You said yourself that he drove that Mexican hit squad over to Jason's house. Picture that heartwarming little scene for a minute. He opened the door and saw Jason and Rebecca sitting in the living room with two other people he didn't even know. And he stood there in the same room with his hands in his damned pockets while some scum he had brought in from Mexico painted the walls with their brains."

Sanchez groaned and gasped, then fell silent.

"And he'd a done the same thing to your little girl in a heartbeat if he thought he needed to," Jimbo said.

"So you're not going to take him to the hospital?"

"I didn't say that," Jimbo sighed. "But it's a long way from here. Might take a while." He looked back at Sanchez. "Besides, I'll bet he ain't got his insurance card with him. And it's pure hell to check somebody into a hospital without one of them things."

TWENTY-SEVEN

The first front of autumn came through lower Alabama that night, a full month too early. The cool, dry air was too heavy to hold any haze, so the next day the horizon was sharp, the sky was a rich royal blue, and the clouds were fat and round and bright. The gum trees and hackberries and water oaks still had dark green leaves, but if you looked real close you could see a sprinkling of yellow ones. The sunlight became clear and golden, the kind of light that is the essence of autumn, clear but without glare, deepening every color and sharpening every image.

Summer wasn't through with us yet, but this early taste of fall had changed the spirit of the place. It now actually felt like it was time for football games, for packing away the white shoes, for draining the fuel out of the Evinrudes. It doesn't feel like time for the beach unless it's so hot you sweat even in the shade and so bright you can't see anything without squinting, so this early touch of fall had its effect on the Labor Day crowd on Dauphin Island. It was the smallest gathering in years.

I sat on the ocean side of the big dune, the one near the public pier, across the street from the Neptune. I was waiting for Jimbo and watching the last, bright slice of a glassy yellow sunset over the western end of the lonely beach. Even the last dawdling TV camera crews had left the island, for the story of the beach house murders had run its course. A police beating in Bedford-Stuyvesant had become the new national outrage over the past twenty-four hours, the new topic of Sunday-morning television blatherings by that same group who gets paid to have an opinion on everything that happens. And even in Mobile the story was getting a little stale. Carolyn was never going to get her chance to tell the world the story of her daughter, but then, she never had a chance to begin with. I think she knew it the whole time.

I had stopped by Easy's that afternoon to catch an hour or two of the last party of the year, but nobody was home. Easy was no doubt up at Tuscaloosa for the game, and Missy was probably back in school or on her way. And that was just as well. Most people, except for the Easys of the world, only have so many hard-party summers in them, and I could tell this had been Missy's last one. She would be clerking for some law firm in Atlanta or Washington when summer rolled around next year, trading in her flip-flops for a pair of Guccis.

Jimbo had called Darla and Lila from the phone on the jet when he was on his two-way trip to Nashville the night before. They were going to meet up with us at the Neptune in an hour or so. Jimbo said they got a real kick out of getting asked for a date from a phone on a jet, especially Darla.

He had called me from that same phone after he set things up. Told me he didn't want to hear any arguments, I was going to stay on the island at least one more night. Billy Ray Cyrus was playing up at the Mobile Coliseum and Jimbo knew a security guard who was going to let us backstage. Darla didn't put Billy Ray on quite the same plane as Harrison Ford, but it was close. Jimbo assured me she would be most grateful for the backstage visit.

That sounded like a first-rate plan to me.

I didn't ask about Sanchez when Jimbo called. A phone call from a commercial jet isn't the way to talk about such things. Of course, I planned to ask him that evening. I was going to ask one time, and one time only. I'd get whatever answer Jimbo's code dictated that he give to me. And I'd live with that answer, even if it was nothing more than a grunt and a shrug of those big shoulders.

The night before, I had turned over to Jimbo not only the effort to save Sanchez's life but also the very choice of whether or not to make that effort. Next spring, I'd have to pay special attention at Easter service to the part about Pontius Pilate, because when I stood on the Fort Morgan shore and watched Jimbo drive off in the van with Sanchez laid on the floorboard, rapidly losing both blood and life, I, too, had washed my hands.

Or had I?

Is that really what I did? If Sanchez were alive, we still had no case against him. So did God mean for me to bust my ass trying to save Sanchez's life so he'd have another chance to jam an ice pick down my ear, or set off a bomb at my house, or think up some way to bring the *Fantasmas* back for one more job? Or maybe wipe out four more kids the next time he needed a way to save his own skin?

No, I had not washed my hands of it. I had made my decision. There was no passing it off to Jimbo. Whether Jimbo had raced like a maniac trying to save him or had done nothing at all didn't matter. Whether Sanchez was still breathing or not didn't matter. I had made my decision not to try to keep him alive, regardless of any choice Jimbo had made. And even if all efforts to keep him alive would have failed, even if he had died before the van had gone a hundred yards down the road, I had still made the call.

Right or wrong, I'd have to live with it. Just as I lived every day with all those other decisions I've made throughout my life. Like the decisions that led to Sandy and Peyton living in Memphis while I remained on the Mississippi Gulf Coast.

Ole Miss was playing a game up in Oxford that night, and it was almost time for the kickoff. Sandy and Varner had driven down to the campus earlier that day, I knew that for sure. That east Memphis group never misses a game. They always set up their table in the Grove, across from the Law School under a hundred-year-old oak, and bring barbecue from Corky's and chicken from this truck stop in Batesville that they pass on the drive down.

Peyton would be dressed in her little red-and-blue Ole Miss cheerleading outfit. She would probably get on Varner's shoulders so she could see the football team on its pre-game walk through the Grove where fifty thousand fans would be cheering on the Rebels.

I wasn't even going to get to listen to the game on the radio.

But that was okay. I needed to give that whole scene a rest. I'd go back someday; I love the place too much. But right then there were just too many old ghosts walking around the Grove for me to deal with.

Knowing that I wouldn't be there with Sandy and Peyton, knowing that it would never again be the way it was for those few magical years, didn't hurt now the way it had for the past six years. For the first time since the divorce, there was no inner voice tormenting me, teasing me, telling me she'd be coming back. When Sandy took off from the Dauphin Island airstrip in Varner's plane, that voice died for good.

I stood up and brushed the sand off my jeans and walked up to the crest of the dune. Jimbo's truck was in the parking lot. The front door of the Neptune was propped open and the band had started playing. It was a loud rendition of "Way Down Yonder on the Chattahootchie."

I was going to have myself a great time that night. I was going to plunge head first into a honky-tonk evening with a good-looking, fun-loving, lower-Alabama country girl who got a kick out of little things, who had dreams about movie stars and country singers, who had never even heard of the damned Winchester Tennis Club in Memphis, Tennessee, and was a hell of a lot more interested in seeing the gift shop at Graceland than anything in Goldsmith's or

Dillard's or any of those shopping malls out toward Germantown.

And for the first time in six years I wasn't going to let yesterday, or all those yesterdays, enter my head.

Not even for a second.

Not one single, solitary time.

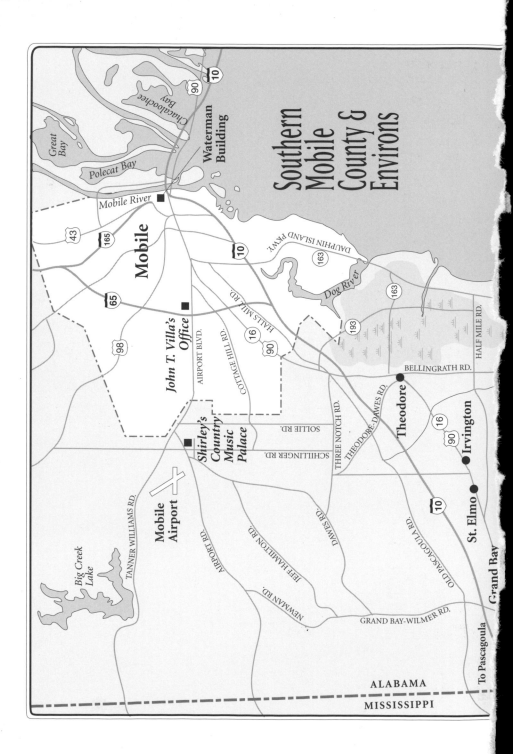